90024

Keane, molly

F
KEANE

Time after time

DATE			
	OCT 1 0 1985		

Time After Time

TIME AFTER TIME

Molly Keane

ALFRED A. KNOPF   NEW YORK   1984

ALSO BY MOLLY KEANE

Good Behaviour

THIS IS A BORZOI BOOK
PUBLISHED BY ALFRED A. KNOPF, INC.

Library of Congress Cataloging in Publication Data
Farrell, M. J.
Time after time.
I. Title.
PR6021.E33T5   1983   823'.914   83-47966
ISBN 0-394-53280-5

Manufactured in the United States of America
FIRST AMERICAN EDITION

Contents

1   In the Kitchen   3

2   In the Dining-Room   22

3   Bedtime   38

4   Separate Pursuits   52

5   The Revenant   84

6   Rediscovery   113

7   Time Translated   137

8   Revelations   171

9   Time After Time   188

Time After Time

1 ✑ *In the Kitchen*

Jasper Swift, owner although not sole possessor of Durraghglass, was back in the kitchen where he belonged. He had been
on his weekly shopping expedition. Today he had forgotten his
shopping list – something that could happen to the most
efficiently equipped person, even to his sister May. He was not
going to taunt his own memory, or his age, on the matter.

His elegant, lengthy figure was bent, like a reed in a cold
breeze, over the bags and packages in the basket he had put
down on the kitchen table. He lifted up his handsome head and
cursed – he had left the meat behind. That was a bit senile, he had
to admit. And April's prescription – no harm. Far too many
tranquilizers going down that silly throat. There was something June had wanted, was it for the farrowing sow? Well, too
late now – let her get on with her farrowing in her own way. At
least he had remembered to buy, for himself, a new hot-water
bottle. He wasn't altogether dotty.

Dottiness was the last thing from which Jasper suffered.
Uncertain and nervous perhaps, but that was to be expected in
the elderly owner of a large and encumbered estate and a house
burdened with three sisters, one widowed, two unmarried, each
of them with a right of residence. That was the way darling
Mummie had left it. Jasper had always accepted her wishes
devoutly, even more devoutly since her death.

Now he took off his cap, a dark checked cap – Mummie had
bought it, perhaps thirty years ago, from that most classical of

hatters in St James's. It was as graciously becoming to him as any hat dreamed up by Proust for Odette. He wore it with an air and at an angle that saved his blind eye a little from the light. Mummie had chosen the stuff for his tweed coat too. She had purred suggestions to the tailor during the fittings and the resulting coat still moved in a flow of perfection, giving grace with austerity. Perhaps the cuffs, grafted and integrated with their sleeves and serving no more useful purpose than that of pleasing the eye, were its most touching and elegant feature. An ageless antique and needing care, it could fall to bits on him any day now. But Savile Row – he shuddered: three hundred pounds for anything proper today. Forget it. Horrible. Horrible times.

He put his cap on again because the kitchen was cold. The Aga was in a dispirited mood because the wind from the west was blowing towards the mountain. He accepted such natural facts and allowed the Aga to take its own time to revive and recover.

There was a time when kitchens in the afternoon held their distance. Cooks and kitchenmaids used to tidy up the kitchen at Durraghglass, perhaps take a little rest from their duties until it was time to make the Sally Lunn for drawing-room tea. Not any more, naturally. Times change.

In the big kitchen, where Jasper now ruled, nothing was ever tidied up, stored, or thrown away. Cats were the scavengers. Cardboard wine cases that had carried more groceries than wine to the house were piled and heaped and thrown in corners. Cats had their kittens in them – mostly born to be drowned. Jasper's great tiger cat, Mister Minkles, was the sire of them all. Strangely, he was clean for a tom cat. No dog ever had a more loving heart. Jasper returned his love and respected him as a person. Now he sat with majesty at the centre of the white deal dresser – sat on the breadboard. Behind him tier on tier of chipped and unchipped dinner services (Mason's ironware mostly), rose upward to the hook-studded ceiling, barren now of hams, and covered in dust thick as ashes. Large calendars from the Allied Irish Banks, year after year of them, hung on a brass hook. There were pictures of duck flighting, stuff like that, which Jasper didn't want to throw away. His close vision was all right.

Jasper hardly ever looked out of the tall sashed windows, or below them to the slope where he cleared briars and ivy from azaleas and camellias planted long ago, and nurtured his own more recent plantings. Red Himalayan rhododendrons grew like banyan trees behind the choicer subjects; and behind them again wild ponticum formed a second barrier to winter winds from the Black Stair mountain. Jasper had larger horticultural plans that milled around like dreams in his head – expensive ideas which he felt just young enough to develop and direct. Money was the hopeless problem. Lack of it kept everything in a state of dream. But at least he could keep the briars in check down the steep bank with its broken stone terraces falling to gold reeds, blue flag leaves, and low, unseen mountain river.

Across the water and beyond was an infinite distance of sun-filled untidy gorse-grown fields; some fields bent themselves round small lakes for wild swans, or moorhens, or water-lilies. Jasper maintained his lack of interest in all this, he had other things to occupy him. There was the constant unremitting fight he must keep up to maintain his authority and position as head of the family. His most important offensive and defensive here was present, as always, when April, his eldest sister and the only married and widowed Swift, spoke to him.

April glided in. A tall and elderly lady, still beautiful, she stood near the Aga, shuddering a little while her eyes avoided their usual disgust with the kitchen. Her expensive clothes became her very well. They had ease and length and fullness.

Some contrivance nipped them always in the right and prettiest directions. Violet, wanda, or dark brown were her favourite colours. She was big and elderly and she swayed gracefully on long thin legs. She had the defensive aloofness of the very deaf. A fierce chihuahua clung and buried his face somewhere under her armpit. She stood apart, humming and murmuring, while the fingers of one hand were devotedly busy round her little dog's ears. Her eyes rested on Jasper, distantly unconcerned with his work, as though plucking pigeons was some sort of unnecessary amusement. When she spoke it was a different story.

"I just wanted to let you know I'm going off my diet to-night."

He had to contradict and deny even though it meant more trouble for him: "Nonsense – you're horribly overweight. Yoghurt and hummus for you."

"I'm glad it's pigeon pie. My favourite. And could you let me have my pills? My head's been more than splitting."

"O'Keefe's were shut."

"No need to shout. How much were they?"

"The chemist was SHUT."

"I don't care if it was raining."

"I said –"

"If you took your cap off in the house, Jasper, you might hear better. At least it would be rather more civilized."

"Do I have to write it?" He put down a pigeon and crossed over to the dresser where, ignoring the cascade of bills, cooking recipes cut from Sunday papers, keys of all sorts, as well as hoarded sardine tin openers, he looked without hesitation into a two-pound marmalade pot (Coopers of Oxford) and turned from it quite pale with annoyance.

"Now who has taken my Biro? I'ld like to know who has been in the kitchen while I was shopping and taken the kitchen Biro."

"Ah! Biro!" She was for once abreast of the problem. "Every

Biro in the house is dry. It's a contagious disease. I tried the library and the drawing room and the morning room and the gents' loo, all the same story. Here's a Biro. I found one here at last."

"My own personal, red, private pen! How dare you? Damn you."

April smiled and spoke indulgently: "Write it down if you can't hear me."

"Librium OFF" he wrote on the back of an envelope and handed it to her with a slight air of triumph. He gave back the pen too, as though he too were deaf and she must answer in writing.

"Oh, NO! And I'm down to my last, my very last."

"Not a bad idea, if you are. Horrible stuff."

"You forgot on purpose," she went on, her deaf voice as isolated as echo in a cave. "I know that perfectly well. I know you and your utter selfishness."

"Steady yourself, dear girl," he spoke in his most sensible voice, "and may I have my pen? My pen, please – I said: MY PEN." Jasper knew she couldn't hear, but in his necessity and annoyance he snatched awkwardly and roughly at the pen in her hand. As he did so the chihuahua raised his head from her armpit, screamed twice, and bit him sharply. Jasper yelled too. "Little bastard – bitten me to the bone."

April looked at his hand with satisfaction. "Oh, he's drawn blood. Mum's own Tiger. Who looks after Mum? Whose does? Zooze does."

"Give me back my pen and get out of this kitchen, both of you."

"Who's afraid of the wee-twee wolf –" she swayed towards the door – "you utter stinker!" She retreated in language to the schoolroom. "What's more, this kitchen's filthy – just a dungeon for dysentery."

Holding her dog to her heart and skirting the kitchen debris with a sort of mournful delicacy, April left the room and went up the stone staircase leading to the ground floor of the house. The curious thing was that the smell on this floor was rather worse than its origins in the kitchen. The old breath of human dinners and dogs' dinners, chickens' and pigs' dinners too, combined with cats' earths and dogs' favourite urinals, all clung to the air like grey hairs in a comb.

April had grown accustomed to her tolerant disgust with most things in life except herself. Resigned and lazy in her private world of deafness, she sailed now, lone as a moon, past and beyond tall mahogany doors to drawing-room, library, morning-room, without a thought of turning a brass drop handle or looking for company. Only, on the landing beneath a window where the staircase paused, turned and went on up, the shadow of a memory, from years that lapsed into nowhere, refused denial. She still saw, rather than heard, the footsteps tearing down the long flight from the top landing. Leaning over the upper bannister rail, dressed for that summer ball, she had watched and agonized for darling Leda, her cousin from Austria, her best friend. Leda's hysteria had been aroused by Mummie's surprising refusal to bring her with April to the ball. A partner had failed. "In any case you aren't *out* yet," Mummie had said with chill decision.

Standing there, in that previous time, April had seen Daddy waiting while Leda clattered and leapt down, half-dressed – her great white dirndl skirts with their ribboned hems flouncing and billowing behind her: the knob of yellow hair drifting from its hairpins, strands smeared to her cheeks by tears; red shoes jumping and balancing and never stopping until she sprang, like a leaping cat, into Daddy's arms. And Daddy, always so distant and unloving, held her closely. Were they whispering? April could not tell.

To remember Leda was to be in two worlds, the earliest that of childhood – Leda's accounts of life in Vienna were vivid and bright as Christmas cards. With her you sped down ski-runs, you skated while waltzes played, you drank hot chocolate through floating cream. Winter came, but it never rained in Vienna as it did so obstinately at Durraghglass.

Leda's strange, pretty clothes which Mummie disapproved of and Leda wore with such panache, came, not from D. H. Evans, but from Vienna, "city of dreams", where Daddy's wild sister, Star, had married . . . unfortunately not a Count nor even a gentleman. He owned a restaurant, a very famous one. But his name was not often spoken at Durraghglass or other country houses. It was Jewish.

When they were nearly grown-up Leda paid another visit. April was too lazy to admit the possibility that she still came – a perpetual ghost of happiness. That summer Leda had just left her larky finishing school in Paris, and April her sober family in Basle. Happily set apart from their juniors, they whispered together, sighed for unspoken blisses, screamed with laughter at new unseemly jokes (better in French). Romantic novels (*Strangers May Kiss*) were under their pillows at night and locked in blue leather writing-cases by day.

"Nevermore" – the word belonged to Leda. She was as unreal now as any old dancer in a forgotten ballet, and as sad. Why harry remembrance for her? Half-Jewish and married to a Jew, she perished in some cold unnamed camp, most likely. Who wants sordid details? Better leave Leda's face as indistinct as a drowned face seen under water. It was simpler, too, to ignore that grey question about Daddy and Leda. It had nothing to do with his death. Shooting accidents can happen to the most experienced men.

9

In her seventy-fourth year April possessed a fortunate forgetfulness of youth and its strivings with happiness and sorrow.
Now she found (or invented for herself) practical importances which fully occupied her mind and her days. Preserving
her looks from the hungry years; maintaining her position as
the only married – if widowed – member of her virgin family;
keeping her secrets; holding her comforts close and her money
carefully gave her objects enough about which to think and
plan. Grossly over-familiar with the house and the lives it enclosed, she had an absolute refuge where she could scheme out
her activities and ignore the penalties of her deafness. She was
the eldest. Her bedroom looked south. She put Tiger down
gently, unlocked the door, and followed the cheerful little dog
inside. Her key turned again in the lock, and from the wide
passage-way her door looked as obdurate as the door of any cell.

Irritated and shaken once again into the state of annoyance in
which April's absurdities cancelled out any appreciation of her
looks or sympathy for her deafness, Jasper was bending over the
kitchen sink (quite a grand affair in stainless steel), pinching the
pin-prick bite in his thumb under the cold tap, when his
youngest sister, Baby June, appeared: a further worrying interruption.

Baby June came from the farmyard. She wore two old Husky
jackets, jeans and gum-boots and a beret as round as a penny.
She had stayed Baby June all the sixty-four years of her life on
account of her tiny size. There was nothing babyish about her.
She could do the work of two men on the place and loved doing
it. Her eyes were a pale jackdaw blue with whites as bright as a
flag. She was the shape and weight of a retired flat race jockey –
too heavy for her height. In her day she had been the terror and
success of every point-to-point meeting in the South of Ireland.

June approached Jasper without much confidence. She worked for him and for Durraghglass day-long, and year in and year out, as diligently as though she expiated guilt of some kind. She did too. She could never forget the hurt she had inflicted. But, secretly, she was happy. Happiness steals through you.

"What happened to the poor hand?" she asked.

He didn't tell her. "April was here, hysterical as usual."

She looked at his hand again. "I thought I heard Tiger letting a roar out of him." She was the only Swift who spoke like the people. There had been no English school for her. No one could teach her to read.

"You heard April screaming, I expect. I forgot her Librium."

"Oh, Jasper, the poor thing! To tell you the truth, I took a couple of tablets myself."

"You did?"

"My poor Sweetheart is having such a nasty labour."

"Librium for farrowing sows? You'll drive me insane between you. How did you know I had a reserve? I forget where I put it myself."

"In the Colman's mustard tin. I knew you kept a few back."

"It saves driving nine miles to O'Keefe's if April runs out."

"You'ld never spare me another couple for Sweetheart?"

"No. Try her with an aspirin."

"Don't joke, Jasper. Remember it's her first litter. How would you feel? Imagine now, how you'ld feel yourself."

"Of course I know just how I'ld feel. Oh, do go back to Sweetheart, Baby, and let me get on with cooking dinner."

"Christy Lucey's with her. He put a blanket on her and said four decades."

"About all he's good for – more utterly useless every day, every hour. *And* you spoil him."

"What's for the dinner?"

"Pigeon pie."

She looked doubtfully at the birds on the kitchen table. "Won't they be a bit on the tough side?"

"Yes. I hope they choke you all."

"Oh, aren't you naughty?" She wandered out.

Mollified by solitude, Jasper wondered for a dull moment how it was that so utterly silly a woman and so small a person was able to drive a tractor; deliver a calf; perhaps, if absolutely necessary, kill a lamb. He had seen her glittering, satisfied eyes after an assistance at some birth, blood on her hands and on her clothes. The thought of her versatile abilities, while he accepted their usefulness, made him shudder. He never suspected that her devotion to Durraghglass was not entirely the quick and mainspring of her life. They knew almost less than nothing about each other.

With the acceptance lent by hindsight Jasper saw the place as it used to be, fully staffed in house and gardens and farm, losing money year upon year while a full social life continued undisturbed. He could still see four different puddings displaying themselves on a side table before a Sunday luncheon party, and sweet peas arranged by May in two silver baskets. His mother invited pretty daughters of the County to excite his fancy. They frightened him and he bored them. Besides, he could sense their curiosity about what nastiness went on behind his black eyepatch. He loved only his mother .... darling roly-poly Mummie – always wore violet (her colour), and a mauve hat for luncheon parties on Sundays or before Clonmel Hound Show. Occasionally the judges came to luncheon and when that happened the mixed grill was superlative. Sometimes now he would make one for his own lonely pleasure – his midnight feast a secret from those inquisitive sisters. He sighed, both in retrospect and anticipation, for at least he was greedy – memories of the delicious food of other days were romance to him.

Those were the young, lazy days when widowed Mummie held the reins at Durraghglass, her courage and competence legendary now. Then Jasper had no further responsibilities than a pretence at the life of a country gentleman. For him a day's shooting or a day's fishing was far preferable, in its season, to a day's hunting. When Mummie died (too young and too cruelly) death duties depleted the whole structure of Durraghglass, and afterwards a miasma of overdraft and mismanagement abetted Mummie's wishes, holding brother and sisters captive for year past forgotten year, locked in inviolable small conflicts and old adventures.

Sighing still, Jasper picked up another pigeon and ripped away quietly at the myriad breast feathers. No need to pluck the wings and legs. He would discard these, of course, treats for Mister Minkles and his wives. A righteous feeling of peace and busyness in creation came over him. Everything to do with the pie was forming a quiet importance for him when May came in. He disliked her, perhaps, a little more than the other two sisters put together.

"Quelle odeur – what a smell!" She arrived, as usual, on a tide of protest. "Grips – Gripper – 'ware cat! 'ware cat!" Gripper was a miniature Jack Russell terrier.

"Pick him up for God's sake."

"No. It's discipline. SIT. Did I say SIT! Good boy! What *is* that smell?"

"Hearts boiling for all your damn dogs, if you must know."

"Rotten, too. Why not open a window? The whole house is steaming."

"Open it yourself. No, don't. I must think about my cat. Traps up and he'll wander."

"Why can't you have that animal fixed and be done with it?"

"Why not castrate your own dog? Embarrassing little displayer."

"Don't be so squeamish – and that cat box is quite scandalous. Weeks of filth. Flies. Diarrhoea for all."

"Look – I'm only just back from Wednesday's shopping. Give me time."

"Time? Organisation, that's what's missing. I've been to Ballinkerry twice already today. Once for the Country-women's Association, back again for the Flower Arrangers. I'm their President, after all."

"Yes. Poor things."

"Now it's almost the six o'clock news and I need Radio 4. I asked you to get my batteries. Did you get my batteries? One of us must keep up with world events."

"Keep up with the Archers is what you mean. Your batteries are in the bag with the light bulbs, and you own me £1.70."

"I owe you nothing of the sort. I put £2 in the House Pool after my win at Scrabble last Thursday. It's in my account book – check if you like."

He knew she was right so he didn't take the matter further.

She rummaged deftly among his parcels. "They're not with the light bulbs."

"Try the bag of cheeses."

"Yes. Got them. And what are you giving us tonight? Not those birds? Far too fresh – look – wing feathers tough as old rope."

"Dinner will be at nine o'clock." His voice was icy – ice on the verge of starring and breaking through to black, angry waters.

"Nine o'clock? Good show! Time to finish my tweed picture. Look *out*! Your cat's got a pigeon. Gripper, leave it, sir! Leave it!"

The noise that an angry, frightened dog and a furious, greedy cat can make together blazed hysterically through the kitchen, and May's doggy-discipline voice rose to a wail: "Grippy,

sweetie, come back to Mummie." Only the Aga stayed calm,
everything else vibrated until the warm air rifted apart. Fear was
in the room. The two humans were afraid to interfere with
Nature, Nature, red in its usual places; until May, recovering
her nerve, seized a moment when Gripper was noisiest and
furthest from the cat, to grab him up and praise his courage.
Jasper's hesitation in removing the pigeon from the possessive,
growling cat did not escape her comment.

"Same as ever, aren't you? Baby June to civilize your pony,
and who was sick before the Members' Race? Afraid of your
own cat, now!"

"If you must look back forty years – who cried before every
Hunt Ball? No-hope May – and now it's china mending and
tweed pictures and the Irish countrywomen's floral club."
It was infamous of him to jeer at her skills and frenzied
occupations. But he kept his eyes away from her gloved
hands.

"Thank you," she said. "Thank you very, very much. At
least I've got both my eyes –" there were tears of wounded fury
in them. "Take care what you say to me. I know something you
don't know I know."

Jasper's hands paused almost imperceptibly as he plucked. "I
can talk or keep quiet too, remember," he said, "so shut up, and
let me get on with dinner." He didn't know what he was
threatening her with.

Left in mid-air for an answer, May hesitated. Could he know?
Quite impossible. But she turned towards the door, accepting
dismissal.

So there must be something, Jasper thought. He had certainly
lit on some small private guilt, too small even to guess at. Her
suspicion of him had only touched a nerve for an instant. For
what could be more secure than present business done with a
Trappist monk? The Silent Order.

*　　　*　　　*

May walked briskly (youthfully was the way she thought of it) up the kitchen stairs. Gripper came behind her doing a faithful four-legged-friend imitation of her purposeful steps. She was hurrying away from what Jasper knew of her life and its unkind imperfection. Her teeth chattered like an angry squirrel's when she allowed herself to think about that. She even preferred a snide cruelty like Jasper's to the wonder, the admiration and the unspoken sympathy her skills provoked. May knew she was wonderful without anybody telling her so. It had been to please Mummie, to keep a special place with her that, as a child, she had worked so devotedly at her hand-writing and needlework, and had striven jealously to excel April in eating neatly, never dripping the softest boiled egg, or slopping the hottest cocoa. As she grew older, aware of conscious looks averted, she put intense effort into achieving every skill possible to her in Hand Crafts. Her flower arrangements were balanced and poised past perfection. Prizes fell automatically to her tweed pictures. They were the neatest, prettiest works of art imaginable and sold like hot cakes at Church Sales and other important festivals. She could stuff a doll, she could trim out a dog. She never asked anybody to do up a button or zip up a dress for her. She was adept at making chamois-leather gloves, adjusting the patterns for herself, and making others as Christmas presents for her friends – inexpensive and ever welcome. Nothing was beyond her will to prove super-normal dexterity. Some enterprises trembled on a thrilling, scarifying knife-edge between success and disaster. "Of course, I'm a very fulfilled person" – she was fond of saying this to herself. That was what she was saying now, blotting out the ugly moment with Jasper.

She waited, sniffing distastefully in the long smelly hall, before she opened the nearest of the two high doors of the drawing-room where, beneath the dark gilt fringes of an early Chippendale mirror she would create a Chinese arrangement with the grey-green catkins, *Garrya eliptica* and early white narcissi – quite an œuvre, she expected it to be.

The drawing-room, its four windows facing back towards the north and the mountains, was tall and cold – the narcissi, soaking in a bucket, hardly made their scent known on the air. To make quite sure of her privacy May turned the long keys in the locks of both doors. Then, before starting work on her flower arrangement, she loosened her glove, the better to deal with stripping leaves and balancing stems and branches. She looked aside as she peeled off the glove. She had never grown used to the sight of the hand she had been born with. It needed three and a half more fingers to complete it.

Jasper's cat, having eaten as much as he was able of the pigeon, returned to the breadboard where he sat at his ease, making the noises of a sated tiger. "All right, sit there if it gives you the smallest pleasure," Jasper spoke in a different voice from the nipped-in tone of patient or impatient dislike provoked from him by his sisters. His love for that fierce cat and his predecessors set free in him a benison of indulgence, objectless since little Mummie's death. Seated on the breadboard within the wreath of carved wheatears, Mister Minkles not only supplied an object for Jasper's affection and carefulness, he embodied his enduring defiance of those sisters with their clinical, dainty ideas. They were afraid of Mister Minkles, afraid for themselves as well as for their dogs. Not one of them would have dared to lift him off the breadboard. Jasper looked his respect for his cat without touching him. Then he opened an oven door of the Aga to hold his arthritic hands in its level heat. Cooking, cats, and the nurture of exotic shrubs had for a long time provided the shields and defences behind which he evaded interference with his thoughts or his days. No present importance equalled the dream and the possibility which the near future held – a possibility about which his sisters were happily ignorant.

When his hands were warmed and limber, Jasper resumed preparation of the pigeon pie. His mind floated forward in inspired construction . . . . there were a few mushrooms somewhere in a paper bag, and he remembered rashers of streaky bacon, stiffening in age, too salty for breakfast, perfect for pie. Beef? He shook his head to himself. Wait, wait a moment – where had he put them away, those perfect leftovers for the dogs' dinners? Actually he had put them in the dogs' dinners. What went in could come out and go under the scullery tap, perhaps. Yes, certainly, why not? A purist in his cooking, he stood out against stock cubes. Black pepper, coriander, bayleaf, hard-boiled eggs – what had Baby June said about her hens going off? Two hard-boiled eggs were a necessity in a pigeon pie. He gritted his teeth at the thought of that idiot, Baby, and her barren hens. He entirely denied to himself his own lapse in leaving the shopping list behind. Blame fell where he wished it to belong. He screwed up the list and threw it away. Neither he nor anyone else was going to read that again.

Far along a driveway the farmyard was held at a distance from the more civilized policies of Durraghglass. The mountainy fields rose quietly outside it towards gorse and heather. Below its nearly slateless cow-sheds and tumbling iron-gated piggeries, a steep slope drained liquids from all ordure down to the pretty river.

Not in the tumbling piggeries, but in a warm corner of a sound old cow-shed, Baby June and Christy Lucey looked with happy satisfaction at Sweetheart, the long white sow, and her eight piglets, safely delivered. Outside the shed spring rain was falling coldly on wild cherry blossom and through the evening songs of birds. Christy Lucey and June had neither eyes nor ears for these other springtime events. Christy Lucey was finishing a short prayer of gratitude to the saint he had been propositioning through the whole affair. Baby June laid the only unsatisfactory member of the litter on sheep's wool in a shoe-box. She had plans for its survival.

"I'm going up to the house now with this little fellow," Baby June said. "Keep an eye on Sweetheart for me the way she won't lie on one of them while I'm away."

Christy Lucey lifted up his lovely dark head and listened. Not to Miss Baby. "Do I hear the Angelus?" he asked. "Will I make it, I wonder?"

June could never deny Christy the time off for his religious exercises. He was the support and stay of her every farming activity – without him, what should she do? Life would fail her – she would be so deprived the beat of her heart would stop. "Oh, well," she said, "I expect she'll do now."

"She will, so," he agreed, "she'll do all right." He took his bicycle and rode away from June. He would get out onto the mountain road through the farm gateway; its stone archway, crowned with a bell-less belfry, was not quite high enough for present-day lorries and trucks.

June must follow the long drive that ran below a demesne wall and on past the house for a further half mile, skirting the road every yard of the way. Durraghglass had been built at the date when one of the marks of a gentleman's ownership, dividing his property from the vulgar public, was a long quietness of avenue.

June walked the distance, back and forwards several times a day. She was familiar with its potholes and long, stony depths and she ignored the riot of briars and nettles on its once orderly verges. Close to the back of the house, a different and more precise archway from that of the farmyard led to the stableyard; a now derelict clock in the archway's face had once told the time. It still looked pretty. The stableyard was built round rather a grand semi-circle. Loose-boxes, weedy cobblestones to their doors, were empty – all but one. June's brown hens scratched about on the wide central circle of grass round which horses had been ridden and led and walked and jogged, or made to stand as they should, to be admired by afternoon luncheon guests on Sundays.

Pig in hand, June crossed the yard to open the gate of an old dog-kennel. She put down the pig for a moment while she unlocked a small door and called softly. "Tiny," she called, "Tiny, Tiny." After a prolonged rumble and shuffle and heavy sighing an enormous, pale Labrador bitch came sadly out. Her back was dipped, her muzzle was silver, but she was still on heat. June knew that anything was possible, at any age. She trusted no one and mistrusted one person in particular where Tiny's welfare was concerned. "Sorry, love," she said, "were you lonely?" She clipped a lead to her dog's collar, picked up the shoe-box and proceeded along the flagged passageway, deserted offices on its right and left sides, which led to the kitchen.

Before she was quite inside the kitchen door Jasper turned from assembling his pie to ask coldly: "Any eggs? I need a couple for this pie."

"My little hens are all off laying. I asked you to buy some."

"Too much trouble to write it down?"

"But so I did, Jasper. I did, so I did."

He could see her childish writing on the list as he answered, "I wonder where? Not on *my* list."

"I'm sorry. I thought I did." He could always make her feel uncertain.

"Too busy with that precious sow to consider anybody? Or remember anything?"

"I'm very sorry – I am, really. Look, Jasper, put this little fellow in the low oven for an hour or two, will you?" She held the shoe-box and the new-born out to him.

Jasper showed no surprise. This often happened. Once she had brought in a premature calf in a tea-chest.

"I most certainly shall not. The low oven is waiting for my pie."

"And the smoke blowing towards the mountain? You know the old oven wouldn't warm a plate."

"Why don't you let the little misery die? The sow won't miss him."

"Sweetheart? Ah, she'ld guess. She's such an intelligent pig."

"If you bother me any longer I'll stick him in the hot oven. Roast suckling-pig – delicious."

"Look – don't joke. It's life and death. Give him an hour in the low oven with the door a crack open – and I'll tell you what I'll do – I'll rake every manger in the place for an egg."

Jasper was a little mollified by her offer. "Only an hour, remember. He's not here for the night. I don't want the kitchen stinking of sour milk and pig shit, do I?"

"Of course not. He's too young for that in any case," she knelt down to the oven, solid as a stuffed toy in her Huskies, and pushed the box quietly into the mild heat.

"Eggs now," Jasper said, "and quick, too, or I'll put him in the frigidaire."

She could tell that was only Jasper's idea of a joke, before she and Tiny went out again into the rain.

2 ⚮ *In the Dining-Room*

Late in the evening there came a civilized pause before dinner.
Servantless and silent, the house waited for the proper ceremony
it had always expected and still, in a measure, experienced. The
utter cold of the spring light shrank away from the high paned
windows. A steep distance below the house the river gave up an
evening daze of fog. A lavatory clattered and shushed. Obedient
to its plug and chain the contents went down the perpendicular
drain to the open water. Faint pieces of paper floated among the
starred weeds and iris leaves of flags. Very fat trout swam there.
Once there had been an open, not a covert, drain. Every morning housemaids lifted a grille and sluiced buckets into a sloped
stone spout from which the doings of the night flowed down
their paved way to the river. Not any more, of course. Those
were the days of tin baths in front of bedroom fires, of
mahogany commodes containing pos or bidets, commodes with
three steps for the ascent to bed – the days of lots of money.

This evening the Swifts were in their bedrooms changing, as
they always did, for dinner. Baths they took by turns. The electricity for both bathrooms was a considerable expense. Tonight
was April's bath night. Wrapped in a pale Shetland lace robe she
could just feel the elegant tapping of her brocade mules as she
went back to her bedroom. Her Floris bath essence and sponge
and soap were in a bag, she would not have dreamed of leaving
them behind her. She unlocked her bedroom door to the soothing warmth within. Two bars of the electric fire were not left

burning to be spied upon by others. There were many things of a private and personal nature here too – things such as her dividend headings, which were best kept under lock and key. None of the family knew just how much money April had inherited from her husband, Colonel Grange-Gorman. That was part of the married mystique which floated her on a superior cloud above her single sisters and bachelor brother. It was something to balance her deafness – something beside the beauty she clung to and preserved in its tomb of youth. Nothing gave her less satisfaction than for someone to shout in her ear: "Mrs Grange-Gorman, you don't look a day over sixty." The fifteen years' bonus was nearly an insult. She knew her looks to be miraculously unchanged, she willingly endured tortures in their preservation. Her diets, changing down the years, and the difficulties she experienced in persuading Jasper to cook the brown rice, or the seaweed, to hatch the yoghurt or to put the wheat and other germs where they belonged, provided endless argument. To escape their strictures it was no wonder that she slipped off Weight Watchers now and then. A little extra physical exercise would cancel out pigeon pie, she thought, as she took off ("slipped out of" was her phrase for it) her featherweight dressing-gown and put herself through a five minutes' workout at the open window. In his little basket Tiger shuddered and cuddled lower against the change of temperature. April hated to upset him, but fresh air on the nude body was one of the disciplines. She shut the window, and sighing, lay down on the floor to complete her marathon. After that she stood correctly (as instructed by the directrice of lingerie at Harrods) to pour her tubes of bosoms into the cups provided for them at considerable expense.

Every time April dressed it was a careful robing, a solace. She considered and pushed and moulded every garment to her body's best advantage. In her middle years the discovery of tights had been a particular pleasure. Her legs had never looked more lovely. When she unlocked the great mahogany wardrobe that filled one side of her bedroom she was implanted at once in an imperishable world of beautiful, cared-for clothes. They hung on padded shoulders. They lay in plastic bags on shelves and in drawers. Stuff was one of the pleasures to her, touching it, folding it into shape, a delight. She loved putting on her clothes. Sometimes she would dress superbly for a party, only to make a last minute excuse and stay at home in the isolation of her deafness. She had her solace: "We'll have a teeny-weeny wee one," she would say to Tiger, "we owe it to ourselves, don't we?" She said it this evening as she took the vodka bottle, the tomato juice, the lemon and the celery salt out of the corner fitting wash-hand-stand with the Sheraton shell on its curved cheek. Learning about drink had been one of the few treats in her marriage with Colonel Grange-Gorman.

At her dressing-table she lit a cigarette and sat on, inhaling and sipping. The minutes went pleasantly by as she leaned towards her reflections in the three-sided mirror, sometimes one profile, then the other. Last and longest, with her drink half-finished, she drowned herself contentedly in the contemplation of her mirrored full-face.

Dressed at last, in darkest wool and wearing gold sandals, April looked round her room. She saw with familiar satisfaction the lavish pink tulle draperies flowing at the bedhead, the close roses on the window curtains and all the Lenare photographs of herself that Colonel Grange-Gorman had paid for. There was no picture of him, nor of darling Mummie. Photographs kept too many memories awake. Before she opened her door April picked Tiger out of his basket, sat him on a head-scarf and then in a knitting bag – so hidden, other dogs and the cats would not provoke his proud aggression. She left her room satisfied, armoured for loneliness, ready for pigeon pie.

*   *   *

May's bedroom, a size smaller than April's and facing east, was as strictly tidy as a private room in an expensive nursing-home. Every object was perfectly in place, every picture hung dead straight on the ivy-trellised wallpaper. Gripper's bean-bag was covered by a baby's blue cot blanket – avoiding for him the slightest draught from door or window. His bean-bag didn't smell of dog – it didn't smell of anything except for a whiff of mild flea spray on Saturday mornings. Two hot-water bottles in quilted covers hung from hooks on the door. An electric kettle squatted in waiting by the fireplace. The black marble chimneypiece was devoid of ornaments; strangely, considering the plethora of pretty objects made from seashells, snail-shells or any other material her genius could employ, which crowded every table-top in the room. May was the maker of the beautifully composed patchwork quilt covering her bed. One knew that the blankets beneath it must be cornered and tucked-in as though the bed were made under Sister's eye by the best trainee nurse in a hospital.

Coughing in terrible private luxury, May lit her thirty-first cigarette of the day. For her, cigarettes were as necessary to life as the breathing they interfered with. She inhaled deeply, only laying down her cigarette to pull a white polo-necked sweater over her head. That done, she put the cigarette back in the corner of her mouth and kept it there as she zipped up a long tweed skirt and pushed her feet into a pair of Irish papooties, flat leather slippers sewn by leather thonging to brilliantly patterned socks. The effect was quite daring and interesting in its own way. Still smoking, she brushed up her hair – the same grey as cigarette ash and stained with nicotine like her fingers. But it grew prettily, and sometimes, in the evening, it had the billowing, dissolving quality of smoke. She did nothing about

her malleable, cheesy-looking face, which could have responded
happily under make-up. She had marvellous eyesight – close or
far, pirate's eyes, piercing distances and alert for any advantage.
Her body might have been voluptuous if it had ever been
desired. Now it was a robot, programmed and pressured on its
consolation track of busy occupations.

For years May had been President of the Flower Arrangers'
Guild. Her lectures to a loyal audience were popular and help-
ful, and she would have died of shame if her arrangements in
floral competitions had not excelled all others. She was faithful
in her attendance at meetings of the Irish Countrywomen's
Association where she instructed tirelessly in the art of picture-
making from scraps of tweed and wool, sprigs of heather and
dead scabious – blue for the sky. And these were only the fringes
of her activities. Ceaselessly and usefully occupied, she was far
from being unhappy or depressed. Another quality of hers – disapproval – generated in her an unselfish interest and a com-
pulsion to help, and, if possible, improve, what she saw wrong
or mistaken in her friends' lives or behaviour. For their
problems, skills, failures, gardens, children, or husbands she had
an endless fund of unreliable information and advice.

With May there was a time for everything and never a minute
to be lost. She calculated now that there was plenty of time,
before Jasper's pie was cooked to his meticulous standard of perfection, to give herself an infrequent treat: infrequent because
repetition stole the essential thrill out of anything.

First, she took the key from her locked door and with a
smaller key on the same ring she opened a drawer beneath what
auctioneers call a desirable bachelor's wardrobe. Out of the
drawer she took a narrow, hardboard panel. On this had been
stuck, with astute realism, short-cropped sandy grasses with
narrow paths wandering their ways through them. Even before
noticing the lightly varnished rabbit turds, a witness would

think immeditely of rabbits. The thought would grow to certainty when, after she had laid the panel along the empty
chimney-piece, she placed a second, of similar size and length,
upright against the wall behind it. Wonderfully and accurately
this panel represented the face of a rabbit warren. Where a
labyrinth of exposed tree roots gripped the bank the idea of a
sandy warren was suggested with devoted skill. The dry mosses
and starved ferns were all there, truly observed and worked
with minute dexterity. It was the fulfilment of any child's fas-
cinated curiosity about the habitats of small wild creatures. It
was, somehow, a gross out-doing of Beatrix Potter – except that
here was no Peter Rabbit, no Benjamin Bunny.

May considered her handiwork critically. Her masterpiece
was never finished or perfect to her. She tweaked up some tiny
grass heads. She took a snail-shell out of a matchbox, but shook
her head at its effect. Then, shrugging her shoulders with an
artist's resigned acceptance of the "so much less" that fails the
dream, she unlocked the drawer in her writing-desk. The
drawer was lined with a sheet of cottonwool on which sat and
lay a colony of small china rabbits. Peter Rabbit was here and
Benjamin Bunny, too. A pair of native grey rabbits seemed out
of place. Two whites shared a carrot. A brown and white buck
pushed a mowing-machine. The variety in the colony was endless. May lit another cigarette before handling them dextrously
into position here and there around the grassy paths and sandy
burrows. She did it all with her cropped right hand, flipping
thumb and finger together in a happy gesture derisive of in-
capacity.

When the last rabbit was in its chosen place May took an
object wrapped many times over in bruised tissue paper out of
the drawer. This was not a piece of Victorian china sold, long
ago, as a fairing. The figurine was that of a nurse, or mother, or
rabbit wife in fine china. She stood upright, wore double

flowered skirts, and a bodice, finely laced. Her ears came through an important cap, and, beneath the frill, the rabbit face wore an expression of determination and intent. One long fore-paw held a blue bottle, in the other a spoon was extended menacingly towards nothing. It was Nurse and Worse. Obviously Nurse lacked her companion piece, the patient.

In the drawing-room the sisters waited for Jasper to announce dinner. He repudiated any offer of assistance – of this they were gratefully aware. They sat and sipped inexpensive, though not the cheapest, sherry and talked to their dogs. There was an inconclusive disagreement between them freezing amity, and even mutual remembrance. Every memory contained its jealousy. If, for instance, as happened tonight, some splendid old dance-tune from the 'thirties blared loud enough from the transistor radio to touch a chord in April's hearing she might say, "Oh, Roderick took me to the first night of that show, and then. . . ."

"Yes, you've told us that before –" May interrupted.

". . . then we danced at the Savoy," April finished in her dreamy "other world than you poor things" voice.

"Very often," May shouted the last words of her sentence, putting a stop to that particular nonsense. Protected in her deaf-ness from any necessity to reply, April dipped a finger in her sherry glass and offered the drop on it to Tiger, who shook his head.

Baby June leaned back in her chair. She had changed for dinner, though less elaborately than her sisters. Her clothes were a successful indoor imitation of her outdoor dressing. She wore her off-white evening Husky, a blue Viyella shirt, clean jeans and faded espadrilles. One hand was stretched like a star-fish over Tiny's ear, as she sat contented and tired after her day's midwifery. She had spent the day with Christy Lucey. In his company she was a world away from her sisters' and Jasper's fractious living. A cheese sandwich for lunch (while Christy ate the beef sandwiches she had cut for him), and no tea (watching over Sweetheart at a critical moment) had left her hungry for pigeon pie, and subject to the present effect of a glass of sherry.

May, turning disgustedly from April, said with kind officiousness: "I must have that shirt you're wearing for the washing-machine on Monday. It's *too* filthy – you've worn it every evening since Christmas."

June pulled for a moment on Tiny's ear before answering: "Blue for Baby June. 'Blue's your colour' Mummie always said. Don't you remember?"

May was silent. Remembering Mummie was in poor taste. Forget love and grief and pain. Life had gone on. Life should be filled, as she filled it, with useful activities and with creations such as the *Garya eliptica* under the Chippendale mirror. April and June were indifferent to its beauty – presently she would bring it, quite casually, into the conversation and force their notice and admiration. For the moment it belonged only to her, and with it came the scent from the narcissi, fortified by the presence of their bodies and breath – certainly not by the distant heat of a very small fire in a very big grate.

"Well, lots of time for a cigarette, I expect," May opened her case, absentmindedly offering it to June, who didn't smoke and to April, who shook her head and coughed. "Only those filthy asthma fags for you, I forgot. Thank goodness I can enjoy a normal cigarette." She lit one impatiently, and shook out the match. "Come on, Jasper! What can he be doing? We're not having six courses, are we, Grips?" Having quelled all response from the sisters, she turned to her dog for an answer, then, in a movement of explicit exasperation, she jumped to her feet as Jasper came into the room.

This was obviously pleasing to Jasper. To prolong the delay he rather sedately poured out for himself a glass of sherry which he did not want. "Your pig delayed me rather," he said to June.

"He's happy with Sweetheart now, poor lamb," she answered. "And he didn't do anything in the oven, now did he?"

"Not much."

May screamed: "You had a pig in the oven with the pigeon pie? It can't be true!"

"You're not compelled to eat the pie, you know," Jasper told her as he held the door open for his sisters. Waiting courteously for them to pass through he looked distinguished and charming, standing there in his blue velvet dinner jacket, white silk shirt and dark foulard scarf, pulled through a signet ring – all a bit greasy and spotted from kitchen work. He never demeaned his masculinity with an apron.

In the dining-room there was silence for a time. The pie was excellent beyond words. The pigeon breasts married beautifully to the beef from the dogs' dinners, the old rashers of bacon and the eggs. A pile of purple sprouting kale sat on the hot-plate to one side of the pie and pommes-de-terre Anna on the other – all three dishes largely depleted when the ladies had helped themselves.

It was not until smaller second helpings and a salad were being eaten that conversation began. June's Labrador started it off. She heaved herself up from her worn goatskin rug and came to sit between June and May. The gesture of her pale, sad head, as she laid it along June's thigh said: Am I wanted? Then, with benign stupidity, she raised her head towards May.

May put her handkerchief and her napkin to her nose. "You do spoil that animal rotten. Why can't she stay in her corner? Question which smells the worst – your dog or that ghastly goat-skin?"

"Ah, poor old Nancy! She was a great old girl," June glanced reminiscently towards the last of Nancy.

"Send her back to bed. Tiny! to your basket! Dogs like discipline. Look at Gripper, never moves."

Hearing his name spoken, Gripper nipped lightly from his neat basket.

"Tiny's not the only undisciplined one, is she?" Jasper said.

"What can you expect? That old bitch is still half on heat. She ought to be shut up. Out of doors. And her breath smells appalling. All her teeth should come out."

"Your little heart wouldn't stand the anaesthetic, would it, Tiny? No it wouldn't." June spoke and answered for her friend.

"Much better done without an anaesthetic."

"Who says?" June sounded fierce.

"David Doherty says."

"The worst vet in Ireland," Jasper joined in.

"You prefer useless Bryan Brendan, don't you, April? Don't you?"

"Butter, please," April answered peaceably.

Jasper gave up his question: "Rather luck, getting hold of this saltless butter."

"Did you say toothless butter?"

"She must have heard something you said," June put in gently.

"Actually, I heard everything you said. I can, when people don't shout. And I'm not going near any dentist. My teeth are quite perfect, thank you very much." She opened her mouth to show them. They all turned their heads away, and there was silence until Jasper broke it with a curious cry: "What *are* you doing, May? Picking the cucumber out of your salad!"

"You rather forgot my ulcer – I can't eat cucumber."

"Can't eat this, can't eat that. Why must you have such a lower-middle-class stomach?"

"Perhaps it has something to do with your idea of Cordon Bleu cooking."

"It takes imagination and a reasonable digestion to appreciate good cooking."

"You don't usually cook cucumber, do you?" The argument drifted into silence.

Pudding time came. Baby rhubarb and rice cream with a vaporous suggestion of nutmeg.

"I hope the rhubarb isn't too acid for your ulcer." Jasper eyed May's lavish helping.

"My ulcer must take its chance. I've got to know what this rhubarb is like. New stools, and I grew them myself, personally. Stable manure, straw, boxes, pots – everything on a wheelbarrow. No help from Christy Lucey – much too busy composting your camellias or on some far less important job for Baby. *Most* probably doing nothing and doing it well, as usual."

"The day you were after him to cover rhubarb was the same day he was taking Sweetheart to the boar." June had the whole memory of the illiterate.

"You spoil him ridiculously."

"Yes. And now we have nine little pigs." In defence of Tiny or of Christy Lucey June was seldom short of words.

"He's not altogether a bad sort of fellow, as they go," Jasper said, "but as we're on the subject, Baby, do you have to use my cling film for his sandwiches? Wouldn't a paper bag do?"

"Yes, or newspaper," May struck in. "And why do you give him sandwiches? On top of his wages and insurance *and* VAT?"

"It's cheaper than him wasting the day cycling home to his mother for his dinner."

"Why can't his mother make his sandwiches?"

"Oh, God! And she crushing eighty."

"She must have had him at a very advanced age," April calculated. She often heard some irrelevant thing not addressed to herself.

"It's not just a question of sandwiches," May continued. "What about the broken shutes? Can't get a wink of sleep on a rainy night. Take care of your shutes and your roof will take care of itself – that's what I've always heard."

"Easily said when we had men and ladders at Durraghglass," Jasper reminded her. "And speaking of ladders, Baby, I see Christy has taken the only sound ladder on the place to close a gap."

"That was the day Jilly was bulling."

"She's had her calf now, and the ladder's still in the gap."

"I'll remind him, Jasper," June answered as forgetfulness settled purposefully on her memory.

"And what about the overdraft?" May scooped up the last of her rhubarb. "I saw Mr Love in church last Sunday and he gave me a very funny look."

"Mr Love is far too nice a man for that sort of thing," April put in.

"Could we leave the Bank Manager until after dinner? I must concentrate on my pudding. I made a few interesting little changes in the receipt." Jasper never said "recipe".

"Is there nothing in your life except cooking?"

"Well, yes. Eating for one thing."

"Cooking – eating – reading garden catalogues – fiddling in your wilderness while basically there's something ghastly constantly happening at this moment of time." She took a swig at her wine. "Brown and Kerry's account has been in three times. And for this" – she put down her empty glass – "Right? So what?"

"Drink rather less, perhaps."

"Jasper, we have to eat and drink to live. And we have to live here together – Mummie left it like that."

"Yes, all right. I do the cooking. Baby does the farming. Things go on . . . What do you do?"

"Everything."

"What's everything?"

"Who grew this rhubarb? Who netted the purple sprouting kale? Who does all the hoovering? And if money wasn't being flung away on Christy Lucey we could have a daily woman three times a week."

"No." Jasper's tone was adamant. "No," he repeated. "She might start cleaning things up, and she'ld expect tea and biscuits."

"Tea and biscuits – what I love," June said enviously.

"Besides," Jasper enlarged on his objections, "she might talk to me."

"Talk about you and the filth of your kitchen, more likely," May said.

"Perhaps. If I gave her the chance. But shan't's the word." Jasper spoke with unruffled decision.

"I'ld give her tea in a thermos," May promised.

"Do that – I know your tea. She'll be gone in a week."

"In any case, how could I run the place without Christy?" June put in, rather belatedly aware of a danger.

"I'll tell you," May seized the opening. "Let the land on the eleven months' system – right? Sell the stock. Pay off the overdraft – you follow me? And sack Christy Lucey. Are you with me?"

"Sack Christy? And the young horse just about going right?" June's protest was torn from her.

"Well, yes, I suppose we may have to think about it seriously. After all, what do we get out of two hundred and fifty acres? Two eggs from fifty hens." Jasper liked teasing everybody. Even Baby June – at times more especially Baby June. She was vulnerable, and her provincial way of speaking annoyed him.

Of course the village convent school had not given her the same advantages his other sisters had enjoyed at Heathfield. Beastly as they were, at least they spoke English. He looked across at June, solid and elderly in her white Husky, and he could never forget. Bitterly as always he linked her with the accident to his eye – his filthy blind eye.

June, aged seven, his friend and companion in outdoor sports, had shot it out with her air-gun, while aiming at a robin on the clothes line. It had all been a great tragedy and a scandal as well. The bird had been May's pet robin. The crime of shooting robins diverted immediate anxiety from Jasper's festering eye. By the time bathing in boracic lotion failed in its efficacy it was too late for the most exclusive and expensive oculists to save the sight, or the eye. While he was being hurried from one surgeon to another, pain changed him to her and, in his fear of more pain, he accused her helplessly and with an unknowing depth that was nearly hatred.

June had been his pride and joy and joke. A tiny creature, her baby size was made accountable for her backwardness in learning to read and write, and created drama out of her dash and brilliance with her pony. He (curse the day) had taught her to shoot. They lay on furze-grown banks together, and from such secret hide-outs she was a deadly shot on a sitting rabbit or a perching rook. She was the Baby wonder, and mostly his creation. How could he have guessed that she would fire at a robin? A robin – perish the thought!

That was all over, of course. Gone and forgotten long ago. But tonight, and at other times, some vague animosity possessed him. He felt like despoiling her confidence a little – just a little. She was so immersed in the place, in Sweetheart's litter, in the brown eggs or the lack of brown eggs, in her cross Jersey cows, in the *Farmers' Journal* that Christy translated slowly for her dyslexic struggle (she had quite a time maintaining that she could read easily). And, beyond all other interests with her, came the series of awkward young horses that she and Christy broke and civilised and sold, sometimes well, sometimes at a loss. Even without being pinched and goaded by May, he could see the ridiculously uneconomic side of her absurd loving methods of farming

Just lately a new plan had been running through Jasper's mind as to the conduct of the small estate in which they all had a share. It was an idea that rambled rather than ran, coming far behind more accessible and exciting inspirations in his kitchen, in his garden of rare outmoded herbs, in his tree nursery, or among the camellias flowering already in their sheltering bays of ponticum rhododendron and Portugal laurel. These were his refuges from any more complicated responsibilities. Jasper was lazy – "It may never happen" was his favourite motto. Whether or not he brought it to fruition, he must hold this plan, with all its complications, inviolate from the girls.

"Isn't it time for doggie-dins?" he said. But he waited patiently until April had realized that dinner was at an end and rose, gracefully as always, almost flowing to her feet. She went across to a side table where three dishes, in sizes for the three bears, waited for the darlings. She picked up the smallest dish and looked searchingly at its contents. "My woofie-woof's dreadfully hungry and there doesn't seem to be any meat in his dins," she said.

June didn't criticize Tiny's dinner, or even look at it closely, there was too much on her mind. But May moved in to the matter at once: "Where's the beef I scraped all the blue mould off and left chopped up in their soup and brown bread?"

Jasper gave her a nearly rat-like grin: "You've just eaten it," he said. "I put it in the pie."

"Ah, don't mind him," June felt as usual that she must keep on Jasper's right side. "He's only joking."

"*I* believe him," May said stonily.

"And you'ld be right." Jasper rose to his elegant height. "To the sword with the lot of you is what I say and I must get on with the washing up. Then early bed, two hot-water bottles, and a good book." Delighting in May's screams and cries of protest and disgust, he stacked a tray with plates, dishes, spoons and glasses, put it in the lift and from there set off downstairs to the kitchen and the washing up, confident that no one would follow him. Some time previously he had bought, as a particular extravagance and personal treat, a washing-up machine. He wasn't over fond of it – slightly nervous in fact – but he would not have dreamed of allowing a sister to touch it. May, who would have understood and corrected its every whim, was particularly excluded. If he was found at the old-world sink with his hands in Lemon Quix he let it be understood that the new toy had its moods and disorders and awaited an expert from Dublin.

3 🖋 Bedtime

After dinner June was beset by a different worry. Had she remembered to switch on the farrowing light with its faint spread of warmth above Sweetheart and her litter? She had better make certain. Although longing for bed, she pulled on her gum-boots, took her dirty anorak off its hook, clipped a lead to Tiny's collar (you never could tell, she might take a fancy). With a mammoth red torch in her hand she went out of the hall door, delaying for a minute or two on the gravel while Tiny, looking sad as dogs do, prepared to perform her most important act of the evening. As June waited, the sounds of water came clear and insistent about her from the circling mountain river below the house, but custom had deafened her to it; it was as un-noticeable as the square-paned shadow that the kitchen window threw up the grassy area bank, to flatten on the level ground where she stood. The lighted window reminded her that Jasper was still at work. And what was he planning about Christy? Something drastic or he would never side with May. She could protect Tiny from any ugly plan of May's, but to keep Christy, if money was involved, would prove a difficult matter. June had no bank account. Her handwriting was too strange for cheques. She only counted as a charge and burden on the estate, although she worked harder and more faithfully for its life than anyone else in the family.

June was commending Tiny for her regular habits when May came out of the house with Gripper. "And where are you off to,

Baby?" she asked. "Do keep that bitch away from Grips. It's so unfair on him." Her tone changed. "When you've done your duties we're off to bedsibyes, aren't we, old man?"

"Aren't you mad early?"

"Jasper's dinner was madly late – right? So now it's just about bedtime. Right?"

"Right, all right. I'm just going to have a look at Sweetheart."

"The good Catholic boy couldn't possibly manage that, could he?"

"He's paid for a day's work, May. Not a night's work."

"I should have thought his huge wage could cover anything. Wait, Gripper, *wait* – do take that bitch away."

June flashed on her big torch and the sisters went in opposite directions. Their manner of walking was as different as their natures. June accommodated her steps to Tiny's shuffle and mild interests. May's neat and solid behind and out-turned feet promised practical execution of her set purposes. Now it was a rat-hunt for Gripper – anything to divert his mind from thoughts of Tiny, even if it delayed their bed-time.

She went round the corner of the house to where broken terrace steps led down the falling slope to the river. On one side of the steps Jasper had kept careful clearings for azaleas and camellias – here there was a civilized courtliness from other days – although the grass was roughly cut where once there had been mown lawn. On the other side of the steps weeds and nettles, long grasses and Portugal laurels grew, darker than the night. Into the heart of this covert Gripper disappeared, Tiny forgotten. The hunting lust was on him now.

May lit a cigarette and waited, attentive to his sharp excited voice – obviously he had found other game than rats in that close covert. As she stood, solidly planted, patient for her dog's pleasure, a fox crossed over the open space between the thicket of darkness and the grove Jasper kept inviolate from the encroaching deserts of present days. It was a small dark fox and lame as well; a vixen, dark as a crow, marauding from some stony mountain earth. She stopped for a moment, stilled with the calculating confidence hunted foxes show, before she slipped from sight, a creature apart, of another world, a fairy world.

Again, a fox. May coughed deeply, turned her head and spat. The horrid gesture only cleared her memory. Tonight she flushed and suffered as she had when romance first passed by, leaving her apart in her perpetual fight to be as others, better than others, never to be mortified as she had been on that bright day. This evening the past event, untouched by reason because it was too ridiculous, existed for her, fresh as ever in its cruelty. Leda, who had slipped from their lives as completely as the fox that had crossed her path tonight, was at its core.

Tonight, waiting for the dog, looking for him through the double darkness of the laurel grove, that past morning was present for her as though she was still seven years old. Seven was her age when Leda first came to Durraghglass for the summer holidays, the time when Leda and April shut her out from their giggling best-friendship. She hung and listened on the outskirts of their talk, longing to know more about the cream cakes and chocolate of Austria. In love with beautiful Leda, she heard waltz music playing. . . . . Now she was in her secret house again, her house built of bent laurel boughs in the heart of the laurels. In its neat lavatory, intent on a quick out-of-doors pee, she had unbuttoned her white cotton drawers from their anchorage to her liberty bodice when she heard two voices in the sunlight and, through the leaves, had a distant broken vision of Leda and April coming down the terrace steps. They walked in a very ladylike grown-up way. Leda, always so trusted and capable, carried Baby June. They set her

down between them on a blue blanket, and played Mummie and
Nannie, spreading out their skirts on the warm clipped grass.
Far off in her laurels May was possessed by an immense wish to
join them, welcome or not, to belong to the group so near and so
divided from her. She had burst out of the thicket and started her
run towards them when she was brought to a standstill by
a spancelling of her knees, then of her ankles: it was her white
cotton drawers, hanging like two balloons below her navy-blue
skirt. And they had seen. And they were laughing at her –
laughing till they fell over, rolled on the grass with Baby June,
bit their handkerchiefs and screamed again with laughter.

Trembling in a hot brew of embarrassment, May went back
again to hide in her dark house, utterly ashamed and affronted
because Leda had laughed at her. Fumbling with the buttons on
her bodice, her hand impotent to join them to the button-holes
on her drawers, her love changed, a septic wound remaining.
Hidden and comfortless she watched them through the laurel
leaves, heads together, talking, talking. She watched until she
saw Leda pick up Baby June, who wanted to practice her
crawling. She saw a small object fall, unnoticed by the others,
from the baby's clutch and heard her furious howl. Baby June
was still howling as she was carried up the steps. Through the
clamour Leda's Nannie voice came clearly to May in her hiding-
place. . . . . "Icky baby shutty-uppy or Leda pinch her icky
botty." Baby June screamed suddenly. Leda laughed and
smothered her with kisses.

When she knew she was alone May came out of the laurels
into the sunlight. She crossed over the terrace steps to the place
where the girls had sat. Smelling round the site like a small
animal, she found what Baby June had played with and
dropped. Her hand pounced down, her thumb and finger
gripped pliers-like round Leda's mascot and treasure. It was a
fox, a fox from Austria so small and perfectly made it could have

fitted in a match-box. The fox had a name – Fritz-Max-Hans. Immediately May knew what she was going to do with him. She set out for her garden, the third of four box-edged plots inside the walled kitchen gardens. She dug a hole between the fairy-rose bush and the mustard and cress. When she had buried Fritz-Max-Hans she felt better, stronger. Even tonight she was happy to remember she had yielded nothing. She had kept her own reserves when, late on that evening Leda, her darling, aware of a day of pain and sulks, came to sit on the edge of her bed, to say: "You know, don't you? Leda loves little May." Leda took her hand gently. She took the wrong hand. Her fingers explored it, more curious than caressing. May took her right hand out of Leda's and gave her the left – Leda patted it absently and went away.

Confirmed in her sense of defenceless outrage, June walked along the familiar wet track to the farmyard.

To her left the white cherry blossom flowered smokily in the half-darkness. On her right a grove of laurel and rhododendron hid the lean old house and its troubles. In the close shelter she heard the dive and chuckle of a bird, surprised out of its sleep. As June smiled and listened, and then walked on, the true importances of her life – and tonight Sweetheart and her litter were of first importance – came to comfort her, in her thought for their necessities, and her power to give them relief.

The farmyard was darker than its approaches – a well of darkness inside its high broken walls. A keyhole of starless sky showed through the empty belfry topping the archway over the gate. Water dripped quietly and constantly from broken shutes into the black depths within buildings. Manure, old and fresh, fumed peacefully in the cold air. June went her uncritical way, between pools and lesser puddles, towards Sweetheart's shed. A small light beamed weakly through the top of the door. The farrowing light must be failing. Anxiety came back to June and she hurried forward.

"Is that you, Miss Baby?" It was Christy Lucey's voice, sounding to her full and happy with its assurance of help and companionship.

"Back again, Christy? Jesus, child, good man you!"

"Ah, no distance, Miss – I wasn't real happy over the old light. I got a fizzing out of it, and a murmur. Would she be as good without it, I wonder would she?"

"I wonder would she?" June echoed.

"My mother says she would," Christy delivered a statement from his mother – she was his oracle in almost everything.

June pushed open the low half-door and joined Christy. Together they turned the light of their torches (his was a bicycle lamp) on the long pale sow and her piglets, pink as the insides of wet sea shells.

"The small fellow is doing great now," Christy commended the frail runt of the litter.

"You couldn't beat the old Aga," June said.

"And I made five decades and sent up a short one to St Francis for him." Christy's reproof was unintentional, but June recognised it.

"St Francis should be *it*," she agreed, allowing credit where it belonged. They had a second agreement over the fizz and murmur in the farrowing light. It would be safest to turn it off, leaving June's powerful torch to shine down from the cleft, hollowed high up through the wall to hold a lantern, or a bottle, or just to let in a shaft of light.

"My mother says she'ld be as good without too much of that old electricity in the air," Christy quoted his mother again as he closed and bolted the top and bottom halves of the door and stood with June and Tiny and his leaning bicycle, all together in the deepening night. "I'll light you back to the house," he offered. He mounted his bicycle, balancing and wavering along beside her until she was through the dark trees and laurels. Then he put on speed and rode away.

June ran both her hands lovingly down Tiny's dipped back. In her gesture she seemed to be acknowledging all the solace that came to her through Christy Lucey's usefulness and companionship in everything that mattered most. "Four miles here, Tiny," she said aloud, "and four miles home. Four and four is eight, isn't that right, Tiny?"

In her pleasure at tonight's devotion to duty June was happy to forget how often Christy might neglect his work in hand at Durraghglass to cycle home, obedient to some trifling necessity of his mother's, or, perhaps, to attend the celebration of the Mass on some obscure saint's day. In spite of these negligences, usually noted by May, Christy's value to June was immeasurable. Eager and ignorant he had come to her, and she had schooled him and put manners on his horsemanship, and skill and knowledge into his stable management. Everything that was expert in him came from June, as his dark, nervous good looks came from his mother; but his unshakeable nerve – due to lack of imagination coupled with unquestioning trust in his favourite saints – was his own. This nerve and courage June had not taught or transferred, and the reason for this shamed and distressed her. In middle age, and after many falls, both had left her. "But, Jesus, child," she told herself, "keep it quiet. Play the buggers along." "The buggers" was her collective name for her family, or for any group unsympathetic towards her.

Much of her alienation from her sisters stemmed from those early days after Jasper's accident, when the two older girls were not displeased to see the baby wonder toppled from the importance that her abilities, her tiny size, and her funny ways had given her with both Mummie and Jasper. After the accident, if she asked a question, the answer was short and cold. If she made a joke unsmiling faces told her laughter was unseemly. Under orders from Mummie, they were silent about her guilt, but their eyes showed what they thought of her: murderess of robins and blinder of brothers.

Her refuge from the chill and change was in the stableyard. The two stable lads Marty Cullinane and Robbie Ryan had no consciousness of her guilt, only of her bad luck and her misfortune. They had, of course, a proper respect for the disaster, sending up occasional prayers for Master Jasper's recovery, but their sympathy and warmth went out to Baby June.

Her happy hours were spent in the stables or on the farm. Cats bearing kittens in the hay-loft, squealing mares in season paying mysterious visits to the stallion and back again, no one explained these things to her, but she gathered all essential knowledge by listening to vague comments. After all, who wouldn't guess what the bantam cock was up to? Once she stood on a wooden bucket and looked over the door of a loose-box at a mare foaling, absorbing facts without any hidden excitement. Always, her pony and other people's unruly ponies were there to be got ready for children's classes in local shows. In those days before pony clubs she learned from the lads how to trim out a pony and plait it up; how best to catch a judge's eye in the ring. Often on a dark evening she would sit on Marty Cullinane's knee in the saddle-room, embroidering a tray-cloth for Mummie, leaning back in his arms and yawning. At other times the lads cleaned their tack and talked about greyhound racing, while a coal fire burned in a small iron stove, and an oil-lamp hanging on the wall filled the place with the shadows of saddles.

All this was clouded in half remembrance, but it had shaped June's whole life at Durraghglass. For her education she had never gone further than the convent school in the village.

Mummie was too conscious of her disability in reading or writing to send her away to that famous school for the upper classes that educated her elder daughters. Being what was called "a little slow" was a more subtle deformity than May's hand, April's growing deafness, or Jasper's one-eyed state.

Mummie spent herself in lavishing comfort and protection and absolute love on all her children. They must have only the best, and the best cost money. In spending money and selling off land when the banks got nasty, she was regardless of future years. Although she had longed for their happy marriages, and often visualised such blissful states, only April's – brief and perhaps not ideal – had consummated that wish. Through the years she was contented and fulfilled to have them round her, loving and subservient to her loving will; adorably distressed (hide it with what confidence they might) by her long, cruel illness. The word she never spoke, "cancer", goes slowly with the elderly. For her own sake and for theirs she refused its reality. But there were many times when she could envy their father that lone shooting accident on the mountain, where he had been found dead with a brace and a half of grouse in his game bag and an empty whiskey flask in the heather beside him. Her silences had been as protective as chain-mail against any murmuring of rumour about his death: no other cause for it than accident was considered. They all sustained the legends and memories of him – a marvellous shot, a brilliant horseman, and April had his looks. Darling Mummie, in her many widowed years, engrossed herself entirely in her children's lives, ignoring while protecting their various incapacities with such considered and perfect tactfulness that she possessed them as though she was within the cage of their ribs, measuring the beat of their hearts.

June never forgot how Mummie had refrained from blaming her about Jasper's eye – only a mournful head-shaking over the robin that escaped. She remembered, too well, those dreadful returns from the oculists' to Durraghglass – Jasper silent and avoiding her, Mummie cheerfully despairing. When, a few years later, even the kind nuns treated her as slightly abnormal (dyslexia not thought of then), Mummie had been wordless in her acceptance of another maimed child. Forget all that, let her get on with her riding.

The baby wonder was provided with ponies to show, and ponies to hunt and sell. Later came the years of that wonderful little mare Magic Flute, by Sorcerer out of Bird Song. Together she and June became the terror of every Ladies' Race in the South of Ireland. When Magic injured a fetlock so badly that she had to be destroyed it was June, her heart breaking, who led the mare out for the vet and the humane killer, and saw her drop. Such close contacts with the hard realities to be met, endured and accepted, gave June a stoic ability in her conduct of stables or farm. She was a true part of the land, but her farm accounts, almost a tally of stones, were intelligible to herself alone. She could, however, translate them with minute accuracy for the income tax forms, over which Jasper fought a sick delaying action with the accountants. It was her illiteracy that gave June a peasant's clarity of memory. She forgot nothing. The past was hers, and its voices. Only the future, with its hazards and terrors, ran back and forwards through her mind, the mind of a cute little animal.

"Bedtime now," she said to Tiny, who slobbered affectionately along beside her, "and ready for the fray in the morning – isn't that it, love?" She left the cold night for the cold house, for her bedroom and its kettle and cocoa, its blue hot-water bottle and its blue pyjamas. "Blue for you, Baby .... Mummie always said."

*   *   *

In the kitchen Jasper, too, boiled up his nightly kettle. While it simmered to a boil, he opened a crack of the window so that Mister Minkles, that knight errant, might get back to bed when the fancy took him. Still waiting, while the Aga gave out its slow heat, he looked around. Unperturbed at the waste of disorder he had as though spewed and forgotten. The white fish mites, that came out from warmth and darkness to speed about the floor, were a matter of indifference to him. The same indifference ignored the floor they darted on. He simply did not see the tiles, blurred with kitchen and outdoor dirt, nor did he smell the cats, nesting in their cardboard boxes. His mind was, for the moment, fixed on the bedtime drink he was about to create – in the most trivial cooking task he looked only for perfection. Now it was Complan; Complan in the one large cup remaining from the Good's breakfast set, decorated with wandering violets. In any other cup Complan would have seemed undrinkable. He added a strip of orange peel (cut thin as lemon zest for a Martini) to the white paste mixed in his cup; then the careful stream of boiling water; after that a capful of whiskey, a coffee-spoonful of brown sugar and a very light grating of nutmeg. Every night he reached the same exact repetition.

When he had filled two hot-water bottles, bed and Hillier's catalogues, old and new, seeds and shrubs, were waiting to lull his mind from daily unfulfilled and irritating responsibilities. No dog followed him up the three flights of stairs to the level of the old nurseries where he slept. On his way he switched off all the lights that his unthinking, uncaring sisters had left on. He looked forward to bed. Bed was the only place where he cared to take the patch off his blind eye and wear his spectacles comfortably. Tonight he was frustrated in his pleasures. The bulb in his bedside light gave out a wavering click and died. Furious with annoyance, he decided against the agonizing decision necessary before going downstairs to find a new bulb.

Rather than do that, he lay sleepless in the dark, while documents relating to secrets of his own and matters to confer with Brother Anselm were scattered in his special disorder on the tables to the right and left of his pillows. Tomorrow would be another day, and he could do something about everything then.

Bedtime for April meant a continued discipline. It was her pleasure to rule her body so that she might dress it for her private eye's delight – her clothes must retain their elegance and meaning. She loved to feel beautiful stuffs in her hands and would buy lengths of wool or silk that pleased her though they might lie for years, folded away on a shelf in her cupboard, before the idea for their proper employment came to her.

When she had patted nourishing creams into face, neck, arms, feet – a different kind for each and all expensive – April put on her crushed cambric nightdress (she hated nylon) and, smelling sweetly and freshly, got into bed. Pushing Tiger gently away from the hot-water bottle and down to her feet, she leant into her pillows and sat sipping and burping her way through a health drink before picking up *Mansfield Park* from the top of the po cupboard.

April had got into the way of reading Jane Austen less for pleasure than as a counteraction to those French books and Chinese and Egyptian prints and pictures which Barry liked her to study before he tried to follow out their instructions and illustrations in bed. After his death she never knew how to get rid of his books – too thick to burn and quite inappropriate for Oxfam – so they remained, parcelled up in their dreadful privacy on the top shelf of her wardrobe. Hidden there they were as lost to her memory as were any occasional gleams of pleasure in past experience. Happily now, she knew the value of her own bodily privacy. She even enjoyed the privacy of her deafness, ignoring what she did not want to hear, even when she happened to hear it. In the same way she could contentedly block remembrance.

One thing from which her memory never skated away was darling Mummie's delight in her marriage – a marriage with a man from the right family, popular in the Regiment, who went well to hounds. How alertly in the courting days Mummie had protected her deafness, answering while April smiled. Silence did not seem to matter during the engagement. Barry only wanted to look and kiss, with gentleness and restraint and a sort of wonder.

April herself had been in a trance of wonder. At that time marriage was the enviable and only true goal. Every morning she woke with something like birdsong in her heart as she realized again: I'll be married, I'll be married. There was absolute joy, too, over the assembling of the trousseau Mummie and she bought, with unconsidered spending. Its culmination was a bridal gown of such plain beauty that her looks shone out undiminished by decoration when, her veil lifted, she walked down the flower-filled aisle on the arm of her handsome (if forty-five year-old) husband. Behind her came May, settling the train to rights with a gloved thumb and finger and marshalling the pages and June in a furious whisper. The bridesmaids' dresses did not really become either May or June – Mummie had decided that nothing must draw a moment's attention away from the star of the day. All the same, her own dress, muted mauve and pink with a soft plumage of clipped ostrich feathers, had cost more than April's. Mummie's tears were pretty, too – everything she did was full of understanding and charm. Later on April was to wonder whether those brief words on the loving obligations of marriage – "It's a thing men do. You won't like it" – might have been more explicit. April had thought she knew exactly what men did, and rather looked forward to it. Now, years later, and knowing better, she pressed her back contentedly against her hot-water bottle and putting down her empty glass and Jane Austen she picked up a leather-bound notebook (she never handled anything ugly or cheap). The pages of the book were filled with lists – lists of china, silver, small period pieces of furniture, craftsmen's samples, baby chairs, clocks, French watches. She turned the pages slowly, giving careful thought before marking some entries with a cross and ticking off others. Business completed, she laid aside her notebook and, with Tiger fumbling contentedly at her feet, she re-opened *Mansfield Park* wondering, not for the first time, whether Fanny Price had not been rather more than an idiot to refuse Henry. Perhaps so. Perhaps not. Henry might easily have turned out to be an earlier Grange-Gorman. She poked Tiger with her toe and read on peacefully.

4 ⚜ Separate Pursuits

Early the next morning, having decided to lecture on rather abstruse Japanese lines to her flower ladies, May walked for miles along the river in search of willow with only the most immature pussies. She was able to combine her quest with exercise for Gripper. Gripper only liked walks when he was going home. He cheered up when May turned upwards and homewards towards the mountains – ravished to blue by the sunlight, turning to slate under the shadows of passing clouds. Nearing home, she delayed to nip a few branches from Jasper's nut grove. He was religious in his protection of his young filberts, so she had to use stealth and care in their pilfering. Before she reached the gates of Durraghglass (gates of spare ironwork always standing open owing to the delicacy of their rusted hinges) she saw Jasper and, quick as lightning, she masked the embryo filberts with embryo willow.

Jasper, who at that hour should have been cooking luncheon, was standing by the roadside, his dark head illuminated by the sunshine and unstirred by the mountain air. The shape of his hair survived even the scissors of the local barber. In spite of his bare head he looked, as he always did, the idle squire. No blue jeans for him. He wore old, but knife-edged, whipcords and a mountain-coloured, faintly checked tweed coat – chosen by Mummie, how many years ago? Little as she liked him, May, with her artist's eye, recognised and admitted Jasper's undeniable chic and style. But now it was his companion who stirred her curiosity, malign and vaguely disapproving. She nodded a cool good morning as she passed by.

Jasper had been absorbed in lively conversation with a white-habited monk, a handsome young man from the silent brother-hood of a Cistercian monastery. The brothers of the Order owned land they had rescued from the mountain. Their farm marched with the fields of Durraghglass. These fields, their quarterings fenced by walls loosely built of stones picked long ago off the poor mushroom and thistle-grown grassland, con-trasted miserably with the well-husbanded property of the monastery.

Walking away and still listening attentively to the voices behind her, May, although she could not distinguish a word that was said, was aware of a tone in Jasper's speech, an indulgent, less than serious note very different from his usual sharp inter-changes with his family. Suddenly she knew what it was his voice suggested and recalled. That was how it had sounded when he and Mummie talked together – talked happily and con-fidentially about some interest from which the girls were ex-cluded. May called Gripper back to her. She felt the need of company. She took a cigarette from her case and zipped a flame from her lighter, sheltering it masterfully against the breeze.

When Brother Anselm had gone back towards the mountain, the wind flapping his belted habit against bare legs, Jasper stood for a minute, slightly bent, elderly hands on his stick, evidently contented and unhurrying. The nervous rigidity with which he opposed his sisters' least harmful, but always annoying, projects seemed melted from him. Then, a suspicion overtaking him, he turned back along the road and went into his nut-grove to find out what May had cut from the young trees in the sheltering bay he had made between alders and wild hazel. Sure enough, he found where she had ignorantly clipped and stolen from one of his choicer subjects. With the ball of his thumb held close over the wounded bark he stood, resentful and dispirited as he had been once before. In familiar places memories are never absolved – they contain perpetual unkindness.

This morning the subdued unchanged voice of the river, running low beneath where he stood, was the same as on that summer evening when he and Daddy, escaping together the awful clutch of school-term tomorrow – Mummie and the girls sewing on name-tapes and packing goodies in the tuck-box – had gone down to the river with their rods – men together, seriously considering the right fly for the water. Then Leda came running after them down the terrace steps . . . . "Take me too – I want to watch," she was calling. She looked like a foreign doll in a box – blue and white striped dress and a little muslin apron. "Please let me," she said. She had never been taught to leave men alone on their sporting occasions. She was green bones in a grave now, but that evening she stood, twisting the ends of her yellow hair, and pleaded, and won.

Again he felt sullen and bereft as he had when Daddy, leaving all the best pools to him, said: "I'll fish the wood stream. You come with me, Leda." Why the wood stream, when there were nearer and far better beats? But they left him. They had gone into the woods together; where the river ran, brown and slow through the close screens of alders and hazels.

Familiar places, keeping their constant hold against forgetfulness, he sighed briefly for that awkward, handsome boy fishing companionless through a long summer evening. Then, back in his present ageing self, he turned his attention towards luncheon, and how little he might cook for his sisters. His mind failed to clinch into anything fully – absurd income tax demands, the annoyance of leaking gutters, these things were the present, and by nature he lacked resolution to combat them.

Unfulfilled dreams suited him better, such as the one he shared with Brother Anselm. His only practical legitimate peace lay in cooking. Using his hands and his brain and its inventions he could forget most things – even Mummie's loss and death – although, for that, memory had no abstinence.

When he quickened his steps towards home and the oblation of cooking, the change in gait to a more free and youthful rate of walking sent his newly roused memory back again to that other world in time when he had been in the inconsolable age of fifteen . . . beautiful April eighteen? nineteen? . . . May – his dislike prevented consideration of May at any age . . . Baby, who had so lately destroyed him, seven? eight? . . . Baby – that was the hoist in his mind. Not to her, back to Leda and the last hour of the last memory of those summer holidays. The passing thought of a mass grave and her unclaimed bones gave him very little concern, so why should the remembrance of that morning, before the journey back to school, still turn his heart, and sicken him just a little?

It had been a morning of goodbyes to the men on the place, falsely cheery goodbyes, the last exchanged with old Mary Kelly in the gate lodge. Her business was to open and shut the gates at any hour, and keep the gravel sweep raked to perfection. Today, as he walked away from the empty lodge with its pretty broken windows, there was still no escape for him from the embarrassment he had felt because he was eating a large unyielding piece of chocolate, Mary's present, when Leda came running to him out of the trees into the sunlight. She was swinging a basket in her hand. It ought to have had ribbons on it; she made such a drama out of everything. Now the drama was mushrooms. "You must come with me, Jasper – I am so much afraid of the bulls."

"Only bullocks."

"All the same, come with me – please!"

He should have been cleaning his gun and taking his rod to pieces. Why hadn't he kept these rules?

The exuberant delight of finding mushrooms put guns and rods and cool goodbyes, and the prospect of the horridly familiar dark journey back to school, out of his mind while they quartered the closely grazed fields together in intimate rivalry. He stooped silently when he found a mushroom; Leda screamed with delight and knelt down to lift her mushroom carefully with both hands. Wind blew in their faces, blew out her yellow hair. Their only thought was for mushrooms. Scarcity made them more precious, made competition keener. Here one, there three, a black, dark patch of grass promised, and gave nothing. Then the find of a grouping, fine dark grasses laced across their half-born heads, embryos tacked to their stems, no matter how careful the lifting. Striding fast on his stalk-like legs, he was doing too well, finding more than she did. He missed hearing her screams, and, feeling very grown-up, he left mushrooms behind him for her to pick. He was the author of her pleasure. Soon it would be lunch time. They must go back. He carried the basket. She took his hand and swung it as she had swung the empty basket. "Oh, but what fun we have had," she said. Then, reaching intimacy without pausing: "Jasper, tell me something – tell me about your eye."

"Leda," he said, and swallowed as he had swallowed chocolate, "I haven't got an eye. You know that."

"I want to see it," her voice was secret to them both. They were standing where the road turned into the shelter of the hazel-grove; the low wall, rounding the turning, was made of loose generous stones, rounded, worn to silver and yellow through years of weather, darkening to a peaty base, where loose-strife lifted up purple spires from the ditch. The sun, the luscious September sun, glared on their backs.

"No, Leda."

"I have to kiss it," she said. The luxury in her voice reached him in its absolute acceptance of his deformity. It held deliverance from all the hatred and disgust that possessed him, while washing his eye-socket, caring for it, covering it up. He freed his hand from hers and raised it uncertainly to his elegant black patch. Still delaying, he bent down to meet her eyes – cold, rabidly curious eyes. Just for a look at his disfigurement she would have kissed. He pulled back from her, back into his own defended world. And she had laughed good-humouredly, the sporting loser in a little game. They went in. It was past lunch time.

Today luncheon was far beyond its proper hour, and May, her wood and river gatherings deeply immersed in a square glass battery jar, straightened spoons and forks twice over on the dining-room table, bit her lip in annoyance and, to fill in time, turned her transistor on to Radio 4 – only that terrible Robin Day. She never knew which side he was on – always the wrong one, according to her understanding of politics. Soon it would be the still more terrible Archers. There were times when they had their moments of interest for her – she could have sorted out most of their problems. Not today.

April came in. The ladies did not assemble for luncheon as they did for dinner. They drifted unhopefully in and away again, to pick up the *Cork Examiner* or turn on their transistors and wait for the appalling news from Ulster.

"No sign of lunch?" April sighed her impatience. Unlike May, she did not fidget ostentatiously, but it was obvious that she had a plan for the afternoon. She was wearing her tweed suit, a suit which could equally have lunched at the Berkeley or walked through a bog. Tiger wore his cunning little matching jacket. "I rather hoped lunch would be in time today, Tiger has an appointment for his toenails and I'm meeting Ulick at three o'clock. It's his Thursday at the shop."

Ulick Uniacke was the chic antiquarian whose Dublin-London-New York activities had an offshoot in Ballinkerry. Behind the small and pretty shop was a mildly heated and well-ventilated store room. Here objects bought privately or at auction awaited complicated face-lifts, while operations nearer to age and sex changes were performed on others. Ulick stayed on the innermost spin of every ring in the sale world. He was an old Etonian, and a funny, charming and suspicious character. He could appreciate April's style and they were happy friends in their less than honourable collaborations.

"Jasper must know it's my Lecture Day – my lecture at Bally-nunty – and I shall need the car."

"Yes – wasn't it?" April replied.

"The Club will be on its toes," May was almost shouting.

"Yes, I do agree." April gave her entire attention to Tiger, murmuring such words of love as lured Gripper from his basket, trustful that they were addressed to him.

"Gripper, basket! To your basket, sir!" May realised that April had neither heard nor wished to hear what she had said. Later she would sort the matter out. There was no question as to who should have the car. The employment of her afternoon was not a matter of convenience of amusement – it was a matter of obligation and duty.

June and Tiny joined the waiting group. As yet there was no grinding of the lift ropes, so May had time to spare for June's problems; while Tiny settled herself in a sitting position on her goatskin, rather like a pig, forelegs stretched straight and senility written over every inch of her. May got ready to fill the waiting moment with sound advice. "I was wondering," she began, "if we might burn your dog's bed? That old goatskin smells like a badger's sett –"

"Ah, poor old Nancy," June sighed her usual response. She had spent a happy and profitable morning with Christy, Sweetheart and the young horse. And she knew what Jasper was cooking for lunch. She wasn't looking for trouble.

"It's quite a question which smells the sweetest? – your dead goat or your live dog."

"Between them it is," June agreed, still peaceably, "isn't it, Tiny?"

May came closer, her purpose firming as Tiny sighed and sank slowly to rest. Tiny's sighs rather poisoned the air. "I don't want to upset you, Baby, but don't you think it's a bit inhuman keeping the poor old thing alive? The RSPCA will be after you soon."

"Let them come," June was roused at last. "Let the bastards come." She stood over Tiny's bed as though defending her to the death.

"It needn't happen like that," May reassured her nicely. "When you do make up your mind to put her to sleep, I'll do it for you. It's perfectly simple – first, you give them a tranquilizer – that's important. Then, one little pill and they're off."

"Another little word out of you," June said, "and there'll be something in your coffee and you won't know about it till *you're* off."

The whole air of the big room (as yet without a whiff of Jasper's cooking) was stilled, as though it waited and accepted June's threat. "Do you hear what I hear?" April asked the silence. She did not look towards either sister, and there was no further sound until the groan of the lift, bearing luncheon upwards, broke and distracted the hatred in the air.

A quiche, lamb's lettuce, and a blackcurrant fool, the contents of the lift came as a happy interruption to a tension absurdly stricter than June's ridiculous threat called for. Jasper arrived soon after the lift. No one but he was permitted to interfere with his dishes or their arrangement. He liked taking things slowly; he stood, licking his lips and sucking the tips of his fingers (he had obviously been enjoying some private pleasure in the kitchen) before taking today's masterpiece out of the lift and dividing it into four wedged portions – exact as a sundial. "Now, girls," he said and sat down at the head of the table while they helped themselves. They did not quite push each other out of the way, but their eyes spoke for them. It was time they were greedy for, of course, not food.

There was silence while they gobbled away, almost contentedly. April was the first to lay down her fork and speak: "The only time that I can't hear the radio is when I'm eating toast."

May looked scathingly at her transistor – she didn't bother to say that it was not switched on.

"Too bad. And it's almost Woman's Hour," Jasper was not at all ashamed to admit unpunctuality.

"And I have to be at Ballynunty by four o'clock." May sprang from her chair, and dug into the blackcurrant mousse. "Alys hates the flower club ladies hanging about. She doesn't know what to say to them."

"And she's so rich. Mustn't annoy Alys, must you? How are you getting there? Bicycle?"

"Bicycle? With cherry blossom and pussy-willow and –" she hesitated, remembering the filbert catkins.

"Yes, dear, I happened to see you coming out of my nut-grove this morning."

"Oh, well, I just cut a few twiglets. I only took them from the back of the tree."

"That's quite all right, of course. You'll kill my tree quite as easily from the back as from the front."

"That's what you were discussing with your friend, the monk, I suppose."

"Not a great horticulturist, my young friend, but pretty, don't you think?" Jasper's smile was maliciously non-committal.

April spoke decidedly from outside the matters under discussion: "Must bring my Tiger to the vet for his teeny-tiny pedicure."

"I'll cut his toenails – too easy – two minutes. Vets are only a waste of money. Right? Get it? You hold him. I'll do it." May sounded loud and brisk.

"Thursday's his day. I'll take the Renault."

"Just an excuse for meeting Ulick – Thursday's his day, too."

"Poor old girl," Jasper spoke with exceptional tolerance. "If she fancies him, let her. He's her treat."

"A most unsavoury treat. He and cousin Rowley were thrown out of Eton together. Remember?"

"Oh – that." Jasper dismissed the idea lightly.

"Not 'that' at all."

"Oh, never look back," Jasper sighed. "Keep yourself up to date if you can."

May took no notice of this, although she fancied there was a defence behind the gibe. What was he up to with that monk? She had read enough to hazard a guess. "I suppose I could drop her off in Ballinkerry and go back to Ballynunty."

"Only twenty miles longer, and what about the petrol? You girls never think of that." He shuddered as he crumbled a biscuit. "Gold, dripping away –"

June came in on the same note: "And it costs fifteen pence now to send a letter three miles – well – your guess is as good as mine."

"Better, perhaps," May agreed. "All the same, my bicycle is never off the road, and the hatch-back's a must for the cherry blossom – right?"

"If we had the wheels back on the governess cart, we'ld save a lot of petrol." No one listened to June. But when she went on: "I saw quite a nice sort of pony with the tinkers yesterday," their attention was arrested.

"Tinkers back on the lower road? You locked up your hens, I hope," May advised.

"Tinkers always make trouble –" Jasper was with May again – "snaring rabbits and disturbing nesting birds."

"Ah, Jasper, what birds? Only moorhens on the river."

"There's a nesting swan there, too."

"And she'ld eat them if they went near her," June defended the tinkers conclusively. She was fond of a chat with the travelling people. Their cures and charms for horses' ills interested her keenly. "And little Mummie always gave them a free run for their donkeys on the mountain."

Silence fell as they accepted the memory; then May perked up again: "They don't have donkeys any more. Fast cars and antique junk today."

"They have a nice pony today too – and Mummie was really fond of the tinkers." June's voice was ponderous with memory.

June's references to Mummie always sounded in the poorest taste. Guarding and keeping their own separate memories, no one replied to her. When they spoke again, it was together, and with separate changes of subject.

April said: "Then that's decided. I'm to take the Renault."

Jasper said: "Only instant coffee today. Call at Mahers for the high roast – and for God's sake don't forget eggs. I'll write it down."

May said: "Someone get it into her head that she's not to start without me." She hurried away, coffeeless, to arrange her branches, her Oasis, her wire netting, her secateurs and a collection of flower vases in the back of the Renault.

*　　　*　　　*

Later in the afternoon, divided from each other and following their several pursuits, each one of the family felt a different and happier person. June and Christy were happy as they extracted a late lamb from an old ewe. On the farm, birth, death from natural cause, or from slaughter, took their inevitable turns and were dealt with as their turns came round.

Jasper, when he had washed up the luncheon dishes, paused to scratch Mister Minkles' ear while he considered how best and most usefully to employ the afternoon. Clearing the briars, creeping from the meagre wood like wolves on his azaleas, was the most attractive idea – he loved brambling. It was quite a sport with him. Then there were the seedling conifers, choking under a spring growth of weeds, but such a bore to weed. Rain decided him; rain driving in to the slated side of the house, into the cold cheek of the mountain behind – the most important thing was to write up the garden diary, and work out and elaborate his new undertaking.

Alone in the house, empty of voices and welling with its captive smells, Jasper went upstairs. Coming to the window that looked down the flowerless slope to the river, he waited, considering, visualising what he might grow, and where. Given shelter from the screaming mountain winds, his plantings would survive, even thrive. Energy possessed him delightfully. His idea was born. He went on up the stairs two steps at a time in his haste to reach the nursery floor before the idea lapsed into futility. He was tolerant of his own limitations; he quite liked skating about on them.

Jasper's present bedroom domain had been the day and the night nurseries. Mummie had made the night nursery into a bathroom, his bathroom, where he could tend his eye uninterrupted by his sisters' necessities. The water did not run very hot up here. He always meant to put in an electric heater. At least it was his own masculine preserve, as Mummie intended it should be. In no extremity could a sister get in; the outer door was bolted firmly on the inside; and he kept his bedroom door locked as religiously as they did theirs. The short way between bedroom and bathroom, padding with the footsteps of Nannies long buried, was his private privilege.

Jasper took two ruled school copy-books, one blue, one red, and a hard-backed diary for 1981 out of the hinged box-seat below an iron-barred nursery window. The other window-seat housed the very expensive train set which he sometimes set out on the floor to while away an hour or two. Now, settling himself comfortably and carefully in the armchair where Nannies had dozed away before him, he opened an exercise book, the red one, to study the plans and drawings it contained. There was something he was going to add to them; it had been clear in his mind as he ran upstairs; now, diffused and blunted, the brightness that had filled the air stayed sullenly unwritten. Accustomed to such a hiatus between an idea and its setting out, he sighed resignedly, put the book down and, opening his diary, wrote: Met Brother Anselm. He agreed . . . . What had he agreed, or suggested, or promised? Jasper could not remember fully, so, giving it all up for the moment, he turned to the *Leinster Examiner* and its Woman's Page – the cookery receipts on this were always open to criticism. Today "Meringues of which you may be proud" filled him with pleasurable scorn. After musing for a while on their probable disasters, Jasper fell asleep.

April, through a series of calm manoeuvres, had remained mistress of the afternoon's proceedings. She was seated at the wheel of the Renault, Tiger on her knee, safety-belt adjusted, before May appeared carrying a basket of mosses, a bunch of Mummie's double pink primroses and a rusted wire wreath-frame, picked up in a wayside graveyard. She had lost control of the afternoon through her delay to adjust the binding of wool and bass on the handles of her secateurs – a non-slip device for her thumb and short fingers.

"Get in," was April's only response to all protests as to who should drive, or which road should be taken. As the engine started and the accelerator added its voice to the one-sided discussion, May, moss scattering from her basket and primroses dropping from her hand, was forced to clamber in or be left behind.

As the car bounced its way into and over the potholes and fissures in the drive she retrieved everything neatly; she put the primroses back among their leaves; perched the skeleton wreath on her knees and, after they reached the road, was still talking uninterruptedly to April, to the air, to herself. . . . "How right I was to nip into the churchyard and pick up a couple of these wire jobs. . . . Everyone manages to die in Lent so I'll fill up a few minutes of my lecture demonstrating a pretty wreath for a grave, people love anything to do with death, don't they? . . . . Steady, April, steady up! Look OUT! We're coming to the tinkers' camp . . . those ghastly children . . . we could do with less of them, actually . . . all the same, take care, awfully expensive to kill one. I wonder which pony June fancied? They all look terrible. And what about that mobile home? – cost a fortune. . . ."

On either side of the road bedding and bright clothes blew out against the further blue of the mountains. Pieces of furniture, old wash-hand stands, garlanded jugs, milk-glass, oil lamps, stood for sale – indoor stuff, indecent in the cold spring air. A beautiful young woman, with dyed blonde hair and strong bare arms, emptied a dish of water onto the road and walked slowly up the steps of an expensive caravan. A boy sat on the lower step trimming a stick. Well-dressed children wandered abstractedly, silent as their dogs. Here time had lost all its measurements. Untouched and unimpressed, May held to her principles. "Fancy, hens too," she said. "Stolen, you bet. Thieves and pigs they all are, aren't they? And rich as Croesus . . . idle, shiftless lot." She dismissed the Travelling People and silence fell between the sisters until May was deposited with her equipment at the door of a rather grand and trim Georgian house. Sweeps of raked gravel lay before it; early daffodils drifted upwards to well-kept woodlands; far below, visible but beautifully distanced, the river – so mean in its beginnings at Durraghglass – turned magnificently through famous salmon pools and streams, all with their names, all with their records.

Happily indifferent as to whether May was, or was not, with her, April paused cautiously at the monstrous Gothic gates, a grandfather's terrible erection, before proceeding on her long drive back to Ballinkerry.

Ballinkerry had no more charm than most Irish villages. A tidy little stream, neatly bridged, and bordered by pleached lime trees, ran down the centre of its main street before it dived underground to carry the town's drains to the river – in its larger way it followed the same system as Durraghglass. Old dark shops with pretty pillared windows had nearly all been demolished, to rise again as supermarkets. Pubs with snugs – secretive corners for private talking and drinking – were now bars with Lounges where ladies might sit and drink, together or alone, without embarrassment at their lack of an escort.

Of the original shops remaining, Ulick Uniacke's was by far the prettiest. Restored with perfect restraint, its position was calculated to catch any passing trade on the road between Dublin and Cork. Shabbily unpretentious as it looked, visitors usually found in it a treasure-trove of pretty things. Behind the shop was the surgery where major operations were performed on larger subjects.

At the shop-front April came to a halt and set about reversing into a space between Ulick's station-wagon and a tiresomely parked motorbicycle. In her avoidance of the frailer impediment April backed smartly into the station-wagon. Happily impervious to the clang of the impact, she drove out and was about to repeat the performance when Ulick came out of his shop and opened the car door. He was laughing heartily. "That's my girl," he said, "hit me again. Why don't you?"

April hadn't heard the crash and she didn't hear him now, so her composure was complete. "Well, my dear, here I am," she stepped from her car, graceful as a girl in a 'thirties car advertisement – there ought to have been a running-board. Her tiny dog was neatly disposed under her arm, a small parcel was in her hand. They kissed, cheekbone to cheekbone, while he tried politely and insistently to take her parcel. She held on to it decidedly.

"Not yet, pet." He always made her feel so young. "Tiger must have a little runny-runs – he's been round the world this afternoon." Tiger, shivering inside his soft coat, that drifted in colour with her soft tweed, refused to oblige.

"I know he's waiting to do it indoors," Ulick picked him up, he was one of the few who were not afraid of Tiger, and directed April towards the shop. "He does love you," she paused to say it. "Aren't you flattered?"

"Loathe the bugger, actually. If he's not weeing against one of my chairs, he's displaying against my leg – embarrassing little toad." But his smile held complete acceptance of anything April chose to bring to his shop. April gave him back her most beautiful smile. It was nice that he appreciated Tiger.

Secreted in the snug – not unlike a sedan chair for two – which he had bought when the Fisherman's Bar was demolished,

Ulick and April settled down to an interesting trade conference. April produced from her handbag the notes she had been reading in bed the previous night; she referred to them long and silently before opening the parcel she had brought with her. "I know you can't keep your hands off it," she said teasingly, although his: "Let me, ducky," had escaped her.

At last the treasure was disclosed: a china rabbit, night cap on head, flowered gown to the feet, seated on a chaise-percée.

"Heavenly, isn't he?" April said. "Red Anchor, don't you think?"

"No, dear, *not* Red Anchor," he wrote to her on a pad – it saved time and shouting – "but very pretty and quite special – a comfit box, perhaps."

"*Malade Imaginaire* – Molière's date."

"No," he wrote firmly, "but very French. Is that a carrot in his mouth?"

"No. Parsley."

How had she guessed? "Oh, R A V I S H I N G." He put it in capital letters.

"How much?" she asked. When he wrote down a figure she shook her head decisively.

"Well," he wrote, "what do you want?"

April referred again to her notebooks; their pages were closely written over with the astounding prices asked by major London stores for their importations from Italy of astoundingly beautiful clothes. She marked a choice with her little gold pencil and blandly named a sum.

"Darling, you must be out of your mind," he wrote.

"All right, darling, when you feel rich." She took up the rabbit and started to re-dress him in his cottonwool and tissue-paper wrappings.

"Oh!" he said, forgetting to write, "be careful, let me."

"Please. Don't touch him."

Their eyes met. Steel met flint.

"Oh, very well," he wrote, "but you can't expect a bonus on the re-sale."

"I do expect a bonus," April said. She went on: "In the drawing-room at Durraghglass, under one of the Chippendale mirrors (earliest Chinese period) there is a Leeds teapot in which every year a wren builds her nest. I wish you could see it."

"Oh, so do I. Why don't you ask me to tea some day?"

"We can't disturb the wren, can we?"

"You could let me know when she's finished hatching."

"And another thing – Jasper calls you 'nasty Ulick'."

"Rude. And common."

"You did seduce poor little Cousin Rowley."

"Can't he let bygones be bygones?"

"Not just Eton. He knows all about that procury little gaming club."

"Darling, you know I came out of all that without a breath on my reputation."

"Yes. And silly old Rowley's still inside, doing a little time."

"And loving every minute. He's made dozens of just good friends."

"Dirty talk," April said reprovingly. "I must get on. I have to collect May from her flower club at Ballynunty."

"Oh, very well," he wrote, "you can have your bonus."

April straightened Tiger's coat as if he was all that mattered to her in life, before she put the rabbit into Ulick's hands. Evil as he was, he had never failed her over the agreed monies.

"Cheque or notes?" he said. And she heard him.

"Notes," she said. She felt darling Mummie's precious little rabbit deserved something really touchable and countable.

"Shall we have a cup of tea?" he suggested when the notes had been given and counted. One of the pleasant things about Ulick was his supply of really good China tea. Another pleasant thing was his supply of invariably clean English bank notes – no haggle about the Punt and its wavering values.

"What a lovely evening, isn't it?" April spoke on a full, pleased note. She could see the strange colour and feel the airy, silky warmth of that Italian knit which Mummie's rabbit would provide. "And you will remember to collect my order from old Horrids?" She drank some tea in a dreamy languid way; then looked at him mischievously across her cup. He understood the importance and value of real clothes – true couture stuff. Again, age for ever distanced, she was the present moment – young in looks, in heart untouched. She had no heart. She waited. There was something else. At last he said it: "Shall we roll a joint? What do you think?"

May waited, flowers in her hands, flowers at her feet. She looked a composed, decisive person standing there in her dark-brown stockinette slacks and white Connemara cardigan, her strong, smoke-grey hair moving prettily in the breeze, her smile ready to gleam open and stay, fixed open, on her face. She could talk through it, and keep talking, ruthlessly. Nothing vulnerable about May. Only May could guess at the cringing second self she must defend so long as they both should live.

A tall, dark parlourmaid opened the door. She should have been a butler, but those days were finished, even for Alys Croshawe.

"Oh, Elizabeth, good evening."

"Madam," Elizabeth looked coldly and politely at the collection of branches on the wide doorstep.

"Here I am with all my bits and pieces," May went on

blithely. "We'll take the lot to the drawing-room. Right?"

"Her ladyship thought the morning-room, Madam. I have put the vases there and spread the flower sheet ready for you."

"Don't bother about vases. I always bring my own specials. Did you say the morning-room?" her voice changed a little towards regret. "I'll take the stuff in – don't touch it, don't touch it. Perhaps you'ld just carry this and this and this – oh, how kind."

Elizabeth was balancing a mountain of Oasis on a rusting foundation for a death token when May's kind friend, Alys, joined them. She came from some further rich distance within the house and brought with her a carelessness over distance or riches – all one to her, all quite natural.

"Alys. This is sweet of you." May bent across primroses and secateurs and rabbit wire for a kiss. "Quite a thrill for my club – coming here to my lecture."

"I'm rather frightened of your flower-club ladies," Alys had a tiny voice, "but we're going to give them 'tea and cakes and jam and slices of delicious' – what have you put in the sandwiches, Elizabeth?"

"Ham and chicken paste, m'lady."

"Oh dear, can they believe that's foie-gras?"

May, who was well aware that most of her flower-club ladies knew a great deal more about food than Alys, laughed her agreement. "I've brought you some wonderful ground cover," she filled a silence while their footsteps hushed on rugs before echoing again on tiles, as they proceeded through the halls to the morning-room.

"Not any more of that rare stuff you gave me two years ago? The border's smothered in it. Reagan says it's common spurge."

"Oh, gardeners! I warned him it was a wanderer. No, this is

Lamium gobdolba – really rather choice." May so loved giving presents that, even against her own knowledge, she endowed them with rare qualities.

"Well, here we are." The morning-room was pretty enough and large enough to contain quite a party.

"Cold, isn't it?" Lady Alys sounded quite unashamed. "We can't turn on the radiators – the oil! Too impossible. Should we do something about that fire, Elizabeth?"

"My dinner table, m'lady, my silver, my sandwiches," Elizabeth made the ghost of a pause, her expression forbidding further orders, before her scrupulously respectful exit.

May, the hour for her lecture near, began to set out her paraphernalia. She picked up the wreath-frame from a glass-topped table where Elizabeth had set it gently down. As she did so she spared a moment to glance down at the small treasures within. Medals and decorations, earned by dead soldiers and diplomats, were laid on velvet, with pendant miniatures of gentlemen in uniform among them. Surrounding the decorations and miniatures a collection of Victorian marbles ran a ribbon-like frame – a touching idea, implying that soldiers and diplomats had once been little boys.

"Oh, marbles, my favourite things." May seldom missed an opportunity for admiration. "Early, aren't they? Early Vic?"

Lady Alys was quite inattentive. Useful, peerless Elizabeth still held the first place in her mind. "She does bully us so," the little bird's voice quavered happily as she kicked a smouldering log out of place in the grate. "Anyway, it's better for the flowers to keep cool, and your ladies can stick to their coats, can't they?" Alys had kept all the airs of youth. Thin hair, fluffy as a baby's, went with her baby voice. Only the sad crouch, above loosened stomach muscles, and the slightly crooked neck, proclaimed age as withering. She had soft, well-taught manners, through which she was as quick to destroy as to please. "I do hope you approve of my flower vases," she sounded sure of approval. "I washed them myself."

"Sweet of you, Alys, but I always use my own containers," May indicated a chimney-shaped tube from Japan, a flat vegetable dish, a copper mould, green with age, and a brown and white teapot with a broken spout.

"Lovely," Alys commented doubtfully, "but I don't quite see them in my drawing-room."

"But they're not going in your drawing-room, dear Alys."

"The thing is, May – a lot of boring people are coming to dinner tonight, so I thought – what a good idea if you left your décor here! A little fellow for the dining-room table, and a couple of big chaps to go in the drawing-room."

May thought quickly. She had valid reasons for refusing. "I'ld simply love to. So unlucky, I have a lecture at Castle Quilty tomorrow, and I rather need this stuff."

"That did occur to me, actually. I've saved up all last week's drawing-room flowers for you. Here they are, very perky in their footbath."

May looked with disgust at the collection of narcissi and forsythia drowning in their footbath. She picked out a spray of forsythia, shook a few petals onto the carpet, and peered closely at the water-blackened oily stem.

"Take the lot," the kind friend said. "Please do. I know there's not much in your garden."

May felt enclosed in the hermetic little world of the money-less among the rich. Remembering the many treats she accepted from Alys, how, now, to refuse a favour? A slow blush of painful confusion climbed above the polo collar of her jersey. Her eyes grew very bright. She found her situation insufferable; twice over unbearable. That Alys should have offered her half-dead flowers, smelling of nothing but their week-old water, was insulting enough. There was besides that, an arid feeling of neglect in the thought of a dinner-party to which she had not been invited, and for which Alys planned to make shameless use of her unrewarded talents. Most difficult of all, impossible to put into words, or even acknowledge fully to her inmost self, was the problem for her lopped hand, arranging flowers in unfamiliar vases.

Alys's inconsiderate forgetfulness of her handicap left May defenceless against a familiar impulse, welling through her now, as undeniable as her blush had been; the wish and impulse to assert herself dangerously against a loveless world. She knew how to fulfil her wish. She almost welcomed an occasion for the blinding excitement in the dangers she must risk before her nerve and dexterity left her equal again with others. She would be more than equal – triumphant, heedless of anybody's love, in a haven of fulfilment which she had reached before, where she would be again. The planning and timing of the adventure meant as much to her as the first movements in a game of sex to a luckier person.

"I won't promise anything super –" she managed to say it quite pleasantly. "My own containers suit me best, of course. And you won't mind the funeral wreath for the dining-room, will you? I promised them a special lesson on that – Lent is the season for old people, er, passing on, and that gives plenty of practice for wreaths and sprays."

"Oh dear, how sad," Alys said, adding doubtfully, "Make it cheerful, won't you?"

"Watch me," May said, snipping a tough twig so viciously that she dropped her secateurs. She stooped to pick them up. "Silly me – I'm always a bit taut before my lecture."

"Oh, I do so understand," the gentle voice conveyed complete understanding as Alys looked away from that miniature hand. "Oo-oo," she cooed out suddenly, "do I hear a car? I dooo . . . . it's the first of the milk-in-firsts arriving. Shall I let them in? Saves poor Elizabeth's feet." She went away unhurrying. She was the simple great lady now, thoughtful for her servants, opening her own door to the polite mob that she would greet warmly without being quite sure of their names. But at least, boring and unfamiliar as May's ladies might be, the flowers for her party would be arranged superlatively – what a neat idea that had been.

Left alone, May gazed with something near to hatred at the row of vases, most of them glass, though there was one merciful affair in white pottery from poor Mrs Constance Spry. The others repelled and filled her with a sick foreboding of failure to give anything like her best in their unfamiliar shapes, although she was so sure and certain of all she had taught her hand to do for her in its accustomed ways. She was proud of its skills, sometimes thinking of it as a different person from herself, a difficult child she had taught to obey – a child she must never betray through nervous awkwardness. She was the keeper of her own defences; of her powers to survive the monstrous injustice in her star.

Her thumb felt cold, chilled to its bone by her nervous expectations. She knew how to restore its usefulness. The therapy contrasted absolutely with her own neat, fulfilled life. Do the thing you most fear: marry fear to the act; go for the coup that balances courage with its dangers; the flow of peace will follow. Success lay in the proper timing, in the moment between danger and safety. May waited purposely until she knew the approaching footsteps, on tiles, on rugs, on tiles again, were close, and closer still. Then, quick as she was careful, she lifted up the lid of the glass-topped table. Her hand hovered, deliberate as a bee taking honey, before it dropped precisely onto the marble of her fancy – an agate marble, brown and white, rabbit coloured. In the fraction of time left – improvising danger was part of the game – she shut down the lid as gently as she had lifted it, and turned quietly away from the table just as the sweet Irish voices, and Lady Alys's voice, from a different Irish world, were in the room. Happily, warmly, confidently May went forward to meet her friends.

"We've got quite a little challenge here today – Lady Alys has lent us her vases. So we'll create something exciting in an unknown container, shall we? Don't let's forget our measurements – from side to side they must not exceed . . . who can tell me? . . . ."

There was a covert murmur of inches from the chorus of beautifully and discreetly dressed ladies as they clasped their winter coats to them and settled down to culture and beauty, and to wondering secretly how soon Miss Swift was going to drop something out of that poor hand.

Miss Swift dropped not so much as a leaf. She romped through all the awkwardness of demonstration in Alys's preposterous vases, and in her construction of the confections she used quite a number of Alys's own leftovers. As she balanced pussy-willow with narcissi (reserving Jasper's filbert catkins) a neat feeling of victory lent an extra easiness to her hand. Her lecture, as she delivered it, was outpaced by the inspiration and agility of her thumb and half finger. Could this be not unlike dancing with a loved one? Supposing she was slightly drunk? Silly as the catching of a falling leaf, the notion teased and fled. Drunk or sober, she had never danced with a loved one.

"And now," she stepped back from her arrangements, everything balanced to a hair's breadth, firm as a rock, "any questions?" She didn't want questions; she wanted adulation, and she got it. The cheesy white plasticine of her face tautened on its bones as she breathed in their praises. She was a star, in love with her audience, accepting their applause. The moment could not last, but in the warm ease that succeeded it, in the unfolding of her skills, the cunning of her cleverness, she was as one with her flower club; she had answers for their thoughtful questions, and snapped out quite a sharp reply to some ignorant suggestion from Alys.

Elizabeth brought in tea at the appropriate moment and, as almost every lady was on Weight Watchers (refusing sandwiches or milk in tea, first or last), May could let herself go on the chicken and ham paste. One way and another she was in need of sustenance and took it; more and more praise went with it, and a cigarette to follow, before she embarked on the funeral wreath.

"Here we have rather a different problem," she began, "so how do we start? We stuff the wire frame with Oasis, previously soaked in plenty of water –"

"Reminds me, I must let out my poor little dogs," Alys interrupted. Her voice sounded pathetically regretful, a whispered whine. Since she had no curiosity about making a funeral wreath (anyhow, the gardener's job), she achieved a polite escape.

"The whole idea is . . . ." May went on, ignoring the stir of Alys's departure, "keep it simple – we don't want any florist's satin bows, do we?" The club was moved to derisive laughter at the idea of satin bows which, not so long ago, had seemed inoffensive and appropriate on an expensive token for a sad occasion.

When the wreath, quite a joyous affair, more of a south-sea lei than a grave-side garland, had been successfully created and immoderately praised, the ladies (after they had carried May's pots and pans, filbert branches and wire, to the steps) made their polite thanks and tactfully early departure. Cosily re-established in their large, well-heated cars, their comments on the afternoon went much the same as always. "Poor Miss Swift – she shouldn't take it so seriously" . . . "I could have cried for that poor little hand" . . . "Oh, it makes me so nervous, I never look near it" . . . "And what did you think of that idea for a centrepiece on the dining-room table?" . . . "Frankly, in very poor taste" . . . "Oh, certainly, I agree, how true" . . . "And what about the big house?" . . . "All that tat and peeling paint? My Richard would never stand for it" . . . Unimpressed by other people's lifestyles, and filled with kind thoughts, they enjoyed agreeing with each other along every mile of their homeward roads.

The thought of a bath and a little lie-down were uppermost in Alys's mind as she waited for May to say her goodbyes. She liked May more and more at the prospect of her imminent departure. "Let me put some of those things in your car," she said at last.

May rolled the marble in her trouser pocket, fitting its warmed globe into the palm of her hand, "No hurry," she said easily, "April isn't here yet."

"April?" Alys's voice was frail in dismay.

"No sense of time," May sounded quite indulgent.

"Well, do come in and have a drink – if you don't think it's too early."

"Never too early for cocktails," May quoted cheerily.

"Only sherry, I'm afraid. Perhaps Elizabeth has put it in the library."

"And shall we take a look at my drawing-room flowers? The *placement* is so vital – I think I've got it right."

In the great mellow drawing-room, still as a well above its worn and faded Aubussons, and warm as toast in readiness for the night's party, May saw with cries of horror that Elizabeth had changed the positions of her arrangements.

"Actually, she has put the vases in their usual places," Alys's voice was as small as a pinprick and she spoke no word of praise or thanks.

"Unimaginable – the stupidity of it! Thank God I saw it in time." Walking resolutely across the room, heels down first, toes out-turned, May lifted the heavy vases and, without loosing a petal or spilling a drop of water, put them down in her well-chosen situations. So placed, they re-assumed the mysterious and beautiful dimensions she had intended for them. "Tell Elizabeth to leave them exactly where they are," she said, and put her hand back in her pocket. Alys, her voice failing her utterly, led the way to the library.

In the library the master of the house was seated by a poor fire reading *The Field*, drinking tea from a mug and eating toast off a plate on a nearby chair. "Only just got in from the river," he said. "Elizabeth made me some toast. Rather good. I needed it. Lost a lovely fish – broke me in the Tinkers' Hole."

"May is here," Alys interrupted despairingly.

He struggled out of his chair: "Oh, May! Wonderful to see you – it's ages since . . . . How did your meeting go? Wish I'd been at it. Did your ladies behave themselves, I mean, enjoy themselves?"

"Oh, yes, absolutely riveted. Didn't you think so, Alys?"

"Darling May," Alys put a small glass of sherry into her hand, "her lecture was bliss. I don't know how she kept it up for so long."

"Just practice," May said. "Two hours means nothing to me. They do love it so. I get inspired."

"Yes."

"And how is my friend, Baby June? Dear little soul. . . ."

Brigadier Croshawe really wanted to know. His mind went back across the years. "Those were the days. What was that great little mare she rode? Don't tell me – I've got it! Magic Flute. They were a combination, terror of the Ladies' Races. Six in a row, one year, I remember. It must have been '38 or '37?"

May could see herself again, standing cold and unnoticed on a hillside, watching another of Baby's triumphs. She put down her glass and put her hand back in her pocket.

79

"Changed times, Hippo." (Hippo was the Brigadier's pet name.) "One common four-year-old in the yard now, and Baby's afraid to get up on him."

"Can't believe that."

"Too true. She's leaving everything to a useless idiot she snatched out of my garden."

"Can't be so useless if Baby's had the schooling of him."

"Expensive *and* useless," May insisted.

"Nothing like catching them young. My poor old Matty is on his last legs, can't fire him though, can I?"

"I *can't* see the point of not," Alys said simply. Then: "Oh, do I hear a car? Oh, I dooo –" the flute in her voice was in happy contrast to an earlier accent in the afternoon.

"April, I expect," May looked regretfully at her empty glass.

"April? How is the old girl? What a looker, wasn't she? Quite lovely. She must come in and have a drink."

"Oh, Hipp-OH," Alys wailed, "you know she won't hear you. May – shall we? . . ."

"Stay as you are, May. Have another drink. Leave April to me. I'll make her come in." He was gone. Slippers flapping on flags, silent on rugs, as he crossed the halls. And he had meant to give himself a rest after the river, and before the party.

At the hall door April sat in the car, revving the engine deafeningly. She smiled in a world detached from him. As he clasped her hand Tiger flew at him, screaming. "Proper little savage, that's the way to have them. Come along in and have a drink, my dear."

"Tell my silly sister I'm waiting," she answered. A scarf, patterned in pale leopard-skin, was tied loosely, perfectly over her grey hair. Her hair could have become yellow fur. Her great eyes surveyed him as distantly as the Mona Lisa's.

"Alys is longing to see you," he said, "do come in."

"Tell her I shall go home without her if she doesn't hurry," April blew the horn.

"Do you good, my dear, a little drink. It's a long way to Durraghglass."

"No, it's not. It's Thursday," April rejoined brightly and blew the horn again.

"No good," he said as he met May in the hall, Alys having wavered away to her bath. "She simply won't. A bit hard of hearing now, perhaps. Such a shame. Lovely girl. Still lovely," he said it sadly. "Well, goodbye, my dear. Loved seeing you. Come again soon. Thank you for those beautiful flowers – and if I hadn't made such an old fool of myself losing that fish I'ld have given you a bit . . . . Next time . . . . Let's hope . . . . well, bless you . . . ."

All the way home May played little games with the marble in her pocket. In her happy repose of mind, she nearly invited Tiger to sit on her knee. April was happy too. The money in her purse promised blissful hours to be spent choosing and abandoning and re-selecting – money no object. And there was something else in her bag, ten cigarettes, hand-rolled by Ulick and put in a Player's packet. Only ten, she could snip them in half. Half was enough, almost. Perhaps, before she had got to the end of the supply she would talk to him again about the Leeds teapot. Nothing definite, just trail the idea.

Happy though they were in their separate achievements, there was no break in the monotony of their mutual dislike as they sat close together driving through the cold spring evening. Hunched, and hissing nervously in the exercise of double driving, May's disapproval asserted itself on every given opportunity. There were quite a few opportunities on the main road they travelled before turning into the smaller inter-locking roads going their distracted ways towards Durraghglass and the mountain. Everything on the way home was so familiar as to be unremarkable.

It was partly a deliberate avoidance of contact that held the sisters separate, their usual displeasures, each with each, an irritation as unendurable as that felt by the arm trapped in the wrinkling folds of a sleeve within a tighter sleeve. They took no remedy for the situation between them, although occasionally there came an opportunity for agreement.

Such a moment came and went when together they saw, snuggled into the slits of a stony bank and spread across the roadside verge below, primroses – the first scanty primroses, their pale determination lightening the dusk of the cold evening. "*Ah*, primroses," they both said it, pleasure hurrying their pulses together, the snuff and honey of primrose scent in their minds. But, because they feared a trite or sweet comment they turned their heads coldly aside from one another. Because neither spoke again, the faint thread between them failed of any purpose.

As they came back to the gates of Durraghglass the headlights of the grumbling little car shone a brief light into the lozenge window panes of the gate lodge, no lamp light behind them. The empty house was like a pretty, neglected animal that had crouched and died at the gate. As they drove on, under the dark trees and over the broken surface of the drive, they both looked forward with pleasant assurance: April, to her warm bedroom, her careful disciplines, and her little drink; May, to a reunion with Gripper, to the proper placing of marble with rabbits, and to Jasper's dinner. They stepped out of the car, stiffly and gratefully, as elderly ladies do, and went into the house.

Strangely, as though a dinner party was to take place, the hall was warmer than it had been all winter. A perceptible foggy breath hovered over the electric radiators as they drew damp out from the walls. All the lamps in the hall were lighting too. Lights glowed under the red shades of two tall standards; lights glimmered in groups of three from the gilt wall brackets. An air of celebration was puzzlingly evident.

"Doesn't it look festive?" April stood still, smiling in the unusual glamour. May smiled too – a satisfied smile. "All these lights left on, Jasper *will* be furious," she said.

5 ❧ The Revenant

In his wild-wood garden Jasper stayed late that evening, subduing and cutting into the thickets of encroaching briars. He very much enjoyed the work: delightful to slice below the woody knot from which the felons sprouted. It was a destruction of personal dislikes, and at the same time a ransom for objects he considered precious. In gardening, and in cooking, Jasper expended all the carefulness or wish to cherish that was in his nature. When alone he cooked with care and affection – the least audience sent him off his head from nerves. In his garden it was different – his spring fever subdued itself happily and expanded his dreams; he could see himself as an explorer, or plant collector in North China. He planned for, and planted, rare subjects that he might never see mature – just as well perhaps, disappointments were the only certainty he acknowledged.

By seven o'clock, as the long cold light lowered and familiar plants and places turned changeling and apart towards the night, he pulled up his last long swathe of briar, three times rooted lightly in the compost round an ailing camellia, cut it in three with his secateurs, took off his brambling gloves and turned his mind towards the composition of dinner. It was too late for that chicken à l'estragon. Let them eat kedgeree, he decided in a school-mistress mood, although he was thinking of Marie Antoinette. Yes. Although properly a breakfast, or, possibly a lunch-time dish, it would do very well – two ageing kippers in the back of the Frigidaire and a small tin of tuna fish he had found sneaking a hiding place at the back of the sock drawer in his dressing-table would lay the foundations for four hard boiled eggs (yolks and whites chopped separately). Not too much rice, he decided, but plenty of butter, cream and Worcester sauce, all under a lavish shower of parsley – one of the good things May grew with unfailing success in the kitchen garden. Then there was the faithful tin of Campbell's consommé, watered to size from the tap or the stock-pot, enhanced by dried tarragon in a filter-spoon and enlivened by a little sherry.

But now, before changing to domesticity, he was still the lone adventurer, warm in the cold evening, pleased with his work and charmed by the sudden thriving of a forgotten treasure – growth and the new year were together at last. He stood in enjoyment of the moment, filled by an after-work peace of mind among his solitary pleasures – the girls were ignorant outsiders, a small tribe to feed and tease.

The idea for a new tease came to him as he heard a car turn in at the gates and advance glumly through and over the potholes and ruts of the driveway – April and May home again after their day out. He shut his mind almost completely towards their interests or occupations, except when he could be disruptive or destructive about them: he had to allow himself a little fun.

Now as he delayed (he was not prepared to help with baskets and parcels) he heard the car pause and wait at the house, its engine running, then turn on the gravel sweep and go down the drive, instead of to its garage in the stableyard. What had those women forgotten? And what were they doing about it? The unthinkable wastage of petrol really hurt him. There would be more to say about this and less sherry in the soup to compensate for petrol losses. Then, as he walked up the familiar broken steps – even in the dark he could have avoided any unplaced stones – the idea that it was perhaps a caller, arriving and leaving,

occurred to him. Thank God, he thought, crossing the gravel –
one of May's Irish Country Women's Association most likely;
or, worse still, an enthusiast from the Flower Arrangers' Guild.
What an escape he had had.

It was then that he saw the woman in the long dark coat leaning against the door, her arms stretched out as though searching
again some unfulfilled embrace. An expensive-looking suitcase
perked itself up aggressively on the door-step.

"Good evening. Did you want to see one of my sisters?"
Jasper's voice, no matter how petulant he might feel, could
never be other than alluring: an inherited voice, unquestion-
ingly confident. There was no warmth but the music in its tone
was undeniable.

The woman dropped her arms and turned from her curious
posture against the door. She stood silent beside her suitcase. It
seemed as though she was part of the cold, delaying spring and
the excitement in its roots, as she waited, and before she said:
"Who is it? Is it Jasper?"

"Jasper Swift." He spoke as if it was an introduction.

"Jasper – I'm back. I'm Leda."

Her voice had no more changed to him than his had to her. If
anything it was fuller, sweeter, exciting like a whistle in the
night. It displaced all the present anxieties, the importances of
his accustomed ways. She put her hands out as if sure of hands to
take them. Her hands moved uncertainly – then she let them fall
into the folds of her coat.

Jasper was not one for shaking hands. To replace forgotten Leda with this woman was beyond him. A girl who had
laughed and given delight, and laughed and taken it back,
who had cruelly disturbed his childhood and mortified his
agonising boyhood, was back again after the long years of
banishment. It was impossible. Yesterday she was only a
shadow, a stammer in the mind that halts over a word. This

evening the stammer dissolved and the shadow lengthened to present reality.

"Leda?" He said her name with a question mark, putting himself aside from the warmth of her approach.

"The Jewish cousin." She laughed without derision.

"Yes. But the war. Those camps – we supposed . . . we thought . . . ." He hated speaking about such embarrassing places. Places he refused even now to envisage. She answered as if remembering unpleasant schooldays: "Oh, I was *the* unpopular girl. The women all hated me – and you know, my husband died, he was never very strong."

She spoke carelessly and Jasper felt grateful for her lack of emotion. "Rather a long time ago," he said.

"Yes. Everything is so long ago. I've been in America with my friend."

"Is your friend here too?" Jasper looked about him apprehensively.

"Oh no. He's in South America." Her voice went delicately, light as cats' feet. "Things got difficult, so then my daughter –"

"You live with your daughter?"

"Oh no. How could I? She's a high-powered journalist. Have you ever heard of a low-powered journalist?"

"A strong-minded girl." Jasper spoke with distaste.

"Wonderfully strong and so much lovely money," Leda seemed reluctantly grateful. "She arranged for me to live in this beautiful Irish convent, where the nuns look after me. It's so peaceful. They give me so much love and care – I'm so grateful." She seemed resigned but resentful.

"You look very well." Perhaps she did, for an old woman.

"Jasper? I'm blind."

The quietness of her voice made every other word she had spoken into a half-truth. How much had she forgotten? As she had been so long forgotten by them. The clearest memory

Jasper had of Leda, a memory put far aside, was of that moment, bribed from him by a hand in a hand, when she had asked to look into the empty eye-socket, the small hidden space that had meant for him all the embarrassments and grudges of his half-childhood, half-youth. Aware now of the reason for those enormous ski-ing glasses she wore, light shuttered out, or dead fish's eyes shuttered in, behind curving blue-tinted glass, edged light-heartedly by a ribbon of glitter – he felt no more than a curiosity (with an affinity he did not acknowledge) to look her over and appraise what age had done to teeth and neck and legs that had charmed him once and had no successors. He felt pleased after his slow reconnoitre, so savagely rude if she could have seen it, at his unimportant distaste at recognising in an old woman only a travesty of his half-enchanted, half-forbidden memories. It was as though an uninteresting ghost had risen from a dead, absurd romance.

"Oh, Leda," he had to say something, "what a pity. Can't they do anything about it?"

"Nothing at all. I don't care. I can manage. It's an adventure. Tell me about you. Tell me more. Go on – you're not the handsome boy any more, are you? Who did you marry? Will she like me?"

She needed to hear Jasper's voice – sweet as a flute, an uncle's voice. The air was filled by echoes. Blind, she could hear and live the past in his voice.

"No, oh, no. I live with my sisters," Jasper laughed. "You remember?"

"April, May and Baby June." She laughed too. Their laughter had the same musical cadences – a family laugh and voice. But hers was the more interesting, lapsing sometimes into an American way of speech, a quickening towards some other language at the back of her excellent English.

"Won't you come in and have a drink?" he said.

"Yes, of course. But, oh, where did that man put my suitcase?" She sounded bereft. "I thought I might stay," she said, "for a night or two."

Late that afternoon June was alone in the farmyard. Christy Lucey was following a single hen suspected of stealing her nest away in the near wilderness of briars, forgotten currant bushes and rubbish dumps outside the yard. While he searched June turned the heavy handle of an old machine that chopped mangolds for the two milking cows. There would be crushed oats with the mangolds, nothing could be less economical than June's farming methods. Her present contentment was evident in her rhythmic unhurrying movement as she turned the handle through its circuit and saw the slices of mangold fall into the zinc bucket beneath it.

She and Christy had spent a satisfactory afternoon schooling the Wild Man. They had asked him a few big questions, notably one concerning a stone-faced bank . . . . "and Miss Baby, did you see the mistake he made? And the lad to recover and I to stay with him at the same time, did you see that?" Christy had been exuberantly pleased with self and horse.

"Jesus Christ, child," June said, "I shut my eyes." It was a proper tribute to the chance and drama of such a moment. She had known many like it in her time, when there was only a breath between disaster and survival. She gave him credit now for the nerve he had, and she had lost. Now, in the still of the cold evening, happy and not even tired, she did his work for him and waited his return.

Here, in the half ruin of the yard there was no presage of spring as there had been in Jasper's tangled glades. Manure steamed into the air. A white hen made noises not indicative of egg-laying. "Useless old bitch – you're for the chop," June thought without malevolence. She left the machine and the open shed to take a look at Sweetheart, heaving a little in fulfilment as she suckled her family. Even the runt of the litter, that yesterday the Aga had sheltered, was fighting his turn, June noticed with approval. She leant over the half door, her eyes shut, as she calculated possible profits – monies to come from the happy family. If one pig made so much, how much would seven make? The sum was agonizingly beyond her. She put the whole pleasant question aside as she watched Christy coming towards her.

Christy was crossing the yard slowly. One hand supported the wrist of the other, cupped and stretched in front of his advancing steps. It was as though he approached a temple with an offering. June waited, silent in a lull of idleness, until he came nearer and she saw, arranged on his upturned palm, three white eggs, misted in their own freshness.

Christy lifted his eyes from the eggs to June. "The pullet, God bless her," he said, "within in the nettles."

"Good man yourself," June commended him. The practical reality of three unexpected eggs for Jasper gave her a feeling of hope and pleasure. She looked at the eggs with as much satisfaction as if she had laid them herself.

"The thistles and the nettles would go through you and through you." Christy made far more fuss over his latest efforts than he had about the dangers of the afternoon.

"There's nothing worse," June agreed, "only the honey bees."

"My mother says there's a great cure in nettles, you should eat them in the springtime."

"Whenever that is," June put the eggs in a tin basin, sticky with hen food, and went back to her work.

"When I was going to school she'ld give them to me with my tea and a duck egg along with them. In the springtime." He repeated "in the springtime" as if the words were part of a rune.

Looking distantly at his legs, so long and useful on a horse and then at his wide shoulders and light hips June felt a faint jealousy in the admission that his horrid mother was responsible for this gracious maturity. But it was she, June, who had turned an ignorant boy into an able and knowing horseman. He was the inheritor of June's past skills and past courage. She could translate them for him. They had the same use of words. There was an equality between them. She watched him going across the yard with the tea-time treats for her two cows and wondered how she could ever get through her days without his presence in them. "Come on, Tiny," she said, "till we shut up the hens. The fox, you know, Tiny, the old fox." She too set out across the wet yard, Tiny paddling step for step behind her.

Before she reached the cavern that housed her poultry Christy overtook her, wheeling his bicycle. "I have all done now, Miss Baby," he said, "and my mother has a visitor tonight, so I'll have to be off. I'm to call to the Post Office for biscuits."

June was disappointed at his going. "What kind of biscuits?" she asked, only to delay him a moment longer.

"Choc fingers."

"Why? Is your mother's visitor bringing her baby?"

Christy looked confused, even shocked, at the idea of a baby: "I wouldn't say so," he said.

Remembering their afternoon together, June refrained from reminding him that it was hardly yet six o'clock. She knew he was in greater fear of his mother than he was of any living horse. She let him go.

Relieved as she was that May was not prowling about with her spy's eyes on his early departure, June very much wished, as she plodded her way back to the house and the stableyard, that Christy had stayed long enough to help her in the search for thorns or other injuries in the young horse's legs. She spent some time doing this herself, with rigorous carefulness, before she went, by the back door and passage ways, to the kitchen, thinking, late as the hour was, of a quiet cup of tea.

The kettle was simmering complacently on the Aga and toast left over from breakfast perched, limp and leathery, in its silver rack. She had made the tea and poured it into a mug, milk in first and plenty of sugar, when she heard Jasper's voice coming down fitfully from the hall. She had hoped the longer evening light might have kept him later at his clearing and clipping. "No luck, Tiny," she said and gave her the piece of buttered toast while she gulped down the tea and rinsed the mug under the cold tap. Jasper entirely disapproved of any casual trespassing in his kitchen. If so much as a skewer was mislaid, its disappearance would be dated from that stolen time. Each sister had an electric kettle in her bedroom for the filling of hot-water bottles or for the occasional private cup of tea, or bedtime drink. The kitchen belonged to Jasper. June had quite a sensation of guilt as she wiped her mouth and went upstairs prepared to suggest that she had merely passed through the kitchen to deposit the three eggs. She hoped that Jasper had not reserved the toast for any special purpose.

On the hall side of the service door June stopped, hesitant in her surprise at what she saw – Jasper, hand in hand with an unknown woman. To June, who could accept any fact of conception, birth, or death in her material world, this was an embarrassing spectacle. The two linked people looked bleakly graceful, advancing across the cold shadowless hall as if about to venture into some stately kind of dance to which she was an awkward audience.

"Put on the lights and the radiators," Jasper said when he saw her, "and light the fire in the drawing-room, that *would* be kind." His words sounded as ceremonious as the half dance with the stranger had looked. And still he held her hand.

"Is that a sister? Which sister?" The woman's voice was as liquid and easy as if it came out of a bird's throat. June was without an ear for music or she could have recognised Jasper's voice in another key, a different octave.

"My sister June."

"June, Baby June, I do remember, of course I remember! So tiny, and that wicked pony – you were up to all his dirty tricks. What did you call him? Don't say – I'll remember." She was holding out both her hands. Fingers lean and strong as the spring in a rat trap closed together in the blunt paw June offered.

June ignored the half thought of a trap, a trap for rats or rabbits. Something within her warmed in accord with the woman's recall. "I suppose that was Crotty the Robber" – the mad dead pony's name was born again in her mind – "he was a right little sod too."

"It's Leda, Baby," Jasper's introduction came late and awkwardly. There was something else he didn't say. Leda said it for him. "I'm blind, June, blind as a bat." Her admission was so light-weight she might have said "I'm the cousin with a cold in her head – nothing serious."

June stared, appalled. Immediately she felt overcome by a gross comprehensive pity as for an old dog dragging a sightless body across a carpet – a pity lacking in any approach to understanding, belonging only in sad story books – Ginger in *Black Beauty* filled her mind. "I'll make a really good fire," she said, confused and hurrying away from such a tragic state of affairs – a blind cousin now, a Jewish cousin, forgotten even before the times of death camps. It was out of order that she should reappear when long years had quenched her memory, even as a social skeleton in the family cupboard. In the uneasy silences of time there was still something untold and unforgotten about Leda.

June loved laying and lighting and building fires, she had a real hunger for the work, compulsive as eating. To force life into a reluctant or dying fire was to win her way back into a primal urge and necessity. Feeding the need of a present moment suited her abilities perfectly.

"It smells of Easter Holidays – narcissi and wood smoke." Leda took a breath and choked a little in the crackle of newly lighted wood and newspaper. Jasper led her to a chair, pushing it gently towards her – a butler at a dinner party. She accepted his help as naturally as she had taken his hand crossing the hall. There was a cool grace about her lack of thank you's, that prompted a wish to help her more. "I must bring in your suitcase," was all Jasper could think of for the moment.

When his step grew distant: "June, is there a Baby June anywhere?" Leda asked the air.

June's teddy-bear bottom lifted from the grate. "I'm here. Did you want anything?" She felt pleased and ready to oblige.

"Just – the lavatory, if you could help me. Tomorrow I'll find the way myself, really I shall. I promise you."

Like Jasper, June took Leda's hand as one dances with a child and guided her up the long staircase and down the two deceitful steps to the bathroom.

"This is where I'm such a bore," Leda said. "I'm all right now, but if you could come back, just this time. I'll soon know my way everywhere." She sounded confident of staying for quite a time, June thought with just a glint of mistrust.

On the turn of the staircase June and Jasper met; June on her way back to the drawing-room fire, Jasper with Leda's suitcase in his hand: "Where is she going to sleep?" he asked. "The Yellow Room, I expect. Better put the electric fire on, don't you think?" – "And a hot bottle in the bed," June added. It was at the sound of car wheels turning on the gravel sweep that she stiffened to the stillness of a dog setting game, before her eyes swivelled to Jasper's eye. "Jesus, child," she whispered, "the old girls will be killed out." She looked nearly as malign as Jasper while they waited together in the turn of the staircase.

April and May were still waiting, held together in their surprise at the unusual, when steps came down the staircase. June's pounding feet and Jasper's light escapist tread reached the bottom of the flight together. The family met in the hall, and each waited for another to speak. In the oddly ominous pause a flare of dismay went equally through April and May. "Gripper," thought May, and her hand flew to her mouth. April, in a second of panic, doubted if she had locked her bedroom door.

Jasper came nearer to them, delaying what he had to tell: "Leda has come back," he said.

"And do you know what?" June came nearer too. "She's blind."

"Leda? How embarrassing. Leda's dead." May made Leda alive sound like an untidy business.

"She's back from the grave, if that cheers you up at all." Jasper's jibe was spoken absently. He had a worried look. "I must really think about dinner now."

"Must she stay to dinner? Won't a drink do?" May was frostily opposed to a live Leda.

"We can't send her away tonight" – any opposition from May was enough to raise Jasper's resistance. "She's staying in County Monaghan."

"In *Monaghan*." May made Monaghan sound almost disrespectable.

"She is so. She is in a convent with the nuns," June supplied.

"Then why is she here? Have the nuns expelled her?" May persisted.

"Nobody ever tells me anything," April said with wounded resignation. "*Who* is here?" She produced her notepad, little pencil attached. Her eyes quested theirs. For once there was no pursuit of her own calm interpretation of what they were saying.

"LEDA" Jasper wrote. "Your cousin Leda."

"Leda." Trumpets sounded behind April's deaf-toned voice. "Where is she?"

"LOO," June shouted. "Loo?" April repeated the easy word.

"And she'll break her leg on the stairs. She's blind, April, she's *blind*."

"BLIND" Jasper wrote.

"Blind?" April put Tiger down. "She'll need me."

"She can't see you. You won't hear her. Quite hopeless." Though at first un-welcoming, May was not going to be left out of the fun. Out-distanced, she shrugged a dismissal of any importance, for April had almost taken flight up the staircase. She was at the bathroom door as Leda opened it and stood hesitating, her hands feeling the air for guidance.

"I thought I was just an old lady lost . . ." she laughed as if the idea was really funny.

"Leda, darling." April could not hear her own voice, or the jubilant tenderness in her welcome. She put Tiger down and put her hands in Leda's fumbling hands before she looked at her with deep dismay.

Leda's hands were strong, searching and unchanged. "You know I'm blind," she fluted out the news like a jolly bird-song. "Are you still so beautiful?" she asked as though that was what really mattered most.

April laughed – a laugh that could have meant either admittance or denial. No mention of her deafness as she bent over Leda and took her arm. She stole sly looks and looked away as they went together, slowly together, down the staircase where

she had watched from above while Leda sobbed aloud and ran
and jumped into waiting arms for comfort. Now it was a help-
less Leda, feeling her way at every step. "I'll remember when
I've done it once," she promised as though to herself, "I hate to
be helped. I need to be left alone." Her ageless assurance was
almost shocking compared with the heavy undisciplined body,
the swollen ankles that made her shoes strain and tighten at the
insteps. There were no lines in Leda's face, the pale flesh was as
if folded on to its bones. The great blue spectacles swam faintly
diabolic, two mocking eyes telling nothing. Only her white hair
had the same lyrical quality as when it was blonde. Short now, it
clung around her head and face as well placed as feathers on a
bird.

At least April could approve the coat that Leda was wearing –
a wonderful dark blue overcoat, drifting and moving with the
wearer, yet keeping a Napoleonic, a military suggestion. Obviously, to April, it came from some great couture house – but
when? The padded shoulders, a certain neatness and definition
dated it. It had been made in the forties; a world away.

"Tomorrow," April said, "you must tell me everything."
Tomorrow she felt she might hear better.

"Oh, I love to tell All. Only ask, I'll bore on for ever. Now
where are we? In the hall? Now the drawing-room – don't say
it. First door on the left." She preceded a hovering April.
Tiger, wounded by the unusual neglect, lagged sulking behind
them.

The smell of *Hamamelis mollis*, not quite honey, not yet
primroses, met them as they opened the door. June's great fire
had loosed its cold stored restraint. "Don't tell me," Leda said
again. She waited, like someone about to step into a warm sea –
"It's witch hazel."

"Right, first time," May applauded. "Can you get the
other?" It was more than a garden quiz, almost a test question.

Leda walked further into the room. The lily of the valley scent from another of May's arrangements drifted and rose and sank as she moved about. She knew it like a forgotten word, she knew the scent in the room this evening as it had been fifty years before, surreptitious and elusive, distanced from the plant that carried its flowers or from the vase holding them; from a further place, as you pass by, it finds you. "*Mahonia baelii,*" Leda hazarded, almost shyly.

May was pleased at her diffidence.

"Right again," she commended. "You deserve a drink. Would you like a glass of sherry?"

"Oh I would." Before May got to the sherry bottle Leda put out a hand. Her acceptance made a delightful importance of the pleasure in store. "Thank you, May," she said. "I know it's May by the little girl's voice. You've kept it. I love voices."

A tide of warmth lifted May's heart. She knew she looked young for her age, but . . . "little girl's voice"! "You must meet my Gripper," she tried for the note in which she had offered the drink, "Grips, come and talk to Cousin Leda."

"I hope he likes me." Leda stroked the little dog's head, the gesture thoughtful as hand in lover's hand, before she drank, without a shrinking of dismay, from the glass of awful sherry.

"I shouldn't encourage Gripper, if I were you," Jasper came into the room, a bottle in his hand. "He has his embarrassing little whims. And I wouldn't drink that sherry either. I've found quite a treat – of course I may have kept it too long."

"Ever since the sober years of war, all drink has been delicious." Leda took another small sip of her sherry. There was a silence in which Jasper and May felt for a moment back in the unnamed years, in the shadows of a prison camp and among its horrid graves. It seemed indecent to ask a question. Any question. They would refrain. It would be easier.

June came in, Tiny lumbering solemnly beside her – they stopped in the doorway. So framed and waiting they must be going to deliver some portentous news. June spoke for both: "I went up to put a bottle in the bed in the Yellow Room and – do you know what? There's a whole flood of water down from the ceiling and into the bed."

"And did I, or did I not remind you about the broken shutes?" May turned pleasurably on Jasper. "How long ago? How often? Well – there you are."

"And how long since you have inspected the bedrooms, Miss Head Housemaid? If I may ask?" Jasper was drawing the cork out of the bottle with care and ceremony, not the moment for interruption. "The Blue Room, perhaps?" he suggested lightly, as though about to run through a list of guest rooms. June was ready with a good answer: "No, Jasper. That bed is in a mortifying case with the cats."

"I'll sleep with anything. Cats? I love cats." Leda's lie was obvious enough to ask for disbelief.

"You can't," June said, "let alone the bed, you wouldn't see what you'ld be stepping on before you stepped onto it."

"Oh, Baby, I carried you to watch them drowning kittens when you were two – you can't remember?"

"I do so. The kittens scratched me and you pinched me and I yelled," June recalled faithfully.

"Oh, I was naughty," Leda laughed indulgently, "and I'm still naughty. So take care."

"I will too," June said.

"The question is," Jasper took Leda's sherry glass out of her hand and almost closed her fingers on the stem of the wine glass he gave her in its place – "where does Leda lay down her head tonight?" He made her sound like a pitiful vagrant. No one offered their room. No one suggested a sofa.

"What's the trouble?" April sensed difficulty in the pause.

"*Beds*," May shouted. Jasper wrote something down on the back of an envelope. When April read it she said, with the authority of an elder sister – a married and monied sister: "Well, Leda must sleep in Mummie's room." Leda smiled happily; her mind circled anti-clockwise.

"A night or two, I suppose." May was genuinely hesitant.

"And I was so hoping you might let me stay a little longer – of course I must pay like I pay in this convent my darling child has found for me to die in. I'll never be able to die – the nuns take such good care of me. I'll just exist. They lead me everywhere, and I need to find my own way – to smell and feel and touch my way." Her voice was shrill with protest – "Oh, they are so kind" – her voice dropped.

"We shall have to think about it," Jasper seemed unsure. "Anyway, see to things, May, would you? While I get dinner together."

"Perhaps you'ld help me, Baby." May seemed anxious, even pleading.

"And to think you're the first to sleep in that bed . . ." June put a hand against her mouth. "Well, your guess is as good as mine," she amended. Tiny dragged herself up to follow the sisters out of the room.

April and Leda were alone.

April: an old woman, deprived in her infirmity, persistent in the safe-keeping of her beauty, cheerful slave to the disciplines involved and apostle of their benefits.

Leda: in the terrible freedom of the blind exuberantly un-aware of lost beauty, confident, as always, in her ways to women's acceptance and to man's desiring.

April spoke first. She chattered on, veiling her deafness. "Leda, what has happened to you? You've put on weight. You must go on my diet – magical. Where have you been? How long can you stay with us?"

"Oh, I can stay. I'm free. Femme seule – I must tell you, my husband is dead."

"Husband?" April had got the word husband and seen Leda's mouth fall down and tighten, lines from nose to chin gripping sadly into the loose flesh. "Have another drink," she suggested, "and I'll tell you about my breathing exercises – you must follow my régime – you'll get your shape back, you'll see."

What did they have for each other now, divided by sight and hearing? Where did they begin again? Impossible to revive an emotion that belonged only in the strength and pains of youth. After such an absence what could survive? How to communicate? April, from her accepted isolation, her self-made content, saw disaster in Leda's looks. She felt more disapproval than pity. Even in a death camp April would have struggled to keep up her exercises, control her breathing. "Everybody eats too much, anyway," she would have said as she gnawed on a cabbage stalk.

"It's a miracle finding you again," Leda's voice swelled, "after all this time – I've gone through the looking glass. Time's a joke," she stopped, her words wasting into the silent room. She heard someone move a chair. All domestic sounds were catalogued in her mind. "Is it April?"

"I'm going to fill your glass," April's voice came from some distance unconnected with Leda's loving speech, "but tomorrow you must promise to start on my diet. We can't let ourselves go."

"Diets? The sadness of it! Oh April, how we stuffed chocolates. Aunt Violet said they gave us spots. We bicycled to the village and ate chocolates on the mountain coming home. April, don't you remember? Why don't you answer? APRIL!"

April heard a shout. "I must tell you, Leda," she said, "I'm slightly deaf."

"And I'm as blind as a bat." Some vibration from the past set them laughing together – they went on, laughing as delightedly, as irrepressibly as they had when life was all laughter, or all tears – nothing between the two to be suffered, or to outlive.

As if sharing in some unacknowledged celebration the evening changed its sharp weather to a dream of summertime, false as a dream, and as exciting. Indoors it seemed so because the house was warmed by an extravagant up-turn of radiators and storage heaters. The constant smells of yesterday were lifted to colder heights and their vacancies held breaths of May's narcissi as well as the crisp incense of bay leaves Jasper toasted on the Aga. "Herbs on a shovel," he commented to himself, disparaging or excusing this quelling of customary kitchen smells.

When someone opened the hall door to put out a dog the evening seemed warmer even than the house, a warmth with rain to follow. In the starless interval of early dusk lost wintersweets and forgotten viburnums fed the air with their suggestions. The hour held for its own a brief and passing recreation of the time when Durraghglass was warm and clean, well-served and full of flowers from the now shattered greenhouses; a time when life had its comforts and its dignified reserves. Then children were discouraged from rudeness, even to one another. Sharp retorts were in bad style. Then, an obstinate mist of love clouded over their disabilities, accepting them and accepting an impotence towards any change in their condition. Mummie had indulgence for everything. From Baby June's dyslexia ("she'll outgrow it, darling"), past Jasper's mortifying eye, and beyond their father's tragic accidental death, she never yielded in her over-looking; never let go her mortal loves, or her strong religious faith and natural jealousies.

These were the submerged days that Leda's coming rescued from a deep oblivion. Since she could not see Durraghglass in its cold decay, or her cousins in their proper ages, timeless grace was given to them in her assumption that they looked as though all the years between were empty myths. Because they knew themselves so imagined, their youth was present to them, a mirage trembling in her flattery as air trembles close on the surface of summer roads. What more might she recall? What else might she show them of their lost selves?

They sat with her, or left her by turns, imagining, mistakenly, that her blindness was melancholy. April was her most constant companion, her memory a perfect mine of diets and exercises for the restoration of the present Leda to something nearer the girlfriend of the past. May came in to put eucalyptus leaves on the fire, and to advise Leda to pay no attention to April's prescriptions. She lit a cigarette for Leda with dry-lipped carefulness and put it between her fingers where it stayed, unsmoked, until April took it away and threw it in the fire. Jasper brought pieces of hot toast spread with anchovy butter and parsley and sat with her to prevent April's interference with the healthy snack. Leda ate one slice, licked her fingers, and ate another. June came in to stack the broken wood-basket, but said nothing. They forbade her to change for dinner because her bedroom would still be cold. They seemed to have overcome their hesitation over putting her to sleep in a bed empty since their mother's death, and in the room where the cupboards were still full of her clothes and hats.

Oddly charged by her presence, each of them, unthinking of a reason, planned to dress as elaborately for dinner as if she could see and appraise them, or was it a parade for each other?

April curtailed her exercises, swallowed a vitamin pill and a very quick drink. She had a flash of pleasure in the thought of having a bedroom drink with Leda. She too remembered illicit chocolates on the mountain and the idea of a secret to be shared again excited her.

May forgot to chat to Gripper and postponed the placing of the agate marble she had so lately acquired. She could already say to herself "Oh, quite pretty – I wonder where I found it?" The other word for finding never formed itself in her mind: "where I picked it up" came nearest. In the bathroom she gargled lavishly before trying out that little girl's voice Leda remembered.

Only June made no change in her usual habits of dress. Her importances were her own. Leda's recall of drowning kittens and a howling baby lived more vividly to her than the other flattering moment, when she had caught her breath in a splendid lost dimension of childhood.

Jasper put watercress in a wooden bowl, rice to dry in the oven, and his fish medley and eggwhites to simmer in peppered cream. Before he went up to dress he turned back from the kitchen door and put another branch of bay leaves to smoke and blacken on the low ring of the Aga. He smiled a twisted sneer at himself as he put his father's evening cuff-links in the cuffs of a silk shirt. He felt rather defiant over the jewelled links and a Charvet scarf – collar and bow tie might be a bit too obvious – the girls would notice if he overdid it. He must evade their un-spoken comment, the look that recognised a change. He despised and mistrusted them, but feared more that they despised him. Jasper felt curiously elated in the suspicion he allowed himself that Leda was not a fourth sister in his life. He saw himself embarking on the hallucination of a flirtation, a fresh leisure interest, a pretence about which to worry the girls. He expected Leda to recognise this as clearly as he did. She would play at the idea, as he would. But beyond this graceful limitation, in every word spoken between them fixed currents changed course. There was a delving interest in a pause. Her voice salvaged the wreckage of her beauty. In any case her body was of little interest to Jasper, but the stuff of old dreams had a frightening potency, a magic to be avoided.

On his way back to the kitchen Jasper stopped for a minute on the turn of the staircase where from the high, floor-length window he saw a swan rise through the ribbons of mist lying along the river. There is ecstasy in a swan's flying; in the neck leaning lasciviously on air, the body stretched behind the shouting wings. He watched while his swan took her short flight and dropped back through the mists to the water, her landing lost to his sight. It was as much as Jasper asked of any emotional moment: to be, and to cease. He was never one for squandering emotion. He had saved and pinched and scraped on it in so many directions that, finally, there was very little left to squander.

Slightly flown on wine and kümmel with their coffee April and May were in keen competition as to which of them would guide Leda to her room and help her to bed. "I am tired, Jasper." She had said it conspiratorially behind the argument in process between the sisters.

"I know you want to take your dog out so I'll show Leda where everything is." Determination was behind April's cosy hostess manner.

"You can't show her anything," May wrote, "can't you see she can't see?"

"I expect we shall manage all right," April answered smoothly.

"What about your own dog?" ran May's scribble. "Does he never want to . . . . ?"

"Can't read a word. Leda, shall we?"

"Please. It's been such a long flight from the convent." Leda yawned pitifully. Using April's deafness as readily as the rest of the family, she said to May: "Come and tuck me up. Promise."

The door of the mother's bedroom opened wide in welcome to the room sacredly unused but as sacredly swept and dusted. Leda smiled as she walked through it. She went unguided across the floor to the big elaborate bed. "We had our last talk in here, Aunt Violet and I," she said. "This room smells just the same. Always violets. . . ."

"You won't let it worry you, sleeping here?" April was turning back the bed covers. She felt reassurance might be needed. "Nobody has slept here since . . . . but I know she wouldn't mind."

"Oh, I like to feel her near." Leda's voice made the idea into something childish and pretty.

"Your blue nightdress?" April asked, busy at the suitcase, "or the pink?"

"I don't care. Perhaps the blue."

"All right. The pink. And where is your night cream?"

"Oh, I never bother. There isn't any."

"Leda, I can't find any nourishing skin food." April persisted in her search.

Leda made a pantomime of writing and April blushed. "I can hear if you speak very slowly," she said, and knelt, fortified by years of exercises, as easily as any child, to take off Leda's shoes. Leda put out her hands to find April's head, then stooped her mouth level with April's ear. "I was longing for a good talk," she said, "without all the others. Like when we used to escape together."

"I heard you," April said. Leda's sweet voice had touched some thread, for once connecting sound and sense. "Leda, I heard you plainly." She lifted eyes swimming with tears to Leda's unresponding glamorous spectacles and she felt, of the two, far the less maimed. "Sit where you are," she commanded, "while I go to my room for my Cream Vitamin Plus. It's pure magic."

"Will it be worth it?" Leda thought, waiting in obedience. "I was rather comfortable in the convent. And safe."

May came in, her entrance neatly timed to April's exit. She carried a torch and a bell. She kicked gently under the bed's valance till the po beneath tingled. "It's just by the leg of the bed – if you must go to the loo – ring this bell." She clanged it.

"Oh, how merry," Leda said.

"April is nearest. She won't hear, of course, but her beastly little dog will and he'll wake me."

"I *am* being spoilt."

"And tomorrow we'll make a space for you in the cupboard. You haven't brought much, have you?"

"I haven't got much. Not here. Tania didn't give me time to pack when we left America."

"Tania? That's your daughter. Sounds a very tiresome child to me."

"Aren't all children tiresome?" Leda conceded, laughing, "especially when you depend on them?" She took off her coat which she had worn throughout the evening. Under it she was wearing something frail and black and softly pleated, quite unsuitable to the Irish climate; and under that almost nothing. She sat on the edge of the bed, crossed her knees and swung her feet, as lightly as a girl.

"What a lovely coat – shall I hang it up? It's as light as a feather."

"It should be. It's vicuna."

"You bought it in America?"

"Oh, no. Does it look like it? Paris, in the war."

"But, Leda, you know we all thought . . . ."

"*Please.* I try to forget what you all thought." Leda's hands went over her spectacled eyes; long lean hands with fat thumbs, reached past her eyes to her hair. It seemed to May that they changed in a moment from the gesture of defensive protection to a movement lightly moulding and caressing the extravagantly pretty growth round her ears and temples.

Looking at Leda's hands, used so impartially to shut out remembrance or to caress, a wave of relief broke in May's mind, a sense of being whole because Leda could not see and, possibly, had no recall of the misfortune that was May's right hand.

"And you do love my little dog, don't you, Leda?" Gripper was scouring suspiciously round the unmarked territories of the unfamiliar room. "He wants to say goodnight. Grips – come to Mummie." The close relief and warmth May was feeling made her long for some return – she demanded approval for her love-object, as a mother seeks the same, sideways, for an unattractive child.

Again Leda's hand went down to find that vulnerable pleasure spot behind the little dog's ears. "I wonder what happened to my dogs," she said gently.

May would not comment or ask a question recalling so much pain, so long ignored.

"Would you like a hot drink? Or biscuits? Could you manage a thermos?"

Before Leda could accept or refuse the night-time comforts offered, April came back, her interruption simplified by her lack of hearing. "This is the stuff Ulick brings me from Paris." She held, like a chalice between her hands, a small jar. "Just a touch and you must pat it upwards, it cleans and tightens and builds and nourishes."

"Oh, darling, and does it do all that in French?" Leda took just a very little and smelt it. "Ravishing. I bet it cost the earth."

"Don't worry about that. She can afford it," May reassured her. "Have a good go. Take off your glasses."

Leda stiffened in her refusal. "No. I feel naked without them – almost ugly."

For once the sisters looked at each other in perfect appalled accord. They realised together that Leda could have no idea of what she looked like now – an old, pitifully plain woman, blind and in need of their comfort. They found themselves, in their whole health and in their ability to give, in power over Leda, that legendary figure of glamour who had become a victim of a terror and a captivity they had steadily refused to envisage. She had come back to them after their long forgetfulness and they were set to cherish and make amends. They did not want to be disgusted and repelled by tales of terrors and filth they had so long ignored. She was to be their darling and their pet. Already they were squabbling over who should do the most petting. They tried to outstay each other. "You're sure you've got this?" – "Do you want that?" – "Here's the bell." – "There's the po." – "Don't get up till I call you." – "I've hung up your clothes in the cupboard." It was a mistimed duet of helpfulness.

"Where is the cupboard?" was the only question Leda asked. "Ah – straight across from the foot of the bed. But I shan't want a thing. I'm very cosy." She rolled her shoulders in the pillows and pulled her hot-water bottle close. "Oh, such bliss. Good-night, darlings, my darlings, à demain."

Still arguing about her breakfast tray, they left the room together, each unwilling to allow the other a separate last good-night.

When she could no longer hear May shouting at April and the sounds of their footsteps on the stairs had thinned into silence, Leda sat up in bed. Before they left her the sisters had carefully switched off the electric blanket and unplugged the fire. Cold was filtering back into the room as it had done before electricity came to the mountains and to Durraghglass. Now Leda pulled April's bed-shawl round her shoulders and swung her legs out of bed. She sat for a minute, easy and waiting for what she intended to do. She could touch her slippers left carefully in readiness, but she preferred to walk without them, feeling the carpet with her naked feet, the counterparts of her hands. Her feet were flawless, long boned and soft soled; walking, she used them like eyes. She smelled at the air, a gentle dog on a scent. The air of that room, venerated, undisturbed, held the sweet stuffy ghosts of Aunt Violet's violet scent and violet soap and facepowder on a swansdown puff. She could feel the room the same as on that September morning when Aunt Violet had spoken so gently, had said goodbye with tears, had given her that letter for her mother, then taken it back, saying: no, perhaps better post it. Leda remembered everything. She started on a round of the room. Touching the top of a bookcase that stood along the wall by the bed, she knew her hand would find Aunt Violet's large prayer book with its elastic band. Did it comfort her much? she wondered. Beyond the bookcase, the dressing-table stood cater-corner to the window. She guessed its position would be unaltered and she was right. Her fingers felt over the moulded flowers on the backs of silver clothes brushes and oval hand mirror, and found the hairbrush. She picked it up and held it close to her face; years of disuse had not quite purged the human smell of Aunt Violet's hair; not the nicest smell but the most evocative. Near the dressing-table she took a handful of window curtain which gave her a bearing across to the long wall opposite the bed. She stopped at the angular tidy shoe-stand, memory catching exactly at the past as she picked up and handled the little shoes, some old enough for a ribbon rosette on their pointed toes, others with the crossed straps of the twenties. She explored meticulously each token of the past: the suèdes and kidskins, satin pumps with diamanté buckles for evening, flat-heeled brown suède for race-meetings, still carefully tree-ed. The very pointed-toed hunting boots, belonging to the early days of marriage, stood there too, stiff and dry as glass on their wooden trees.

Lastly, Leda reached the vast wardrobe, constructed with

hanging spaces and drawers and shelves for every possible article of dress. When she opened the doors a mixed gush from camphor, lavender and violet sachets, for years suppressed, vomited out into the slightly warmer air of the newly inhabited room. Leda stood and drank it in, as pleasurably as a smoker inhales, before her careful hands fumbled and felt among the orderly hung rows, placed as tidily as a choir on Sundays, of Aunt Violet's clothes. She delayed when she touched the true silks of the twenties and thirties, ran a finger down the accordion pleats of a skirt, laid a tickled cheek to ostrich feathers, avoided tweeds and held fine wool in her hands with pleasure. She had a true sense of touch on stuffs, and a proper value for their textures and prices.

Her hands quiet, their explorations over, she stood for a stilled moment in reverent recollection before, gathering in her breath so that her body seemed to extend and exude power, she spat with virulent intention into the padded breasts of a beaded evening dress – violet she was sure, though she could not see its colour. She shut the cupboard doors carefully before, getting onto all fours like a big cat, she found the electric heater and plugged it in, neatly and competently. Back in bed she touched the ON switch of her blanket, and when she had clasped her hot-water bottle (forbidden in conjunction with electricity) closely to her, she was as happy in her mischief as any child could be.

It was only when she heard a man's distinct unhurrying steps coming up the first flight of the stairs, crossing the landing below the long window and continuing up and on and out of hearing, or contact with any interest beyond his own nightly concerns and comforts, unshared in an endless regularity of habit, that she shut her blind eyes behind her glasses, spread, then curled each hand separately as though they held her purpose in their grasps (but one must not know what the other knew), stretched her body into the lengths and depths of Aunt Violet's bed and then allowed the constant miracle (Leda was a wonderfully good sleeper) to set her free from all purposes on long healthy breaths, drawn in perfect peace.

6 ❧ Rediscovery

In every beginning there is a certain tense excitement, a brief time of discovery before all is familiar, to be accepted or discarded. It was like this in the first days of Leda's return to Durraghglass. Her evocation of a past time was so strong that even the house yielded up its cold poverty as she pulled the past into the present remembering pictures or silver, long ago sold, so vividly that their lost qualities restored themselves, ghostlike, to their empty spaces.

After the first morning, when she had counted the steps of the stairs – three up, three down to the bathroom, twenty-two on the flight to the hall – she refused guidance to the drawing-room or to her usual chair, placed by May at just the right distance from June's enormous fires.

It was a performance, as she crossed the room and set herself down as confidently and provocatively as though she could see an audience. In these ways she repudiated her blindness, insisting that it should be forgotten. Her hands lay along the chair arms, her feet were crossed with elegance. She leaned a little forward, waiting for entertainment, or ready to give it. She was not a weighty or demanding guest. She could neither read nor sew nor play cards, but she could talk beguilingly and funnily. All the memories of their childhood and youth were easily within her recall. The absurdities and successes and lamentable moments came out like toys from a box, alerting them to young forgotten people: themselves. It was a game, which because of her sightlessness she could play honestly: she had not seen age overtake them. In her approaches April and May were shy and dazzled by turns. It was a silly balm of pleasure to which Jasper was only mildly addicted, his politeness distanced familiarity. His pinched expression of avoidance was invisible to her, but she was aware of the forced kindliness of the hands holding only the outside of her arms, as he helped her to a chair, and of how he took his hands off her arms quickly, in a polite recoil, dull and strange. A moment to accept, an approach to be changed.

Leda spoke English as she had learned it from her mother, the Swift English; but her voice had a lush quality that softened the correct accent. The family voice that she shared with Jasper had no autumnal creak. When she laughed the sound hung on the air – the last note of a wild free song, a celebration. There was glory and sweetness in her laughter. Her silences were pregnant with past considerations and calculations for the present.

It was in the dog rivalries that Leda became an intermediary, fostering jealousies. She soon knew the dogs apart – Tiny was the simplest to identify. Leda's hands fumbled the big head, patiently waiting its caress. But it was the dreadful smell which told her precisely who it was she praised when June was near, and belittled gently in June's absence.

"Stinking and senile," May said, "more than time to put her down. Right?"

"You don't think she could have a growth, do you?"

"Certain of it. Sheer cruelty keeping her alive – never off heat, either. So upsetting for Gripper."

"Well, you do have a point."

"The little fellow can't get his mind off her – no, Grips. Not Mummie's knee."

"He *is* a virile boy."

Then, to April it might be: "Lend me Tiger for a bit. I want to warm my hands. Come and be my skater's muff, sweetie. No nasty habits like Gripper, have you?"

"Yes, Tiny man loves a good gallop."

However April translated it, Leda felt that she had said her piece and shown a preference.

When Tiny nearly brought her down as she steered her way across the hall she cursed her, but in German. June near, and not near enough, had no suspicion of the sharp kick so nearly suffered by her darling. "You should have shouted, Leda. I was only setting the drawing-room fire."

"My own silly fault. Come here, darling. Why doesn't Auntie May like you?"

"*Sit*, Tiny," June said, refusing compliance with the stranger.

"And you carry all the wood and turf?"

"When I've cut it up with the circular saw," June stated proudly.

"You clean the grates, too, do you? It's too much for you, Baby. Why doesn't Jasper help?"

"Grates aren't a man's work, that's the why."

With Jasper her true doggie feelings found a proper expression: "Your sisters' dogs – they do love them. A bit like super nannies with rival babies."

"Yes. And I have to cook for their babies. All cooks hate the nursery world."

"Can't the girls do it? The girls should do it. Why don't they?"

"No. They'ld cut each other's throats. Besides, I can't let them near the Aga. God forbid."

"Yes. I see. The kitchen is a man's place. My father's kitchen was a kingdom. A place for creation. A world for invention. I'm glad he died before. . . ."

"I've never been to Vienna," Jasper said hastily forestalling any sad reminiscence.

"Don't go now." Change and regret sounded in her voice. "I'm glad I can't see it. I have to forget – I must." There was a pause. "Do you laugh at the dogs?" she went on, "or are you absolutely maddened?"

"Well," he felt warmed. Her understanding was on the edge of his acceptance. "One can't take it all too seriously."

"The sisters, the dogs, this place – Durraghglass, you can't laugh it all off your shoulders." She couldn't see his face darken. She waited, then let the subject go. "I've been meaning to ask you – would you let me have the receipt for the watercress soup you gave us last night? I could take it back to Sister Agnes – it would be so comforting, when I leave you."

"It's an old Durraghglass receipt," he answered with polite uncertainty.

"All right. I'll exchange it for Papa's secret – the greatest goulash. It's written on my heart. His books are lost." She shuddered, but only just. "Would you allow me in your kitchen? I've been there before . . . but you wouldn't remember. . . ."

He saw her, surpliced and tied in a cook's white apron, sucking her fingers and laughing with the cook while they waited for an Austrian confection to sublimate itself in the oven. The untidy blonde hair was escaping down her neck and over her eyes. He put down the pigeons he had shot and went away. He knew Mummie didn't welcome any reminders of Viennese restaurants and considered the presence of young ladies in the kitchen unnecessary and in poor taste. After Leda's departure that torte had been eaten; he remembered it as an insubstantial happening. Avoiding the thought of Leda's hair then, short and white now, he rather resented the sleight of memory. But the sense of things forbidden rose out of the past. In an odd excitement of fake disobedience he said, "Yes. That would be interesting."

"Oh, when shall we put our heads together?" she laughed.

Jasper grudged himself any certainty. Decisions were not to be captured and dated. "Oh, some day. You aren't leaving us just yet," and he left the room murmuring about something forgotten, a reason for escape.

Alone, Leda bit her lip – the "just" in "just yet" had been disappointing.

As Tuesday merged into Wednesday, then Thursday, and the days past Thursday quickened towards another Tuesday, April and May conspired against each other in their rival love affair with Leda's needs and care. She leaned on their help lightly, gracious and grateful, distancing herself while retaining the half sexual aura of the most popular girl in the school. It was in April's bedroom that intimacy quickened and throve in the evening sessions. April, the deaf but sighted one, the one with the money, was happy in this unison with Leda which excluded her virgin family. Once they had whispered and giggled in curiosity and innocence, now their talk matured into the discussion of marriages past and diets present, health-giving exercises for the body, drinks in place of chocolates, and always clothes, lovely clothes to be displayed and felt and discussed with April's endless knowledge and seeing eye and with Leda's perfect attention and agreement. The other side of this warm restoration was less agreeable, for April insisted, and couldn't hear no for an answer, on celery seeds and other herbal concoctions, to be swallowed before the vodka bottle came out of the cupboard. There was deep breathing at the open window and stringent exercises to be performed on the floor, and directed with all the vigour of a good games mistress, before Leda was robed in some dark benediction for evening, chosen by April from her treasure house. Then, a vodka martini beside her and a note-book on her

knee, Leda would enlarge her tolerance with a good drink and
scrawl comments on yesterday, today and tomorrow. Sometimes there was a joke in the wildly scribbled word, even a
risqué joke. April would bend close into that muffled distance of
hearing she occasionally knew in the tone Leda gave to spoken
words, and they would laugh together till tears rolled out under
Leda's blue glasses and she mopped them from her fat cheeks
and wrote: "What about another little drinkie, darling? Can't
face Jasper's sherry." In such faint tokens of criticism sides were
taken and preference shown.

May was the cousin who had least appeal for Leda. May had
no wish to overstep into the ring of horror where Leda had
suffered, but she could not restrain her curiosity in lesser
hardships: the Convent, for instance. Did Leda have her own
bathroom? Did she attend Mass? Were the sisters very
strict?

Yes, and yes, and Oh, no. They are kind – Leda's answers
echoed her patient acceptance.

"And your daughter Tania – what's her other name?"

"Same as mine. Unpronounceably German Jewish."

"Can't cope with that. She's not married?"

"She's a career girl. She has money."

"And, in America, who paid for who?"

"My friend. She was rich too."

"Then why did you leave her?"

"I told you, darling. Things got difficult for him – Tania
found this convent. It was all her idea."

"Does she know about us? The Swifts. Does she know
you're here?"

"Yes, vaguely. She's on one of her big assignments. Some
kidnap somewhere, I expect – Germany, perhaps. She doesn't
tell me. I suppose she can't."

"Very funny. Rather rum."

"And now, darling, I think I'll have a tiny zizz – lunch was far too good."

Perhaps she closed her eyelids, how could May tell? But in the silence she pondered the "her" and "him" in Leda's replies. She would have liked to hear more, but time pressed on. She had secured Christy Lucey for half a day's work in the kitchen garden, so grudged a moment lost in watchfulness over his work or his lassitude.

The kitchen garden and its greenhouses were, for May, filled with the not unhappy presence of her Edwardian mother, always wearing her hat and sometimes neatly veiled. Her mother had none of the present snobbish form of gardening, of balancing and landscaping even a small area. She planted exactly where her plants would do best. From this principle there grew the wandering bows and tidy knots of box edging, gardens within gardens, within gardens – Russian dolls in their spaces – spaces skeleton now but ever containing small treasures, whether they flowered in spring, summer or winter: gentian, double white violets, cyclamen, double primroses, saxifrage, Hose-in-Hose, May could see them still with some of the avid perceptions of childhood.

Pergolas were the thing too, they ran the lengths and richly enclosed the squares of vegetables. Their arches bent and rusted, now barren of the American Beauty that clothed them once. No more Dorothy Perkins either: May could see nothing in those lush drapings of pink to suggest Coarse Gardening – an expression taken by Jasper from Coarse Fishing. She could remember with pleasure the period triumphs of the rock garden with its awesome torrents of aubretia. Like a person in a long dream she re-established the autumn border, peaches and greengages and Comice pears on the hot wall at its back (narrow glass shelves running ludicrously above their heads) and below grew dahlias and Michaelmas daisies and clove carnations, falling out on the path among their dry, jointed stems.

May still lived on in the imbalances the garden had outgrown to be a wilderness. She could never forget the careful sumptuous days of her mother's gardening – with a head gardener and a helper or two. Her mother's garden had nothing to do with Jasper's wild landscaping of wood and river bank. In those Better Days flowers were grown inside the walls of the kitchen garden. There was little or no planting of shrubs round a country house. Instead there were acres of mown grass; a pony, shod in leather, for their mowing; wide dappling of tree shadows smooth on their surfaces. The gravel sweeps were weedless and stone pineapples had not toppled off the pillars of the steps going down to the river. It was definite as any photograph to May. She resented the present overgrowth and hated the ash saplings taking over the tennis courts – like letting in the tinkers, she thought.

The kitchen garden was a different matter – it was enclosed. Ivy might cloak and drag at its walls, docks and nettles invade its distances, but those parts of it maintained by her vigilance were May's thrust into a conceit of happiness. Every foot of the walled wilderness that could be kept under cultivation was of vital importance to May. It was her province. She fought for its maintenance with all the strength of her immense will. The rotations of peas, beans, spinach; the triumphant hatchings in battered frames of new potatoes for Easter; the continual supplies of parsley, chives, mints (in choice varieties), thymes, oregano and basil were the successes May brought to birth, properly in their seasons or their perpetuities.

The kitchen garden, situated as was usual at a proper distance from the house, had its narrow green door implanted deep and dark in the thickness of the garden wall, a solid cut-stone arch holding it safe from time and neglect. Myrtles reared up giant rusty stems on either side. The lock on the wooden door had a big smooth keyhole and the easily turned key made its own possessive sound as May turned it and went in, like a robin or a fox, to possess her territory.

Gripper hated gardening, but he came along. May brought his bean bag and intended to settle him comfortably in one of the shattered greenhouses before giving her full attention to Christy Lucey. As she expected, Christy Lucey, the unwilling slave, was dreaming over a barrow-load of manure. May looked into the trench he was about to fill. "We must dig that six inches deeper," she said briskly.

"Excuse me, Miss, but I'm killed from digging," Christy stated gently.

"Dig deeper, Christy, and don't fill in the manure until I tell you," May said before she moved off, a garden trug full of seed packets, slug-tox and small stainless steel tools in her hand, on her own busy concerns.

Christy looked less than gentle as he took up his spade. You couldn't satisfy that one, he thought and wished that he was out schooling the Wild Man with Miss Baby to instruct and admire him. Even cleaning out the pigs without a vigilant eye on his short rest periods would be preferable to the heavy employment of this long afternoon. As his day was ending May delayed him for help in lifting and replacing the old pierced pots covering the seakale while she gently explored the mounds of leaf mould and shook her head regretfully at the infancy of the violet and white thongs they blanched and nourished. "Give them another week," she decided and piled the dark mould over them again.

Elated rather than tired by her afternoon spent in today's work and vain thoughts of other days, May released Christy (not an instant sooner than five-thirty) and walked back to the house and tea. Her garden trug with half-empty seed packets clipped together by clothes pegs hung on her arm, a pot of dark primulas was between her hands, her dog snuffled along, interested and contented, behind her. Before she reached the house April and Leda, walking arm-in-arm, drew near her. Leda's head was raised and April was bending down, a smile breaking the monotonous beauty of her face – obviously she had heard whatever it was that Leda had said – or thought she had, May commented to herself. She saw Leda stumble into a stray pot-hole. Her weight, pulling away from April who held Tiger in the crook of her other arm very nearly brought them both down. They laughed.

"That was a near one," May put down her flower pot and hurried forward to take Leda's other arm, "if you must go walking so late, I'll come along too."

There was a pause, like a silence in a jolly party, and she felt Leda's arm a little less than receptive.

April said, "We mean to walk for at least half an hour and we should be jogging if we followed the programme properly." Leda said, "Run home, May, darling, and tell Jasper I shall need a big delicious tea after all that."

May felt dismissed. If the two mature ladies had still been the best friends of their schooldays, May would not have felt that they distanced her further. When they had gone a little way from her she could hear them laughing again. Then one stopped the other as if suspicious of being overheard. Again alone, her hands, the maimed and the unmaimed clasped round her potted primula, May resumed her walk, heels down, toes out, sense and determination explicit in their action. Behind the propriety of this façade, all the comfortable stuff of her afternoon, the proper work extracted from Christy, the seeded drills, the times remembered, her hand forgotten, lessened in their content of importance, giving place to an old reality: April and Leda were together again. Avoided, she knew, or imagined she knew, that they were laughing at her, or about her, as they had done before. But today April was deaf and Leda was blind. May was the one who should do the laughing or refrain from laughter. She experienced the same need to exert her power in some direction as on the day when she had stolen and buried the little fox. Today she had other means of reclaiming love. She put down her flower pot again, lit a cigarette with sharp rasp on her lighter and turned back to the garden. There would, after all, be seakale for dinner. Her seakale. Jealousy and love go hand in hand.

Again in the drawing-room after her walk with April, her voice at rest from strain and her mind replete with April's faultless memories and descriptions, going back through decades of fashion, Leda held her one lovely coat round her – there was always an impression in her mind that she was naked under its timeless grace – and waited to hear Jasper's voice. Hearing him speak she could shudder again in the delight of her remorseless youth. She could feel the tremor of a revival, but as yet no clear way to follow.

"No girls here yet," he said as he came in, "oh, good."

She laughed: a complicity between them.

"Because I've made a Sally Lunn," he went on disappointingly practical, "and we can have two huge slices before they set into it."

"Oh, do let's." She accepted the change to a less exciting level. "Darling April keeps such a close watch on my diet. All for my good, but I do long for seconds."

"I thought the veal we had for lunch was quite a success, did you?"

"Perfect. I cried behind my specs thinking of darling Papa and Wiener Schnitzels – I'm not sure yours weren't better. But he had magical ways with a goulash."

"Can you remember? Do tell."

"Yes, of course. First you. . . ."

"Oh and you had to let my fire go out," it was June, down on her knees coaxing and whispering with the bellows. "Isn't the tea in a bit early today?"

"Not really, considering I have quite a lot to do about dinner."

"Wouldn't scrambled eggs do us? Christy found three more eggs today."

"I thought he was working for May today."

"He found them in his lunch hour."

"Pâté sandwiches, I suppose."

"And what happened the two slices of cooked ham I bought myself for him? Your cat, I suppose, too."

Jasper looked slightly embarrassed. The ham had made sandwiches for a different pet, an outdoor pet.

"A fellow has to get a bit to eat. That's a fact, Tiny. Isn't it a fact, Tiny?" June let the matter drop.

On the edge of the least privacy Jasper was never sorry to be pushed back into the ordinary banalities of life. He dreaded an irreclaimable step of any sort. The edge of anything was near enough for him. But he found edges irresistible. In the same way he found excitement in the creation of a wonderful dinner from forgotten scraps irresistible. He would denigrate its perfection in the dining-room before finishing any morsels left by his sisters when the dishes came back to the kitchen, testing and satisfying his exact judgement.

Leda had been with them for a week now and he could see with malign interest how April and May elbowed each other for her favours – two jealous ladies-in-waiting. He wondered how long it would be before June became a victim. He was glad to know himself outside the spell, amused and well able to resist any advances, to side-step any risky involvement. He saw

exactly how to play a role in the comedy, and found it an unusual diversion to watch those two poor old things in a shadow-
land of sexual combat.

"Oh, Baby-blessed-June," Leda stretched out her hands and
feet, supplicating warmth, "your fire is wonderful. Thank you,
darling."

"Were you cold?" Jasper asked in a surprised, hostess voice.

"I'm always cold, cold in my bones. It's a left-over from . . ."
She stopped. "Not to be a bore. Worse things happened."

"Did they put your eyes out?" June asked stolidly. She put
down the hot poker (a delicate idea) as she spoke.

"Not quite." Leda didn't laugh. "No oculist – naturally. And
after 'all that' it was a bit late. I'm used to it now. It gives me
more time."

"What for?" June was as curious as a vet about a sick animal.

"Oh, shut up, Baby." Jasper wanted to spare himself, rather
than Leda, any details.

Leda's laugh fluted away again. "Oh, you get to know people
so much better. And you miss lots of awful things, like the telly
advertisements. That sort of vulgarity."

"You can still hear the announcers' voices, especially the
weather-men, and the appalling language they speak. 'Black
Ice,' what *is* 'Black Ice'?" Jasper shuddered.

"You see – I feel you shudder," Leda said with intimate suggestion, "and we are nowhere near."

"Let's tremble together," Jasper said loudly as May came into
the room and sat down, "and have some more of my Sally
Lunn," he moved the silver dish gently away from May.

"Sally Lunn? We haven't had that since Mrs Byrne left us."

"Left us? And who sacked Mrs Byrne?" Jasper asked
sharply.

"Need we go into that? You know how it was on her
Thursday afternoons."

"No. Why should I know?"

"Or care – even when the handlebars of her bicycle were literally bending under the loads of food she stole for her friends."

"What a kind woman," Jasper said mildly.

"And who, May, nearly poisoned us putting the hyacinth bulbs in the Irish stew in place of the onions?"

"Quite right, Baby," Jasper commended the memory. "That was when I was compelled to throw you out of the kitchen, wasn't it, May? Cooking not my line of country then."

"If you ever had a line of country." May threw the end of her cigarette into June's fire. "I knocked quite a spot of work out of your spoilt boy, Baby. Quite a good afternoon. He looked rather tired at the end of it," her tobacco-stained teeth glinted briefly.

"You couldn't tire that fellow. He's ready to tackle any lousy job any time you like," June spoke up as usual in Christy's defence.

"No more, Jasper – April will see me being piggy." Leda put out a hand to cover a plate that was no longer beside her. Jasper had just put a wedge of Sally Lunn on it.

"Right. All right. Give it to me." May snapped up the cake.

"Like a dog with a bone," Jasper said to Leda, "can you hear the clack of teeth? Pity falsies don't grind."

Leda held a silence for a moment. Her great ornamented glasses swam in her face, invoking some sort of gentleness.

"May, do you give us seakale tonight?" she said, "you thought it might be ready."

"Yes, Leda," there was a great note of special giving in May's voice, "and I only hope Jasper won't spare the melted butter."

Jasper's face lit. He had thought immediately of the proper sauce. "But it has to be lemon juice and yoghurt," he said spitefully, "because that's what suits April."

"All I want is a cup of tea, *without* milk, please." April sat on a square Victorian stool, shoulders down, pelvis up, ease and distinction united, beauty served. "Tiny man wants a tiny crumb of whatever that is. He's had such a long walk with Mum and Aunt Leda, bless him."

"And my old love can lick the dish," June said.

May screamed a denial, and Jasper said: "Of course. Why not?"

"It seems to me Gripper is the only unspoilt dog in this family," Leda's voice communicated a preference in May's direction. She intended tea-time attentions to soften and still the gripe she had tasted in the air when she and April had passed May by. She would make up for any defection from April later on, when, in the hour before dinner, there would be strong little drinks in April's room. She was thankful that April was able to ignore the connection between alcohol and obesity.

Punctually that evening April knocked on Leda's door. She entered the room at once, assuming a "come in". She smelt warm and scented. Leda could hear the movement of her luxurious, touchable clothes. If April's evening dress had been hanging on padded shoulders she would have been pleased to run her hands over its contrived simplicities. She compromised by saying: "Givenchy tonight? And you smell wonderful – Balmain?" All equal whatever she said, but Leda liked to get things right in her own mind. She was a purist and an exact one.

"Drink time," April answered, but she was aware of Leda's approval and pleased acceptance.

After a week Leda was satiated by the discussions of clothes past and present, but she kept the game going. The vodka martinis were worth the smiling effort. Even the nauseous herbal draught preceding them, and the exercises, the deep breathing and stretching, the invisible contracting of pelvic muscles which April supervised along with other weight-watching austerities, seemed endurable when the moment came

for: "Another little drinkie, darling?" – "I shouldn't, but I will."
Then she could direct April into the past; hear her say the things
that brought moments out of the deeps, their suggestions to
Leda more potent, almost forbidden, because they were outside
April's understanding.

. . . "Your dirndl skirts and all those petticoats – white
stockings. . . ."

. . . "and Aunt Violet forced me into awful knickers . . . I
stuffed one pair into the garden bonfire. . . ."

. . . "I had blue accordion pleats for the dancing class . . .
Bronze sandals, elastic straps. . . ."

. . . "Thank God my feet were too big for your old sandals,
she'ld have had me in them too. . . ."

. . . "Even in children's clothes Mummie had such marvellous
taste. . . ."

"Say that again and I'll hit you."

"My first ball dress – can you see it? *Do* remember: yards and
yards of white tulle, tiny bands of satin and a simple string of
pearls."

"That was the night she said I couldn't embarrass her in my
German fancy dress."

Here they both stopped. April recalled, through the pretty
memory of her own first ball dress, the tears and protests of that
forever unhappy evening.

For Leda their sudden silence woke again the wild pleasurable
memory of her flight down the long staircase, of the arms that
caught and held, the scent of the handkerchief, showing a peak
above the breast pocket of the velvet jacket on which her head
was laid – the surprise enclosed in that embrace was present
always, and with it the sudden knowing of his unwilling
rejection as he set her on her feet and fiddled sadly for a moment
with a whisp of hair, sticky with tears and spit.

That was the evening it began – the all-in-all that was to be the nothing. Adoration violated by every circumstance of propriety, unforgivably dangerous – a flirtation, and a forsaken nymph. The giggling and the guessing with April were left behind, pitiable in their inconsequence beside this new ravishing dimension of living to which she succumbed delightedly in first acceptance. Certain that her darling loved as wildly as she did, sure that his pleasure to touch and caress her matched with her own and that he asked no more, she was without a guilty or remorseful thought. Aunt Violet was sedately plump and old, almost fifty, so love with her must be a comic indecency, not to be considered, while for Leda the immeasurable delight and changing intensities of a first love affair were sharpened through every escapade and escape made to contrive a meeting.

Inevitably it happened – the summons one morning to the quiet of Aunt Violet's bedroom. There love was set aside and denied in fear and shame by a child, derelict and cast-away, beating on a shut door. She could hear Aunt Violet's voice, quiet and sure: "I have your ticket to Vienna, my dear, third on the train, first on the boat. This money is for a little something to eat on the journey. Don't over-tip the porters. Just a change in our plans here. This will be the best way – your uncle wishes it too. My darling child" (she had said my darling child) "you do see we are doing this for your sake, and nothing need be said to 'Maman' – that's what you call her, isn't it, 'Maman'?"

Then the two days of black mistrust, for there was no speaking to him, he had gone to some race-meeting or some shoot, obediently out of the way. After that she remembered best the packing of the black school trunk and April, as un-questioning of Mummie's decision as she was oblivious of its cause, crying and kissing (such childish kisses) and pressing small precious things on Leda, objects that Leda had admired and envied – a pearl choker, blue satin camiknickers edged with écru lace, a photograph of April, softened into nonentity in the manner of the day, all valueless to Leda now, they were squeezed into the black trunk. She could see Aunt Violet's luggage labels, every change on the way to Vienna clearly marked as they were carefully tied to the leather loops and straps of the trunk.

On her unexpected return home there were many questions asked, and sulky answers given. Suspicious silences that were reft apart by Aunt Violet's (perjured Aunt Violet's) letter to her mother. In it was a summary of the shocking things she had felt it right that Leda's mother should know, should be aware of, in her own daughter. They had shown Leda the letter, her mother and poor Papa together, and asked her in frightened angry voices if she could explain or deny any of it.

Far from denial, Leda, stung into utter wickedness, had admitted, she had sobbed out an exaggerated confession, incomplete in her passionate ignorance, but frightening and explicit enough to justify the letter written to Aunt Violet, and another from the wild sister to the vicious brother, a letter of terrible accusations and suspicions requiring immediate verification or denial.

Before her mother's vigilance was relieved by Leda's punctual menstruation the answer came in the news of that tragic accident on the mountain. A man had died on her account. There was grandeur in Leda's desolation – not remorse. No meaner, lesser calculation entered her mind; nothing to include a chaste shocked wife, or the stresses of an estate and a bank balance run into extremities, came into the pictures she kept: absolved from faithlessness, he had killed himself for her only. The remembrance of his charming looks failed from her, but his voice never cheated her memory, capturing and echoing the wild certainty of first love, distancing that from many another.

In April's bedroom, an empty glass in her hand, Leda said: "Jasper has his voice."

"Jasper," April caught the familiar word. "I wonder what he's giving us for dinner tonight."

"Seakale," Leda answered sadly, back in the present. "Would it be terrible if I had another?" She held out her empty glass. ". . . And *then* we didn't even have a glass of sherry before dinner," said April, taking both glasses back to the vodka bottle. "How did we survive it?"

"Don't you remember? We were so happy," Leda answered miserably. Recovering her good manners, she wrote on her note pad, "Tell about your Going Away dress. How was it after that? Did he pounce? Or was he sweet about it?"

"I bet Aunt Violet never told her a thing," she said aloud.

If April was part of Leda's restoration and re-establishment at Durraghglass, May, too, was an important object for sub-jugation to the limitless charm that was Leda's whole trade in life. She could find a use for any person or circumstance even before she knew how such a one or such an event could forward her aims. People had to be kept apart, distanced from one another by small steely jokes and denigrations verging on kind-ness. So, to May she might say: "Oh, you *are* so wise and patient. How do you do it? I love April, but one gets to the end . . . and she can't read my writing." Then there was laughter, first at her own infirmity, then perhaps a reprise of some absurd non sequitur of April's they had heard together. Like fitting pieces in a puzzle, familiarity joined them until Leda could whisper, "Save me, save me!" when April came to insist on some stringent exercise or a direful fast for beauty's sake, perhaps when the incense from Jasper's cooking was falling from the air.

May could seldom rescue, but she could sympathise and join in the fun of saying things that April could not hear. Leda warmed their intimacy with her special skills to capture love in any form that she could use at her own discretion and requirement. And May, the sad pretender to all importances, the stringent avoider of pity, the deviser and maker and restorer of so many lifeless pretty things, found herself borne on a mild tide of sympathy and appreciation. The tide was making, was invading the dry shores of her life, where before its flow only her own courage and fortitude had sown and grown her importances. Her cultivated corners of the deserted garden, her flower decorations, her china restoration, her industry on behalf of The Countrywomen's Association and the Flower Guild – even her friendship with Alys – were all maintained by usefulness alone. Beyond these things it was her secret vagrancies that lent her a power outside herself, a power that she accepted questionless. It was her ultimate protest and defence against her infirmity – it was a power that took her like a spasm, a secret untold even to herself. But to have the other lonely territories invaded, to find warmth and understanding sneaking round her, to have questions asked and answers remembered, woke in her a gratitude and gentleness absent from all her self-given responsibilities and occupations. This was, since her mother died, the first time that May knew a whisper of love to be in the air about her. Appreciation she earned often. Love, never.

The underhand contest with April was another matter. It was a sport without a name, a point scored when she knew herself preferred, points lost in those pre-dinner meetings in April's bedroom. Neither saw that Leda was a doll to them. And she played the doll. They were children scrapping for the favourite doll. In every nursery there is a Princess Baby Doll, the forerunner of the favourite dog. The dog precedes the lover, and the lover the baby. For the sisters, dogs had, for a long time, taken the empty places of lovers and babies; now, with the coming of the lost Princess Doll, even those importances had lessened. The accusations and arguments concerning them were fewer. Leda in her gallant helplessness, with a silent past of persecution behind her, superseded their darlings. She was there for April to diet and exercise, a face to paint and restore into something approaching her recollection of it, which was also a recapturing of her own youth. Because blind Leda could see no change, all April's years of stringency held a proper validity. She had put Time back and now, with eyeless Leda, she truly felt herself again the giggling school-girl, the jeune fille en fleur. Her pleasure in this was lovely and insatiable.

May was the Nannie figure who washed and ironed, folded underclothes and filled hot-water bottles. She was the over-careful guide. Leda resented guidance. If she had to go down on all fours to find her way she would do so. She disliked having too much explained too often. She could smell secrets in a tone of voice, a hesitation told her as much as a change in eyes or mouth told the seeing person. But, suffering May's leading and coaxing as of a blind dog, she played reliance, making small demands, clinging to an arm and laughing if she stumbled, main-taining a lively interest, asking a question as she heard again one of May's accounts of some worthy and successful activity.

Leda needed to balance her favours. Jealousies and priorities were unwise. That was the reason that brought her one evening (when she might have been drinking vodka with April) to May's locked door. She knocked. There was a delay full of May's unattractive cough, and she put a slow sad rhythm into her next knock.

"Oh, Leda, it's you, Leda?" May said through the locked door before she opened it in lavish welcome. "Jolly good! Come on in."

"If you could do up this zip for me – you're locking us in? How mysterious."

"One must have a place of one's own," May stated pontifically, "I do all my porcelain restoration in here, and I design my tweed pictures. This room is very me. I wish you could see it, Leda."

"I can feel it," Leda said.

"Yes, I suppose it's full of atmosphere."

"Choking with vibes," Leda agreed. She felt a little cross with longing for a nip of vodka.

"All my precious things are here," May took her eyes away from the rabbit warren she had been re-arranging when Leda knocked. "At this moment of time, looking back with hindsight, I know where each one came from."

"Do tell."

"Wouldn't you be bored?"

"You're not exactly a bore," Leda said: a caress.

"I suppose I have a fairly good eye for porcelain, I've picked up some rather nice little pieces in my time." It was exciting to tell and not to tell. May lit a cigarette with a snap and a flourish.

"I hear you – another death tube," Leda giggled. "I haven't smoked since – oh, well, I think I'll try, just one."

May put a cigarette between Leda's fingers with as much care and gentleness as if she put a toy in a baby's hand, or an ivory ring to bite on.

"I remember now," Leda said. "Balkan Sobranies."

"Those were Daddy's."

"Of course."

"I smoke Players and they cost exactly four times as much."

"Exactly. Take this away, darling. I don't think I really like it. What a waste."

May pinched out the cigarette and preserved it. She had liked the idea of their smoking together – rather raffish and forbidden with all the anti-nicotine propaganda.

Leda turned her head, questing the room. "Tell me more," she said, "about you."

"There's the garden – that keeps the wolf from the door. And I think up lectures and displays for my flower group."

"And you have your little dog – far the nicest dog in the house," Leda offered the praise as a bone to another dog.

"Gripper. No, Grips, basket! – He's a character. I wonder if he loves me? Do you think he loves me?" They were statements, not questions. "And then, my tweed pictures. I love the work. I've just done something rather special, I'm quite pleased with it. The thatch on the cottage is real heather. And the blue on the mountains, I know I've got it right."

"Did you ever weave a nesting swan?"

"Oh, no. Swans make me think of Jasper."

"Perhaps. And then? Go on."

"My collection means a lot to me. Even the broken pieces I've found – restoration is my worst hobby, I'm afraid."

"Let me hold one – oh, it's a rabbit, how sweet! I'm going to find your mend."

"I bet you can't."

"No. I can't." Leda's finger tip was meticulously tracing the hair-wide scar. "I remember when you had a baby hippo without a head. You took him everywhere with you in a match-box, lying in cotton wool."

"Oh, Leda, you *can't* remember that," May coughed luxuri-ously in her pleasure. "I changed to rabbits," she said in a collector's voice. "I've secured some really interesting little pieces. Junk shops were much easier once." She looked across the room to the rabbits, not yet quite properly positioned in or out of their burrows: her fingers itched to place them, while an urge to tell Leda all, to have her entire attention, ran through her like a flame.

May knew that it was a flame to extinguish before it took possession. Telling would belittle the power lent by her secret. Unless she could disclose the whole reason behind her adventures, a reason she neither understood nor questioned, the tale was purposeless. Never told, its vibrations were hers alone. She left Leda, distancing the danger so narrowly escaped. At the fire-place she picked the agate marble from among the grazing rabbits and rolled it between her thumb and middle finger, thinking affectionately of poor duped Alys.

"What are you doing over there?" Leda knew May had moved away. She could hear her fumbling, noisy and invisible, a mouse in the dark.

"Putting the little people to beddy-byes."

May's silly voice sounded hurried and secretive. Leda heard an embarrassed delight in it. She thought of a girl longing for, and shunning assault. She heard a drawer closed and locked, and her mind was filled with curiosity. There was a confidence to be won she felt sure, and a proper time in which to win it. Not now. Dinner now.

"What do you think Jasper is giving us? He says a surprise."

"It's too obvious. He said he bagged the last cucumber in the supermarket today – got it just before horrid Ulick."

"What does that tell us?"

"Salmon, of course. Madly extravagant, and one thing Jasper doesn't cook very well."

"Yes. What a pity I don't like salmon. I don't know why."

"Don't eat it."

"I couldn't not. Too rude. Poor old boy, he tries so hard." A thread of denigration and complicity was split between them.

7 ✍ *Time Translated*

Now, when they were together, she leaned towards Jasper's voice, an inflection of intention as though she must see where it came from. She heard in it the inherited sweetness of voices in an uncle's generation, the same heights and falls, the narrowness, never a wide sound. Each word was born to its subject, unpremeditated. She enjoyed the level effect, no change to speed or noise, even when he was being nasty to the girls. She knew her voice matched with his. Unaware of age she required of Jasper a response beyond sense or time. She needed him – a bird of youth between her hands.

Evading the sisters' company became a game between them, a game they played together with unprofessed amusement. She would shrug and laugh at the girls' absurdities. For their nonsense talks they chose the times when dogs were walked or fed, or, if it was Tiger, scented and dressed. Not that Leda neglected the sisters; she gave her deep attention to April's spring combinations of stuffs and colours, and obedience to the harsh régimes of diet and exercise. She needed time and she bought it.

May's flower operations and arrangements demanded a more complicated and exhausting response. May could hear Leda's comments, and there was no vodka to alleviate absent interest.

"What has she arranged this time?" Leda asked Jasper on one of May's bustling exits. "Do tell, so that I can say the right things."

"The Taj Mahal in white daffodils, and it's not finished building yet."

"You don't think we could escape to the kitchen before she gets back? I'm crying with hunger too – April only allowed spinach and junket for lunch. Do let's. Please."

She sounded like a pheasant courting in the spring. He supposed it was because her neck was so fat that her voice had neither aged nor roughened. He could listen, but he avoided looking as he took her arm, fearing to let her stumble and crash on the kitchen stairs. "I can do it," she said, and took only his hand, like a child in the dark, as she went carefully, heavily, down the stone flight, an old woman except in her voice and gestures.

In the kitchen they conversed in a language common to both. In the same way that sculptors or writers may speak a little of their work, not understanding their accepted gifts, only the industry that brought the work to – as it were – the birth, Leda and Jasper discussed cooking. For Leda had probed a chink through Jasper's reticence. She stood now where no one had trespassed, and she was sure of her ground.

There is nothing warmer than two cooks confiding. It is a matter of giving counsel and keeping secrets. Hinged to Leda's true interest in food was her total recall of the methods followed in her father's great kitchens, the methods by which they cooked, how they served, and with what accompanying sauces, their measurements simmering nostalgically in her mind.

True to himself, Jasper was a little miserly in imparting the secrets of his own great dishes. Although Leda could cook no more, he felt sure her hostess nuns, when she went back to them, could be guaranteed to make a nonsense of his specialities. Less and less was said about the length of her visit; so far, nothing more about payment during her stay. Jasper didn't want to hear that idea confirmed, he so dreaded permanency. In the mean-time, admitting Leda to his kitchen was a good new tease for his sisters, besides providing interest and information on the subject nearest to him – a subject less difficult to follow than his pursuits in the groves.

"Tell me again about your watercress soup," she might ask. And he would almost tell her, then veer into conger eel soup – he knew the nuns would be hard put to it to capture a conger: saffron, one clove, only one, such a wine, such herbs. "Not *so* much," she would amend a quantity, "only *so* much." There was something less than a tremor of excitement in his agree-ment, but there was the edge of a stir.

"And do your sisters actually like conger eel soup?"

"Hate it."

"Then, why?"

"I must have some fun."

"Of course," she accepted the implication absolutely. "Even with Baby June?"

"June would swallow anything I cooked – after all, I swallow Christy Lucey."

"Do tell, why?"

"Baby's world spins round Christy Lucey. I know her world costs a fortune. We'ld be nearly solvent if Durraghglass was horseless, henless, pigless and the land was let, or –"

"Sold?" She said it quietly.

"Oh, I can't make up my mind to go to those lengths," Jasper escaped even from the notion of such an issue. "Things may never happen." He looked miserable in his indecision.

"You must like your sisters quite a lot."

"Not at all. No more than they like me."

"Oh, they do."

"Don't be silly."

"Then how have you lived together so long?"

"That's the way Mummie fixed it. Charges on the estate. Rights of Residence. April pays quite a bit. June works like a slave."

"And May?"

"Don't let's talk about May."

"I see your point. So," she paused, "they're yours till death."

Some importance between them shrank as she stopped talking to listen, then broke the silence to say: "May's back. Do you hear her? Aren't you aching to know how it went with the flower club? I want to make her say, 'You know, I'm their President' again." She got to her feet and considered the direction of the door.

"You won't have any difficulty in that," he said crossly, as he moved to guide her.

"No, Jasper." She denied his help. "Don't come. I'll find my own way. I need to. I'ld like to."

Jasper let her go, turning back from the kitchen door because he did not care to watch her rather toad-like ascent of the kitchen stairs. Coming down from the hall he heard voices and laughter and felt nonsensically deprived of her company, in which there was neither stricture nor criticism. While she had been there unseeing, a globe of the past held the dirty kitchen in which he stood now, irresolute whether to go upstairs and make his bed before he forgot that he meant to do so, or to take the chicken out of the Frigidaire before it was too late to de-frost it for dinner. Both necessities faded in the immediate beastly task of boiling sheep's hearts for the dogs' dinners, before they went rotten. At least he had postponed that long walk upstairs, as well as the familiar trudge round the kitchen to the larder, until a more convenient moment. Jasper's days were full of such irritating lapses of memory, and the small comforts of their postponements.

*   *   *

Only June stayed uncharmed, outside the circle shrinking closer in the house. She was occupied with her daily work, too early out in the morning, too early to bed at night. She was supported in independence by the live multitude reliant on her; by her ambitions for the hens to lay, for the calves to refrain from scour, for Sweetheart's litter to thrive. Everything living on the place depended on her and her acolyte. June was too guileless to be aware of any competition for favour. That opening flash of memory with which Leda had surprised and flattered her was overtaken by the recollection of kittens moving in a bucket of water. The moment when kisses and pinches and tears had been suffered June put aside, unquestioned and disliked.

One of June's early tasks of the day was the laying and setting of the drawing-room fire. In the morning the drawing-room of Durraghglass was searched through by a cold spring light that had no sun in it. Every damp stain on the wallpaper streeled its evidence of neglect; each worn chair-cover glistened like an unhealthy skin. Wood dust and turf dust were heavy as fur on glass lustres and wall-brackets. Even May's fragile and poetic decoration of white cherry appeared weighted by what the mind knew of unshadowed dust. The room was colder than the day outside. Frigid and fireless, it waited, silent as if locked and left for evidence after a crime, or perhaps in acceptance of some event or change. The most spoilt and cherished room can retreat into this awful distance before the day's services have begun and its solitudes are exorcised.

Unaware of any threat in the chill, Leda came in and made her way carefully and surely to her usual chair – it had already become "her" chair – near the now dead fire. Her coat draped its folds round her, elegant as a Chinese robe; she sat, her knees crossed, her back comfortable in a sort of uncomplaining patience. Presently April would take her for the walk prescribed by the sacred régime. The morning would pass and at lunchtime she would entertain Jasper. There would be absurd intimacies. She was constructing them in her head now as she sat in her darkness.

It was June who brought her ringing ash bucket and kindly rustle of newspaper and heavily breathing dog to interrupt this waiting for April.

"It's Baby, I know. Good morning, Baby."

"Good morning."

"And Tiny? Are you going to talk to me today, Tiny?"

"Ah, she's too deaf," June excused her. "Sit down there, old girl." June knelt down for the proper business of setting the fire. Leda was silent for a moment before making a plaintive suggestion.

"Baby, when will you take me to meet your pigs?"

"Ah, you'd only be all muck." June's answer was strictly practical.

"Hens, then, and a new laid egg to hold in my hand – an egg for breakfast tomorrow."

"I think Jasper wants all today's for his soufflé."

"How sad. I haven't felt a proper egg for years and years."

"Have your nuns no hens? They should keep a few hens." June sounded quite disapproving. "I might gather up a setting for you to take back to them," she offered.

Leda was not looking for that sort of response.

"Would you take me round the stableyard, then?"

"There's a big change there – you wouldn't know the place," June sighed.

"But I could remember. I just want to walk from one loose box to the next. I want to hear doors opening and shutting and bolts slipping in, and horses' hooves sounding different on bedding and cobblestones, I want to put my hand in oats. I want to smell a stable before it's mucked out. I want to feel the strength of a horse when I touch him."

"I didn't know you were that keen."

"I used to go round the horses with Uncle Valentine. He laughed at me – I asked such silly questions."

"Yes." June's "yes" put a stop on the past. "Well, the only horse in the yard today is out in the bog-field this morning under a New Zealand rug."

"But you have a good groom."

"Groom? I have a good lad all right."

Leda heard June's voice soften and felt instantly that her thumb was on some pulse of change.

"He's only young and he can turn his hand to any job on the place, and he's great to ride a school on a young horse."

"You must value him like gold."

"I'ld be sunk here only for Christy Lucey."

"Christy Lucey – lovely-sounding name. You don't ride any more yourself?"

"I've had a few falls too many. Christy's the fellow gets up on them now."

Christy, and Christy again. Leda knew that she had picked up the key to some odd little lock. The time might come to turn that key.

Another Tuesday came round and every day that Leda stayed, the lifts and changes, almost imperceptible in each new day, lifted and changed a little further, a little more giddily.

Through the cooking flirtation with Jasper came inspired memories, back to school holidays, when puddings were all-important; together she and Jasper could recall the delicious horror of an orange soufflé crowned by crystallised violets. Mille feuilles they allowed. Once, she reminded him, there had been four different puddings for lunch on Sundays and four silver vases of sweet peas down the length of the table – violet sweet peas.

When she remembered things like that Jasper could nearly smell his mother's scent and brush with a ghost kiss the faintly mauve powder on her morning cheek. So could Leda. They had this shadow of a share in Aunt Violet. Leda, he thought, must always think of her as she was before any blow struck or sickness dismembered and sucked away all happiness and usefulness. Jasper felt free in Leda's ignorance of such a change. Leda knew she would enjoy that dark place. In time she would explore it.

With May, Leda's endless patience was sorely tried. She maintained it, obstinate in scenting out any possibility of usefulness.

"Tell me about your flower club party. When is it? Next week?"

"Yes. You know, I'm their President?"

"Really? Are you?"

"Yes. They insisted. So I had to agree. Don't you think I was right?"

"Of course. Marvellous."

"Basically, I do feel it's worth while."

"What flowers do you give them for the party?"

"Forsythia and daffs. And we have a show of our hand work. I'm lending my two best pictures and my greatest example of porcelain repair – a very early candlestick I'm doing for Alys."

"I wish I could see your picture."

"I wish you could. I think I've really got something – a ruined tower by a lake worked in grey frieze scraps and – I am quite pleased with this idea – blue jays' feathers woven in for the sky, seen through slit windows of the tower, of course."

"Of course."

"Then, tiny snail shells stuck on, for boulders by the lake."

"And the lake?"

"Well, perhaps a bit of a cheat here, but you have to let go somewhere. . . ."

"Tell me more," Leda said, leaning back and shutting her eyes behind her blue spectacles.

In May's bedroom there was no drink, only a long hour of listening and waiting for some hint or confidence that could be a little dangerous, provoking curiosity or excitement. Leda might have been wanting to write a book about her cousins, but all she wished for was a power over each against each, and to steal even the secrets they didn't know they kept.

"Ah," she said, when May went on to complain of the unfair amount of Christy Lucey's time that Jasper demanded for his wood garden, "does Jasper think he can tame the mountain? What a dream."

"Dream is right, jolly well right. Jasper's not a worker. He spends half his time talking to that young monk, Brother Whosit, I can't remember his holy name. Brother Anselm. *Anselm*, I ask you!"

"What are you asking me?"

"Well, isn't it a bit unhealthy, really, basically, encouraging these so-called ascetics? All they think about now is grabbing land and making money, and the B.V.M. and all that lot are down the course."

"One can't see why he has much in common with them," Leda said carefully.

"Exactly, how right you are, it's just what I said, and Jasper asked me if I thought Brother Anselm was pretty. 'Pretty', rather a funny word, don't you think?"

"Very funny." They both laughed. Leda postponed the discussion. No shadowy suggestion of a homosexual involvement had ever deterred her purposes. "Be a love and fill up a hot-water bottle, my back is rather cold. May? What are you doing?"

"Hottie coming up – just a minute."

Again there came the unexplained pause, a secret diligence in process. Leda heard a breath drawn in, and at the sound her curiosity grew as to the importance of May's absorption. If May was not going to tell it was better to show lack of interest. "What's the time? I think I'll nip along to April. It's warm in there. And she's quite rivetting on her own. Colonel Grange-Gorman must have been a *beast* – the adventures. . . ."

Leda was gone. May stood almost a minute, the round china back of a rabbit warming in her hand. A longing to tell, a shaft of temptation, had pierced her secrecies again, but she still held them close, her own.

It was for Jasper and for Durraghglass, that invisible haven staffed by invisible slaves, that Leda waited, planning her moves with daily increasing interest and optimism. Her bed was soft at Durraghglass, the food delicious; she could see nothing of the damp and decay and age, all mumbling towards their ends around her. In the same way she had not seen her beauty go, and so maintained without diffidence the manners of a beauty, the gestures and tones of youth undefeated. Through the medium of Jasper's voice she was back in the time of her young rapacious loving. Now, calmly, preposterously sure of success, she enjoyed every moment spent towards its achievement.

Jasper enjoyed the game of capturing her attention from the girls. He allowed the kitchen to become their play-ground. She could find her own way down the stairs now and it amused him to stay her hunger, the result of April's dieting, on delicious scraps, it pleased him to feed her like an animal and so undo all April's ruling. Her company did not distract him. As she could not see his methods he was free to construct a dish and cook it as he liked. There was no embarrassment under a critical eye when he sucked a spoon clean, wiped butter off a palette knife with his thumb and forefinger, greased paper with the palm of his hand or rescued the fifth pork chop from Mr Minkles. One prevarication of the awful truths in his kitchen he allowed himself. He slipped the replaced bay leaves onto the low ring of the Aga so that the smoke from their curled blackening leaves might quell other smells. He sniggered a little at such weak-mindedness and let himself call it politeness. Her company enlivened him as she meant it should. While he still avoided any hint inside the edge of flirtation he found this brink, though absurd, rather enchanting. Together with this acceptance of a new sparkle in daily life went his gratitude for her total reticence over the horrors she had outlived. He was too reticent himself, and too idle, to give sympathy or understanding to events that had been and gone, leaving this interesting survivor in their wake.

Cooking was the link he admitted between them. Today it was particularly close, for she held in her head the receipt and method for a classical Austrian cake, a delight from other days. Between them the marvel would be brought to its perfection. Six day-old eggs had been yielded by June's hens, their proper age a prime factor. The right liqueur, the right dark chocolate had been procured, everything was set – even the electric mixer was forbidden, all must be done with an old wire whisk.

"How long do we beat it?" he asked.

"For twenty minutes."

"I'll be dead by then."

"No. Not you," she laughed. He didn't look at her when she laughed, not wishing to spoil his enjoyment.

"You have everything assembled? Quite sure? Delay is ruin."

"Must you be so fussy?" He enjoyed her serious outlook.

"And our oven," she stood up, a blind bird turning its head this way and that, "let me feel the heat, please."

He led her to the Aga and guided her hand into the oven's mouth, holding her wrist level between the hot shelves.

"Oh, good," she said, and he took her hand out carefully. "Well, perhaps," she delayed, "the lower shelf would be a softer heat."

He had to catch her hand again and felt it unchanged by work, as his own and his sisters' were changed. Slightly arthritic, tough nailed, double knuckled. This was a young foreign hand he saved from burning. Once more, as usual, he avoided thoughts of prison camps or gas chambers.

"No. I still think the top oven is right." She took her hand away gently, he forgot how long he had been holding it. Sad that, unlike her other looks, it matched the youth in her voice.

"Oh, hell," he shouted as they turned away from the Aga, "Mister Minkles!"

"Is it the butter? Oh, the scoundrel! Give him to me." He put them together in a chair and looked away from her hands exploring the fierce cat's fur.

"Now, we'll start," a schoolmistress tone came into her voice. "We reduce the butter to a cream. . . ." While he creamed and beat she talked to Mister Minkles, sometimes a German word. The air of the kitchen swam in their warm accord. All the material assembled to her orders on the table was a pattern of the familiarity growing between them. To each, cooking was a matter of serious skill leading to brief delight – neither of them despised or under-estimated their greed.

It was when the fifth egg was being incorporated – "Care! Gently! I can hear you're going too fast – you'll splinter the butter" – that the interruption came and the ceremony was desecrated by May's determined entrance.

"Sorry if I'm interrupting anything. Hold on to that cat, Leda."

"You hold on to your beastly dog," Jasper sounded more fierce than exasperated, "and whoever wants me, I'm busy. They can wait."

"It happens to be a visitor for Leda," May said with quiet triumph. Then, her voice hushed to reverence. "It's Alys," she said.

"Alys? Who is Alys?"

"You don't remember Alys? Alys remembers you. What about the dancing classes at Ballynunty? You can't have forgotten."

"No. I do remember something. I know – Alys and I won the prize for our waltz. God, how long ago?"

"Alys says you were her star partner," May passed on the commendation with respect.

"I danced man," Leda shouted with laughter. "We must meet again, did you say she was here?" She was on her feet, Mister Minkles springing with all his wounded feelings back onto the table. "Jasper, you've got the idea now. Just take it quietly. Don't panic."

Although she lumbered heavily out of the kitchen, Jasper again felt himself left in the wake of a whirling dance. Today, vengeful of her desertion and disobedient to instruction, he tipped the exotic cake's preparation wholesale into the electric mixer. Even so, the practical rapid note of its efficiency failed to obliterate that time of the dancing classes just recalled: when he was seven. When he first fell in love with Leda.

It happened to him on one of the purgatorial Wednesday afternoons that gathered only the upper-class children of the neighbourhood together for a dancing class held at Ballynunty where Alys still lived. A dancing master, Mr Leggat-Byrne, came from Dublin to instruct. That afternoon Jasper wore, as usual, his blue velvet party suit with the frilled shirt, longish blue velvet shorts, white socks gartered below the knees, black strapped shoes, patent leather. Very well dressed he felt when Mummie kissed him goodbye in the hall. His heart only began to sink as the side-car rattled away from Durragh-glass. April and Leda sat on one side of the car, he and May on the other, overcoats buttoned high, separate rugs round their knees. Kelleher, wearing his bowler hat, drove from the box seat.

Much later in the afternoon five little boys sulked speechless at the back of the ballroom and twelve little girls chattered together, commenting on each other's dresses. They wore velvet dresses; dresses with accordion pleats floating out from high cut yokes; India muslins, inset with real lace, stiff blue or pink foundations showing their muted colours through the transparencies. They formed into lines, lines of thin legs in black stockings with lacy front panels.

Now, the schottische. Pointed bronze dancing sandals were raised up to the knees, right arms held above heads as "Weel May the Keel Row" barked out from the piano.

Jasper was all right in the back row, hopping about – a laborious blue frog. Then it was: take your partners for a waltz, and each girl flew to her best friend. The boys scowled and delayed before they took the floor together. Jasper and the last little boy faced each other, holding hands. Then Leda, her partner in trouble with the elastic on her sandal, came between them. "Come and dance with me, little Blue," she said. "I'll be man," she said. In her steel-strong arms rhythm became articulate. One-two-three, *one*-two-three. She led, he followed, they swirled to the music. It was ecstasy – only comparable to his first success on his bicycle. The waltz was over. A gavotte followed. Then it was a polka. He ran to her side. "Dance with me, Leda." Chin held high, smiling up into the air, she avoided him. "Sorry,

I'm engaged," she said in a worldly voice and away she went with Alys. "Come along, come along, find a partner," Mr Leggat-Byrne said and slapped the gloves he held in his hand in time to the music.

Going home Leda sat on his side of the car. Distanced and bound in her separate rug she paid him no attention. She sang. The coachman sang with her. Then they all sang, in and out of tune, under the stars, all heartless and unaware of him. They sang: "Waltz me around again, Willy, around, around, around. . . ." Then a vulgar one from Kelleher: "Sit beside me, don't deny me, Play with the chain of my watch." After that Leda was singing alone, a song about a Miller's Daughter: "don't be cross, dear one, to me. . . ." Jasper, huddled in his overcoat with the otter skin collar, choked on his own silence. Still singing, Leda explored slowly under his rug and held his hand. They both wore knitted gloves.

She's always been a bad fairy, Jasper thought sourly. There was no poetry in the cake-making now. Magic had stolen away. He shovelled the raw mixture together, and shut the oven door gently (gently from habit only) on the work that had been so amusing, done together. Then he put on his wellingtons and picked up his secateurs before setting out on the useful solace of brambling and, perhaps, a conference with Brother Anselm. Poor hungry young soul, he thought, living on Lenten air and prayer in the monastery. He delayed to construct a large beef sandwich. Brother Anselm liked a little chutney, but no mustard.

Quick in vibrant interest, light in betrayals, long in memory, Leda set about another capture from her expended youth: Alys. Alys refused to come into the drawing-room for a cup of coffee or a glass of sherry. She meant to make her escape as soon as

May delivered the Meissen candlestick she had kept, far too long, for restoration. Now May, her heart racing happily in expectation of comment and praise, had gone upstairs to fetch and display her work, finished and perfect.

"We waltzed?" Alys said to Leda. She was not attracted by the idea. "It doesn't seem possible, does it?" She contracted her small stomach's muscles and pulled back her shoulders, grateful for the contrast between her own tidy shape and Leda's flourishing bulk – of the two, it was Leda with her rich sweet laugh and her ageless gestures who was the nearer to those lost springs in time.

"We did," she said. "Fancy! Our first waltzes – were we eleven? You had the sense to admire my dirndl dress. Mummie knew it suited me but Aunt Violet disapproved and all the children laughed."

Alys only remembered her own party dress, absolutely perfect, and straight from Debenham's. "I knew you could waltz," she said, looking at Leda now with more tolerant interest, even curiosity.

"Your voice is just the same as when we were eleven," Leda said, "and I'm no more sensible now than I was then. Are you?"

"No," Alys said, suddenly remembering her first perfect hunter belonging to the fearless years – the years when strawberries tasted as good as they looked and cream was not forbidden. Briefly the idea of her own well-guided life with its proper accepted rules and luxuries failed in importance. It was due to Leda's gift for raising the temperature of the hour that a sudden wish to run off and gossip and be girls together came to her. Looking through the open hall door she saw the day had changed, it was now a morning without clouds, clear-shining after rain. "Come back to luncheon," she said.

"Oh, yes – what a rampage."

"Come on. Let's get off before we have to bring poor May."

"Oh, poor May!" Leda burst into her most beautiful laugh.

"Are you all right? Don't you want a hand down the steps?"

"No. Yes, I do. Yes, please."

"Why *can't* Jasper do something about his drive?" Alys whined, as her car battered through pot-holes and fissures.

"Born idle, that's why," Leda said. "Good about food, though," she added kindly.

"Food yes. But all that cooking is a bit – what's the word?"

"I don't think he's queer. Do you?"

"Hippo never liked Jasper much. Baby June for him every time. Now, isn't this maddening?"

"What?"

"A farm tractor across the gate. Dotty Baby, I suppose. And that ruined gate lodge – too ghastly." The car came to a halt and the expensive horn sounded on both its notes.

"Pardon the delay," Leda heard a man's voice say. "I am just leaving these few willow hurdles I promised Mr Swift for his wind-breaks."

"Who's that?" Leda asked. There was a pause in which she could feel Alys's attention fixed unwavering and away from her.

"Maybe you would let Mr Swift know I'll be around again," the voice went on, and then the engine of the tractor broke into terrible life.

"Who?" Leda asked again.

"*The* most beautiful young monk." Alys let the clutch in smoothly and the new car whispered away. "Queer from the cradle by the look of him."

After a pause Leda discarded the idea, although it had an appropriate link with what had been said before. "What do you make of May-Blossom?" It was a change of subject.

"Blossom? Why Blossom?"

"Didn't you know? Aunt Violet christened them – April-Gaye, May-Blossom, June-Rose."

"Oh, no. What's Jasper's?"

"She could only find Julius for the July baby. She crippled them all with awful old love."

"Well, they were all rather crippled for a start. Odd, when their father was such a beauty."

"Uncle Valentine, was he? I expect I was too young to notice." Leda was hungry for some explicit description, but none came.

"I think May's hand is almost the worst and she smothers it with her industries – oh, those tweed pictures. . . ."

"I'm rather glad I can't see them, but it's almost worse, listening about every thread in their construction."

"That's nothing to the Flower Arrangers' Guild. 'My flower people.' 'I'm their President, you know.' " Alys did a very poor imitation of May's trampling voice. "And she lives on the flower club ladies' worship. If she only knew – they're just watching the drama of that gruesome little hand *not* dropping anything."

"Of course. Why are we slowing down again?"

"It's this beastly tinker encampment and a chap rather in trouble with a young horse. Ooh! I thought he'd gone that time. No, he's still there – quite a tidy jockey." Alys switched off her engine and waited with knowledgeable patience for horse and rider to go by.

"I suppose those were Baby June's two treasures," Leda sighed. "Poor Jasper, he can't make up his mind to get rid of them."

"The boy rides nicely. Not much prospect for him here." Alys sounded thoughtful.

"You ought to hear May on his idle ways. Jasper wouldn't

mind getting rid of him, but he can't take the step. Baby is like a lioness with her cub on the subject of Christy Lucey."

"Maternal, or? You know, your great grandfather did marry the dairy-maid? No one knew the family for a generation."

"And my mother married an Austrian Jew." Leda's laugh rang out.

"Just when your Aunt Violet was busy living down the dairy-maid. A bit unfortunate, I do see."

"Aunt Violet was a cruel woman. Can one wonder about Uncle Valentine? Well, I ask you, can one?"

"I suppose he must have? He was so good-looking, too – Jasper's like him in a depressing sort of way, don't you think?"

"Yes, I do," Leda agreed as if she could see. "It's his voice," she laughed again. "We're all maimed – what a family! Even lovely April deaf as an adder and boring for Ireland, but she's happy with her clothes and her diets and her little booze-ups and a whiff of the grass."

"Does she? Does she really? She *can't*."

"My dear, can't she . . . ?" Leda went on with her entertaining hints and disclosures. There was never a dull moment on that drive through the gentle countryside, invisible to both. Leda could not see it and Alys saw nothing to move or interest her in the mild hills, folded cheek to cheek, unless a fox covert showed its dark and gold on a slope and she could re-live in memory some horrendous obstacle which some long-mourned hunter had leaped at her bidding.

When Leda came back to her cousins, late on that light, Lenten evening, there was a chill in the air, a politeness in the indifferent enquiries as to her outing with Alys. Only April was changelessly benign, unaware of defection. Her afternoon had been spent in the careful separation of spring from winter clothes. To touch, to fold and unfold, to consider and reconsider the properties, colours and textures and to plan their changeable marriages, excited April as the first fine morning excites a child.

"Was this the cake my six eggs went into?" June asked.

"Yes," Jasper said. Even before June said "What happened to it?" Leda knew that her desertion had been calamitous.

"Nothing like accidents in cooking, always best. May I have a slice?" Leda said.

"If you must. But I don't advise it." There was no sour note in Jasper's charming voice, nor any suggestion of their previous intimacies.

"Shall I risk it, May?" Leda asked.

"May's not here," June said. "May's above in her bedroom. She took a toss over her own dog and smashed up a bit of china she was mending, and so now she's at it again."

"A candlestick?"

"How would I know what she would be at?" June said, uninterested and unhelpful. And unwon, Leda knew. She knew too that there is nothing like a disturbance in intimacy for its recreation on a closer level. The fear of loss has its own potency. She felt exhilarated in the thought of a change of tactics in the siege of Jasper. The afternoon with Alys had been a passing flight, a pastime only. But it had suggested two new lines of interest – Jasper's monk and Baby's groom – on both ideas she built mischievously. Neither to be exploited, only kept in mind: in her own mind and in Alys's. And Alys needed little prompting. Leda had been aware of the acquisitive note in her half-expressed admiration of Christy Lucey's horsemanship – an unspoken assumption that such usefulness was wasted unless it served her.

"I think I'll put my feet up and have a tiny zizz. Wouldn't a hot-water bottle be bliss?"

"Get it you, April. I have to shut up my hens." She heard June leave the room, careless that April would not have heard a word. When, a minute later, April said: "All right, Jasper," she knew that Jasper had written down the message. She heard him go, without speaking, and in his silence felt a quickening of her wish to possess the ghost and the live successor to the ghost. In a tremor of certainty she knew that she must hear that voice again: must always hear it.

It was April who woke her up at seven, laid her clothes and shoes ready and went away, saying, "Drinkies soon."

Leda liked to dress herself. It was satisfying to know that only she could put on clothes to the best advantage of the body she had so often known irresistible. The hump on the back of the neck, the tubular sag of breasts and swelling ankles that she could not see were immaterial to her. Ignoring them, her walk would always be a Beauty's walk; her status in any room she came into, a Beauty's right. While all that survived of her beauty was the ashen hair, its growth as true as a child's, its cling as easy and tenacious as little ivy leaves on stone.

"Is the bathwater always hot in your convent?" was the first thing April asked as Leda came in to her bedroom, even delaying the drinks for an answer. Longing for the punctual evening drink, Leda's nod of the head was emphatic. "Ah," April twirled the glass with a little something in it. "And are the paying guests allowed dogs?" Leda nodded vehemently, and stretched out a hand.

"Just a moment, darling. A little bit delayed tonight, I had to give myself an alco rub – the water's never cold on Jasper's bath night."

"I'm longing, rather," Leda said. She looked it too.

"Here's your celery juice and garlic," April said cheerfully. "Choke it down, it's pure magic." She put a glass into Leda's hand.

"Oh, drop dead, you silly old cow." Leda smiled her thanks.

"Now! Shall it be ginny-gin-gins or vodders?" April was at her bar. She felt younger than springtime tonight, perhaps it was the alcohol rub. Pearls of twenties slang fell from her lips. She had not heard any later language. "I suppose we are rather naughty," she mused, "but it's rather fun. After all, we're only young once. Let's have a double."

The two old ladies sat and sipped. April fitted a curious cigarette into a long black holder. As she lit it she felt, in a satisfied confused way, that she might be in a song by Noel Coward. She was happy; her happiness sheltering and burgeoning in the orderly disciplines of her diets and exercises and in the heady release of the evening's lift into pleasure. "You *are* happy? I want you to be happy," she said to her dog. But now she meant Leda. Tiger jumped onto her knees and nestled, but was not allowed a crumb of biscuit. She loved him so much that she cherished his health and figure as ardently and strictly as she did her own. And now, Leda's. "Do admit he's rather heaven. You do like my poppet, don't you?" she pleaded.

Leda smiled and smiled and held out her empty glass.

"I wanted to ask what you thought about this – it's a three piece in three parts – awful old Harrods three years ago. It's all interchangeable, so do you think blue and brown work out together? Even shocking pink, perhaps? I wonder." She dreamed and held the woollen stuff up to her chin.

"I don't remember," Leda said loudly, hoping that the touch of blind tragedy might end the conversation and leave time before dinner for another drink. Her empty glass overlooked, and not from economy or malice, Leda wondered how, when she had won Jasper, she might best contrive to eliminate his sisters. She thought her nuns might suit April very well – they would be patient as angels with her deafness, sympathetic with diets and disciplines and understanding and worldly over the nips of vodka.

"I'm not too sure about the prune and pale blue. Rather too pretty, do you think? A bit 'vin ordinaire' . . . ?" April droned on.

May and June were draining the last drop in their sherry glasses when Leda and April joined them. Jasper was not there with any treat in a wine bottle. As she sat and waited for dinner, listening to the girls arguing about their dogs, Leda felt very sober.

"If Tiny is not on heat," May was saying, "could it be some kind of tumour?"

"Is that the kind of thing interests your dog?" June parried the idea. "And get out, you!" The kick she aimed at Gripper was near enough to its vulnerable mark to earn a scream from May. Unhearing, April put Tiger down to share in the sport.

"And keep him to himself, too, he's forever flashing Tiny and that only upsets her. You're not able for that kind of thing, are you, Tiny?" June picked Tiger off Tiny's patient head. "Your two dogs are the two most over-sexed little bastards going. There's nothing amiss with Tiny."

"Nothing except this awful smell," May repossessed herself of Gripper.

"And who made it? He who smelt it, dealt it," June came up triumphantly with the schoolboy saw.

"Oh, shut up, girls. I could hear you arguing in the dining-room. To the sword with the lot of you." Jasper appeared at the door and without a bottle in his hand. "Shall we go in? It's a soufflé."

Leda touched his elbow and sighed an accord as she passed him in the doorway. She walked as certainly as a girl with wind in her hair. No hesitation, no fumbling as she timed the moment when he would push in her chair. In the bending turn of her head she might have been giving him the next waltz. She misjudged the importance of the moment for him because she could not see that his quickened interest was for his soufflé's proper maintenance. He dreaded a time-fall from absolute perfection.

There were silences through dinner. Silences unbroken by May who ate on stolidly and without comment. She even accepted a tribute from Leda on her purple sprouting broccoli without launching into a history of its seed time and harvest. Leda recognised sulks and reserved a restoration of intimacy for a further hour. Leda felt no uncertainty. They were hers – three bridges back to her innocence. Some she might diminish (destroy was a word she forgot), when her power at Durragh-glass reached its supremacy, when she would live and make love with the voice that belonged to someone else. For the present she held three of them. She was under their skins. The fourth she would hurt when the moment was right, and the hurting would be satisfactory – a more practical vengeance towards the past than spitting into Aunt Violet's clothes, although she had enjoyed that.

May could see no jealous absurdity, only well-justified grief in her reaction to Leda's desertion, a desertion with Alys, her own acclaimed friend. That morning she had come down to the hall, candlestick in hand, ready for wondering praise and gratitude. And there was no one in the hall. She could hear the car turning, just turning on the gravel sweep; Alys was waiting for her. She hurried across the hall. Gripper, excited by her speed, ran in front, yapping idiotically: ran back and crossed her. In her natural effort to avoid falling on her darling, she fell on the candlestick.

It was June who picked her up and with June she heard the

car's slow, quiet exit. "They've gone without you," June said with true, horrible sympathy.

"Oh, yes. My idea. Makes a change for Leda," May managed gallantly.

"Did I hear a crash?" Jasper came delicately onto the scene. "You look rather dazed, May," he said with remote distaste.

"Sure, they left without her," June's appalling sympathy repeated itself.

"Swirled off on a last waltz," Jasper gave his rat's grin. He took his gardening gloves and secateurs off an oak chest, put on his graceful hat, and went on his way.

May knew he knew, and her comfort was that she had taken Leda away from him before she herself was deserted.

"If you're all right," June said, "I'll go back to the yard. Christy should be in now."

Left alone with her shattered candlestick, the forceful habit of May's life asserted itself. Habit and courage can go together. On her knees she picked up every morsel and chip of china. Like a child about to do a puzzle she considered how best to fit them together again. Lacking Jasper's hindsight, she made no feasible connection between this morning's desertion and that cruel day when her knickers had betrayed her and she had stolen and buried a little fox.

"I've been so bored all day. And now I think I've hurt you somehow. You do know what happened this morning? All my rotten eyes. I thought Alys was just turning the car and waiting. I thought you were coming with us. . . ." Leda was sitting on her bed, Aunt Violet's bed, later that evening.

"May," she had said, "could you help? This zip always beats me." And May had come unwillingly and pulled down the zip in silence. Leda had caught her good hand and held it. "You understand, you *do* understand? I can't bear you to think I was rude."

"Oh, nonsense. Rot. I was enchantée for you to have a little break from us all. You must be bored stiff."

"You never make *me* feel a bore or a nuisance, and I'm both, twice over. Darling, would you, could you help with this suspender clip?" Leda's thighs, once elastically hard and strong, were now a welter of flesh in which May's thumb and finger sought diligently for the suspender.

"Oh, bless you!" Leda sighed her thanks and relief. She held May's finger for a moment. "I wish I could see you," she said sadly. May took her hand away, glad of Leda's blindness. "And it makes me so cross that I can't see all the lovely things you do. You're so creative."

"Only in my own small way, perhaps." The word "creative" had unbound May a little.

"Alys was telling me about your pictures and your porcelain restoration. And what about that flower club?"

So they had talked about her. May warmed a degree further, she felt re-assured. "Alys is too silly about me, far too kind," deprecatingly she invited more.

"Yes. You mustn't let people make too much use of you."

Of course Leda meant the Flower Guild. "We both love a good game of scrabble," May went on. "It's a hoot really, neither of us can spell. She loves winning, bless her."

"She told me you practise in private – left hand against right," Leda laughed. "You're so versatile."

May blushed unseen. "One must take a game seriously, or it's no fun."

A small grey silence fell between them. Leda broke it. "May, perhaps you ought to know this – you did the flowers for Alys's last dinner party – yes?"

"Yes."

"Well, her parlour maid – a jewel – re-did the lot."

"Alys told you that?"

Leda evaded the question which she could feel was loaded with belief – Alys had not told her that exactly – but their talk of May and her "flower people" could stand embellishment. "Oh, she was so amused with the flower ladies you brought, too. Ghastly afternoon with a dinner-party pending."

May remembered the cold morning-room, the cross parlour maid, and the offer of old flowers in their stagnant water. She thought with satisfaction of the agate marble.

"You're such a very trusting person," Leda felt for a hand to stroke, then stroked her own. "That's why I feel you should know that Alys really is not quite the most loyal friend in the world."

"Alys and I have always been friends," May's voice shook in her obstinate loyalty. "Alys is pure gold."

"Of course, and she's so fond of you. It's all a bit the Prefect and Betty in the Lower IV."

May had a mortifying suspicion as to which of them was in the Lower IV.

"She's certainly not like your ghastly flower ladies," Leda went on softly. "She says they are all simply avid to see you drop a twig out of that brave little hand."

May felt cold, as though she had stepped without warning into an ice age of absolute nullity where all triumph froze. "Brave little hand." She laid it across her mouth and bit into it with hatred not for her hand, but for those who pitied it. Leda could not see her hand and she must not pity it. May would have no pity. She knew that pity destroyed all that she had put into subduing her handicap. All that she had attained, all her energetic skills, fulfilled in their public displays, were distanced and distorted now through Leda's hints of betrayals by kindness.

There were other achievements that kindness could not touch
– those untamed adventures and triumphs, matchless and apart,
irresistible as love, taking the places of wild moments she had
never known. The thought of them overcame her and, nearer to
love than she had ever been, she was overcome by a wave of lust
to tell and to prove herself to Leda, distanced from any slight or
pity. Here was an act for which there was no pity. Leda must
know. And in the telling May would blot out, even out of her
own mind, the suspected shrinkings from her deformity – eyes
turned on and away – together with the waves of sympathy and
help rejected by her since her hand hemmed, with stitches
smaller than April's, the first cambric handkerchief for Mummie's
birthday.

In the overwhelming luxury of confession and display to a
loved one, anything so meagre as discretion forgotten, May's
adventures lived again. Riveted, even amazed, Leda perceived
in each event the never-mentioned hand on its gallant escapades.
At one moment she was in the dark expensive spaces of
Harrods; hardly escaped and hurrying towards Knightsbridge
Station, when the narrative sped on, and an ugly moment in a
supermarket froze her in expectation of disaster, but lightning
thinking and matchless dexterity outpaced detection. The
breathless rampage continued in defiance and defeat of all
respectable principle. It was so far beyond the ordinary that
Leda, as she re-lived the capture of each rabbit or other object
now caged in May's collection, felt in her own pirate's heart
nothing but admiration for such ruthless and useless adventure.
When May's story ended with the agate marble Leda wondered
if she heard sobbing, but decided that it was more of an ecstatic
gasp that broke between the words. Elated and curious, she
groped the air again for May's sad hand, before she accepted the
other on which to swear secrecy.

When, calm after the reckless chastity of her confession, May had at last gone on her way to bed, Leda sat on, her bare feet on the floor under the black skirts, sure and contented in her ascendency. May was hers, April equally so. It was neat and convenient that they rivalled each other for her favours. She heard May's brusque and meticulous movements in the bathroom; tap turned fully on and sharply off; even after tonight's emotional confession habit prevailed. A towel was tartly flapped, then came a double flush for the lavatory. She was sure the bath would be left sparkling as crystal. It awed her to know the wild side of this domestic paragon. Such a good story – who should she tell it to?

Leda, still sitting on her bed, was waiting in the solitary patience she had learned in her years of blindness for the sound of Jasper's footsteps passing her door on his way to bed. Her obsession with his voice, sweet as a whistle splitting her darkness, took her senses backwards to her ravished first acceptance of love. If a man might sleep with a stranger and invest the act with his desire for another, a distant love, so might she. And, if this was a fetish substitute, Leda, as she waited to hear Jasper's voice again, knew its potency.

Jasper was sitting up in bed – rather a little-boy-home-from-school look about his austere pyjama jacket. His eyepatch was off and his hair was turned freakishly upwards by the pillows in their valued habitual arrangement. His mind was concerned absolutely and entirely with the propagation of azaleas; a manual on the subject was in one hand and the violet-patterned cup of Complan, with its powdering of nutmeg and its bottlecap of whiskey, was in the other. He was absorbed in the pleasures of reading about things he would never do, when his door opened and Leda came in. She waited, standing with her back to the dim white door, a dark figure from a dream.

"Speak to me," she said in a very ordinary tone of voice, "say something, so that I know where your bed is."

Jasper put down his Complan and reached for his eyepatch, determined on an immediate evacuation of his bed. But she had located him. She was coming across the room, her head forward-seeking: a blind earthworm.

"Do sit. Have some eiderdown," was all he could think of to say.

"I couldn't sleep, Jasper."

"So I see, dear. What a bother."

"Jasper," she said, "I'm sorry I ruined our cake."

"Don't let that worry you. I thought my failure rather an improvement. Less goo-some. What did you think?"

"Awful. Awful."

"Perhaps you're right. We must try again."

He felt her hand on his knee, above the blankets and the electric blanket. He thought again of the knitted gloves and the blue face-cloth carriage rug. He thought of an evening's unhappiness by the river, and he thought of a mushroom field. He wished he was back in total forgetfulness. He was glad that he was no longer young, or suffering. Even as a good tease for the girls he did not want Leda in, or even on, his bed. It fidgeted him to think of her weight on the electric blanket. He leaned forward, the battery was on the floor, to click off its switch.

Very quietly Leda slid along the bed to where she thought his arms waited for her. There were no arms waiting. Jasper's hands were clasped, embarrassed and protective, over the somnolence of his private person.

"Dearest girl," he said, "let me offer you half a Mogadon. It's all I have."

"Oh, thank you. That will be a help."

When he put the half tablet onto the fat palm of her hand and the tooth-glass of water into the other hand, he congratulated himself on his diplomacy and felt grateful for her tactful accept-ance of a non-event.

"Thank you so much. I'm sure I'll get to sleep now. Awful of me to disturb you, but May was asleep and I couldn't wake April and June's not one for pills. So there was only you." She stilled her voice on the last words. She waited another moment.

"I should get back to bed before the Mog wears off. It was a rather small half," Jasper said uneasily.

"Yes. So it was. Night-night."

Jasper felt he should get up and help her downstairs. But he wasn't wearing his patch, and only the top half of his pyjamas, so what if they should meet one of the girls? . . . . No. It was better to leave well alone. Not that it was very well either – a miserable distraction from his reading; and the Complan, disgustingly cool now, was less soothing than usual.

On the wrong side of Jasper's door, turbulent in the certainty of her rejection, each step she took a small purgatory of delay, Leda went slowly down the unfamiliar staircase. She must fumble her way now, where once she had gone running and crying. Some part of that furious disappointment was with her again tonight, but she could not match it with youth's violence.

Hearing a footstep – was it on the landing below? Was it in the bathroom? Whose step – May's? April's? – she stopped, not certain how near she was to the bottom of the flight. Perhaps if she moved across to the wall she would be less noticeable. For it did occur to Leda that she would look pretty silly creeping down from Jasper's sacred precincts in the middle of the night. She stretched out an arm, feeling with the back of her hand for the wall. Then, its irresistible distance enticing her, she leaned a little farther from her hold on the stair rail and, unbalanced in her darkness, stepped into air, and fell.

It was April who caught her as she pitched forward. April with the lavatory flushing thunderously behind her; April in her beautiful nightgown, nourishing creams and astringent plasters distributed over her face, her hair in careful clips; April, whose arms were a nanny's loving arms, and distant from any loves that Leda valued.

"Leda, Leda, are you hurt?"

"I lost my way to the loo," Leda wailed.

"Thank goodness I was here. Thursday is the night for my herbal purge. So lucky – you might have been killed."

"Oh, go back to bed and leave me alone," Leda was shaking and gasping.

But April heard nothing. She only saw that picture, always in and out of her mind: Leda tearing down, leaping the same steps of the staircase, her white skirts in a billow, her tears falling. Tonight it was a blind woman, shoeless, in a black dress. But for April their youth was constant.

"Get undressed, darling, and hop into bed. I'll bring you a magical herbal – you'll be off in a trice."

"Oh, for God's sake! Fuck off in a trice yourself, you old fool," Leda shouted. April smiled encouragingly and hurried back to her bedroom and the electric kettle.

While Leda waited, impotent to refuse the draught in process of concoction, one certainty lived for her: the voice she was in love with was monstrously embodied. In it she had suffered a second expulsion: time translated – Aunt Violet was here again.

Mogadon totally ineffectual and herbal tranquiliser in the po, Leda sat on, still in her black dress. She sat very quietly, measuring the present with the past, accepting in the stillness of anger the balance between the age she could not realise and the youth that caught up with her so unkindly. Jasper's polite and certain repulse could have been spoken by Aunt Violet. The

two situations were alike and each had been quietly para-
phrased, words were used belonging nowhere, implying only a
polite ending to an unacceptable situation.

In her own darkness, daytime was as present to Leda as any
other hour – tonight she was living in a September afternoon.
Corn-coloured sun invaded the luxurious purity of Aunt
Violet's bedroom, warming and fading the glazed chintz chair
covers – violet and lilac. Sun splashed over the great padded bed
with its lace counterpane, and blotted its warmth into the basket
where Aunt Violet's pekinese stirred about, mottled in the sunlight. She heard Aunt Violet's voice, sensible and kind: "It *was* a
silly letter to write, dear child. Of course, nothing need be said
. . . of course not. . . ."

Leda, fifty years older, a survivor, got off the bed and
undressed, riotously throwing her clothes about like an angry
girl – the banished schoolgirl. Naked in her blue spectacles, her
body was unknown to her, its changes distressed her not at all.
Tonight, mind and body refused to admit or accept any reason
for Jasper's rejection other than his untried – could it be? –
virginity. She sniggered at the idea and instantly replaced it by
that of the pretty monk.

Unwinding her nightdress, carefully coiled round the hot-
water bottle by May, Leda reconsidered her prospects at
Durraghglass. Where did advantage lie? Whom should she
betray to whom? How long could she endure April's implacable
routines – and for what end now? Or the constant lesser
purgatories of May's recitals? Or June's obtuse refusals of
confidence? It had all seemed worth the exercise of charm; in
any case, for Leda to exercise charm was to exercise power. She
needed victims and through her life she had found them. She had
no remorse, for she felt no guilt. Lying at last near sleep, in the
bed made and warmed by loving May, a sudden rift of laughter
came to her, briefly dispersing the sullen disappointments of

the night. She remembered May's extraordinary story and thought how much rich Alys would enjoy it. Alys had a warm house. But the cooking was far below Jasper's standards.

8 ❦ Revelations

May laid the dining-room table for breakfast. Shafts of daffodil-yellow sunlight slanted in through the high narrow windows. Spring was here when the sun first beat the mountain's shadow. May lifted a big flat dish of primroses; the sudden scent of primroses caught the breath in her throat – she was in love. Festive, she swept up all the quite clean place-mats and, with reverence and pleasure, laid out the six she had embroidered last – blue linen with white button-hole edgings and daisies with pierced centres. There was waltzing in her blood as she poured out lavish glasses of orange juice and wiped the crumbs from the tray beneath the electric toaster.

The sunshine grew constant, dazzling back from the table and its silver. With May, a dazzle of hope and pleasure responded. She and Leda were bound in friendship now. In the secrecy between them no one else could have share or part. May's heart hurried in the ripe thrill of such trust and confidence. In this new ascendency she was ready to be bright and pleasant when April came in.

April carried a basketful of healthy breakfast foods. Tiger followed her closely. He went at once to Tiny's goatskin.

"Good morning – oh, stop him!" May cried out too late.

"It's going to be bacon and eggs," April sniffed at a waft from the lift. "Poison. If only you and Jasper knew what's going on inside you."

A patina on the air, the aura of a thousand breakfast times,

171

hovered. Still there were silver dishes on the sideboard and a mixed clutch of china cups huddled round tea and coffee pots. Napkins were linen, never paper. Once kedgerees and kidneys simmered and waited. Family prayers were read, where now there was silence. But in the present, as in the past, a new morning briskly advanced towards its difficulties.

May put an extra spoonful of tea into the pot. She was feeling exorbitantly giving as she filled it with freshly boiling water and clapped on the tea cosy. Jasper followed the grumbling ascent of the lift and took out of it the swollen glass bulb of the Cona coffee machine.

"Good morning. Why coffee? It's Friday."

"Good morning. Didn't Leda say something about coffee?" Jasper was making a small gesture of accord. "April, what are you up to with that doll's teapot?" He pointed, and April got the idea at once: "Our rose hip tea."

"Our" stood for Leda and April. Yesterday May would have flinched at the implication. Not this morning.

"China tea – Earl Grey – is what Leda likes," she said to Jasper.

"Poor Leda."

May's thoughts flickered pleasantly in the untried places and promises that were part and structure of her life now. Jasper was hardly worth an answer.

June, a solid twelve-year-old schoolboy in faded jeans and old espadrilles – wellington boots politely discarded – went straight to the lift in search of a proper breakfast. She had her day's work to do. Tiny was not with her.

"I'm glad you agree the old thing is on heat," May said.

"There's nothing wrong with Tiny," June took a meticulously fair share of scrambled eggs, bacon and mushrooms. "I left her outside. The way your two nasties wouldn't be shaming me over my breakfast – and that's *it*, and all about it."

They were all eating in a morning silence when Leda opened the door. With her usual extraordinary calculation she carried her body, smoothly as though through water, to her usual chair. She was wearing her beautiful coat and swathed it round her and pushed it closer to her neck as if she invented the cold.

Jasper felt a shade of relief that those sweet fat arms and piercing elbows were hidden away in dark sleeves. He need never see them again, or fear to see the blind blue eyes.

"Coffee?" he asked, getting up at once to bring it over to her.

April waved him back to his chair. "We're having rose hip tea today," she almost sang the words as she poured it out.

"Oh, please," Leda said, "I was thinking of Earl Grey."

". . . And she's going to love her cereal and some rich, ripe yoghurt."

"Does she take sugar?" Jasper asked.

"I don't think *that's* very funny." Leda's forehead filled with sudden lines as though she strained up her unseen eye-lids to keep back tears. Looking across at her, Jasper wilted, horrified at what he had said.

"For goodness' sake, April, let Leda have a proper breakfast for once." May had a cup of tea in one hand and a plate of bacon and eggs in the other. She put them down in front of Leda, pushing April's goodies onto an outer circle.

"But I've only cooked enough for three people," Jasper peered into the dish where one portion, his own, he hoped, remained.

"Would it be within the bounds of possibility to cook some more?" May asked perkily.

"That's the last of the eggs," June stated, "so your guess is as good as mine."

"You see how it is? You'll have to eat cake." Jasper looked nastily at May and helped himself to everything in the dish.

"It's all right, Leda. I'm not one bit hungry. You have mine."
May's voice revelled in the sacrifice.

"Take that poison away," April spoke with authority, "eat it
up yourself and put on another pound or two, why don't you?"

"Because I seem to be the only one giving a thought to Leda's
breakfast. Shall I cut it up for you, Leda?"

"You'll kill the woman with kindness," June said, helping
herself to marmalade.

Perhaps it was this remark, satirical and uninterested, that
broke through all the defensive calculations working in Leda's
mind, stripping down any wish to charm her way forward.

"For God's sake," she said, "I don't want anybody's breakfast. I don't want any breakfast."

" 'So take the nasty stuff away. I *don't* want any soup today.'
Struwwelpeter, wasn't it?"

Unaware that Jasper quoted the lines directly to May, Leda
took real and absurd umbrage at the light indifference they
conveyed. It was a continuance of last night's polite dismissal.
She stood up, tears rolling out and down from behind the blue
spectacles, hands flattened on the table to each side of her plates.
Suddenly she lifted them and swept both offerings to the floor.
Nothing could have looked less like a disastrous accident befall-
ing and embarrassing the blind.

"Everything under control." May squatted down to scrape
up the disaster.

"Will you watch the woman, she's very saucy this morning."
Baby June's comment, reasonable as usual, was enough to set
Leda's tongue terribly free.

"There's a mental defective in every old family," she said
quietly. "Some of them can read and write, others can't resist the
charms of their stable-boys."

"Not at all a bad idea," Jasper hoped to lighten the implication, "if it gets any more work out of them."

June looked round the table at each member of her family. "It'll be your turn next," she said, "you wait."

"My darling's eating the bacon," April wailed.

"Your darling has just made the most horrible smell." May held her nose and indicated Tiger.

"That's your brute, May. I know the difference."

"Shall we put them both outside?" Jasper glimpsed an escape for himself from the difficult scene.

But it was April, in touch with an undeniable reality, who swooped down on both dogs and carried them to the hall door. Back again, she set about reconstructing Leda's healthy breakfast.

There was silence round the table which April broke, saying: "You all seem very talkative this morning. Anyway, I'm not going to waste this perfect yoghurt, Jasper can put it on your carrots for lunch." She sat in a sunbeam spooning up a pool of yoghurt from the table.

Leda lunged towards her: May too uttered a cry of protest. Jasper said, "Don't worry, I shan't use it."

"Now," April handed the cup of yoghurt to Jasper, "a squeeze of lemon juice perhaps, and it's perfect."

"Oh, *Christ!*" Piercingly sweet, Leda's voice rang out. "Can no one stop her starving me to death and boring for Ireland?"

They all shook their heads in submission to April's deafness.

"Deaf as an adder," Leda proclaimed to the silence, "but she makes up for it. What about all that vodka? And you ought to hear her when she's on the grass."

"She's deaf, all right, but she's not a horse," June said.

"All right, perhaps not – horses are tidier about their sex lives."

"Must we? . . . ." Jasper flinched.

"You don't want to know about that old satyr she married?

Just one of the things he loved was doing it on trains. He died doing it on the Flying Scotsman."

"Well, why fuss? People have their little hobbies. What's wrong with trains?" Jasper spoke in a worldly way.

"And another thing. Shall I tell them, April? What the guard said? Shall I tell them?"

"Yes, do. It was a very fine morning."

"Oh, do I have to write it all down?"

There was a pause, appalled but interested, while Leda scribbled wildly on her pad, ripped off the page and threw it on the table. "Read that and give it to her," she said. Jasper picked up the small square of paper and spilled coffee all over it. "Oh, look what I've done. I am sorry, April, it's for you." He wrote on a corner beyond the spreading coffee: "You were never lovelier" and handed it to April. For a brief moment he felt something like being the head and protector of a family. April read, then squeezed the wet paper together and threw it in the slop bowl. "Thank you, darling," she smiled shyly at Leda.

By now Leda, beyond all sense even for her own advantage, was trembling and shaking, provoking in May distress that was as fulsome as it was abject.

"Of course you're on edge – you're in shreds, actually – all that ghastly health food, your nerves are stripped down – right? Am I right? I understand. We know each other in and out, don't we? Don't we, Leda?"

"Too damn well we do," Leda flung at her. "I ought to know every rag in every tweedy bloody picture you ever made, and the thought of your flower life makes me vomit. Perhaps," she turned towards June, miscalculating Jasper's position at the table, "you all ought to know about the dangerous thrills in that flower life."

May's terrible blush spread down the neck of her shirt to her sweating breasts. "Don't listen, don't listen, it's just my fun," she cried out.

"Fun?" Leda paused and purred, prolonging pleasure before revelation. "Funny name for shoplifting," she spoke mildly as though of a delinquent child, making her indulgence the more insulting for May. "Did none of you know? She's been stealing her little fancies for years. Harrods nearly caught her. Now she sticks to supermarkets. Well, Jasper, how do you like the idea? Amused?"

"I really don't know whether to laugh or cry," Jasper waited; then, speaking with difficult hesitation, he said: "My dear May, in my whole life I've never felt in such sympathy with anyone. Cheer up. Don't get caught. That's all I ask."

"And another thing," Leda was insistent, "wait till arthritis sets in. That terrible little mole hand is going to let her down badly."

"Shut your dirty mouth," June said suddenly.

"D'accord, absolutely," Jasper poured out a cup of coffee and pushed it towards May. "Pay no attention. I've always understood lots of respectable people are martyrs to it."

May, very white now, sat entirely disestablished and betrayed. Every picture she had seen and shown to others, every comfort and satisfaction built on her desperate efforts deserted her. She was back where the efforts had started, in the time when they fed her with a spoon until she was six; when Jasper, so much younger, had his own fork and silver knife.

That he should sympathise now brought that lost time into close perspective. If he could be kind, she must be finished. She stared forwards into nothing.

Jasper glanced at the untouched cup of coffee and avoided looking at May. If he could not help her, he could at least avoid upsetting himself. It quite startled him to think of the three sisters he had so long teased and tolerated in their cruelly uneventful lives, so exposed. Here was Baby June in thrall to Christy Lucey (he had always thought those sandwiches a bit excessive); April, once happy prey to a dead pornographer, and now a secret lush and besotted in absurd vanities; while May – an extreme example of propriety and the sister who annoyed him most – had, it seemed, a career of successful shop-lifting behind her – well behind her, he hoped. And wondered. He looked at his three sisters out of a new distance, a distance from which, for the first time, he saw them as objects of curiosity.

"Well, tell me more," he said chattily. "What about me? Don't leave me out, will you?"

"Oh, fire-up, fire-on," June said. "I'm late already getting on my tractor."

Leda took a breath: "Don't you want to hear about that brother you maimed, Baby? Between you and Aunt Violet you've left him a one-eyed, sexless virgin."

"Leda, dear, don't mince your words" – whatever Leda was going to say about him, he felt it would be fairer to the girls to leave it undenied – "Aren't you trying to say homosexual?"

"Yes, I am. And I hear the Lord Abbot is on to that hedgerow romance. He's heard about satyrs in woodland groves. Have you?"

"Yes. In old school ties, too," Jasper answered agreeably. "But aren't we, all five of us, a bit old for these gambols?"

Leda turned her head away as though in refusal to see or imagine change. "We're not *old*," she said in a different voice, forbidding the subject.

It was June's laugh that rang out, pitiless. "Take a look – oh, sorry, you can't. There's hair on our chins and humps on our backs, our ankles are swollen up with the blood pressure and our knuckles are knotted backwards with rheumatism."

"Forgetting the name for it . . . losing our spectacles . . .

impotent without them," Jasper's voice made a melody of the list.

"Your voice is the same," Leda drew a breath and her eyelids dropped behind her spectacles.

"Really, dear, don't exaggerate – I was in the school choir when you saw me last."

"It's not your voice I'm hearing, Jasper. It's your father's voice."

"Can't we leave him out of this?" A flicker, lighting long silences, flared in Jasper's mind.

"You do know he was my lover? I suppose he seduced me."

May raised her head, bent low over her hand, crumbling toast. "He couldn't possibly have done anything so common," she stated. "After all – he was in Pop at Eton."

"And he rode the winner of the Grand Military," June put in.

"For God's sake, girls," Jasper protested hopelessly, "can't we stop this total recall? Breakfast time, after all."

"You aren't interested, are you? You don't want to know why Aunt Violet turned me out of the house – all care and kindness, and a friend to meet me in London – extra money for the journey, you don't want to know why? You cousins should see my daughter. She's very like her father."

The silence round the table was appallingly polite. Only April, in her own silence, was outside it. Toast lay on plates, coffee and orange juice ignored beside them. Only the innocent scent of primroses reassured the air from which bacon and coffee had failed, as though in shock.

"Didn't you know?" Leda said. "I came back to find you. I was so happy, once I was so happy." She burst into tears, covering her spectacles with her hands.

Not a Swift moved to comfort her. April didn't hear the sobbing. Jasper heard a distant, a welcome sound. "Your dogs are fighting," he said. "Can't you hear them – nip to it, girls!"

The noise that even quite small dogs can make when at each other's throats sounded an appropriate, a horrifying release, and an acceptable interruption. In a moment June, May and Jasper were off their chairs and out of the room, dragging April by the hand along with them.

Leda's crying stopped while her hands felt about the table for toast, for butter, for honey. The relief and satisfaction she had experienced in her breakfast-time exposé led to a sort of post-orgasmic peace, as when she had spat in Aunt Violet's dresses. That had been nice too.

Outside the window the dogs' voices quietened, allowing those of their owners to renew the skirmish. In the dining-room Leda, honey on her hands, on her coat, felt piteously that May at least should return to help her. She did not actually regret her outbursts, but felt they were forgettable – an outlet after weeks of irritation, sustained with charm and patience; a reprisal for the repulse and disappointment of the night before. Footsteps came and went on the gravel. Voices sounded in the hall, but no one came back to the dining-room. "Heartless beasts," Leda thought as she ate her toast, "people are all the same, disloyal to the core." She sat on, soaking in her grievance; thinking of much sharper things she wished she had said. She heard a car drive up to the house. She heard someone trying to make April hear. She knew the voice. She stopped eating toast, and waited: old, pale, powerless.

"Good morning, Maman," a clear little squeak of a voice, small as that of a mouse following its secret ways behind cupboard doors. The woman who spoke crossed the room, came close to Leda, sat down in May's chair and looked round her shyly, slow in her observations as one who must be careful in their retention. She was a little creature, elegantly made and inconspicuously dressed; she might have been attractive if her big handsome head had not looked so out of proportion with the skimpy, shrimp-like body; a mouse's head has the same heavy quality.

"What are you going to tell me this time?" Leda said. "Have they caught up with him?" She sounded only mildly curious.

"Not just yet." There was a pause. "But they're getting warmer."

"Oh, don't fuss," Leda said. "He won't talk!"

"You don't think . . . . under interrogation?" The hesitant voice faltered over the word.

"Oh, please, must you? You just like to frighten me about nothing," Leda said crossly.

"Why did you leave the convent, Maman? All the nuns know about you is that you're old and blind and in their care. Why did you come here to the cousins . . . . after all you've told me?"

"I thought I might find something again," Leda said sadly, finally, as though she was deeply hurt. "I didn't."

"Then you'll come back with me?"

"I suppose so."

"The old lady I met in the hall said she would see about the packing. She asked about the convent."

"Stone deaf. Doesn't get a word."

"I wrote it all down."

"I much prefer to do my own packing." Leda stood up and walked across the room with almost boastful certainty, then, turning back at the door: "I wonder if they'll want to say good-bye to me?" She was asking herself a light, informal question.

"Yes, I wonder if they will," her daughter answered in a voice mistrustful of the simplest gesture or event.

She was standing in front of the Sargent-like portrait of his father when Jasper came back for another cup of coffee. He had seen a woman get out of a car and thought, as usual, that she was one of May's avoidable ladies. Unfair, that May should have left her to bother him in the dining-room; there had been quite enough bother for one morning.

The little person turned away from the picture as if she had been caught doing something private and impolite.

"Please excuse me," she said apologetically. "Isn't that Valentine Swift?" She added, as explanation: "I'm Leda's daughter."

Jasper flinched. What hideous embarrassment was he to be involved in next?

"That's one of Maman's fairy stories," she said, quietly, catching his thought. "I was born two years afterwards. If she was seduced. . . ." coming from her the word sounded indecent – "but I doubt that very much." She stood in profile to the picture and ventured a tiny laugh: "I'm a Jewish girl," she said.

A modifying wave of relief comforted Jasper nearly into friendliness.

"We're second cousins," he said, "or do they call it 'once removed'?"

"Whichever it is," she said, "from what I know of Maman I'm not very keen on my Swift blood."

She was no clinger to family relationships, Jasper realised with approval.

"Well. . . ." to give himself something to do, he began to clear the breakfast table, May's proper work. "Your mother has been a charming guest. A few difficult moments . . . . everything passes, yes. Of course. Can we put you up too?" He asked despairingly.

"No. Thank you very much. I have a business appointment. I flew in yesterday from Brazil."

Looking at her in her cosy knitted suit, beige and belted, Jasper thought it unlikely; but he swallowed the absurdity with gratitude.

"Another time?" the hospitality in his voice warmed a little.

"Thank you. But I only came here to take Maman back to the convent. The sisters were so worried when she flew the nest."

"I wish you'd come yesterday," Jasper said, "we'ld have been spared all this . . . fuss."

"Has she hurt anyone?"

"One of my sisters does seem a bit upset."

"Yes. That happens. Maman loves to charm and she loves to hurt," all uncertainty had left her voice.

"A bit rough on Leda, aren't you? We do realise what a ghastly time she went through in those camps. We thought, you know, we thought. . . ." he refused to say "gas chamber". "Of course she can't speak about it all," he ended, relief in his voice.

"No. She can't. She's only read about camps and gas chambers. She had a very comfortable war. In Paris, mostly. She had friends, very good friends, in the Occupation."

"Oh, had she? Did she. . . ," he failed to bring out the word "collaborate".

"She was useful. Her mother wasn't Jewish, so you can understand how. . . ."

"But your father?" No sooner was the question asked than Jasper regretted it.

"Papa?" The mask of understatement slipped. "Oh, he was on a list. He saved them the trouble of coming for him. Il s'est suicidé, avec son Browning."

Her escape into French seemed more funny than pathetic. The curiously filmic bang-bang effect of her phrase made Jasper turn his head to smile, before the calculated desperation implied in the words provoked his well-submerged memory of a different suicide; a decision to die taken in less dignified circumstances than those encircling Leda's Jewish husband. While he avoided even a glance towards the indifferent portrait of his handsome father, he had to allow to himself that Leda's woundings could be mortal.

"Then what about you?" he asked, turning hopefully to a lighter subject. "Weren't you rather young for all that?"

"Thirteen, fourteen. I was in Switzerland, in a convent. The Abbess was a wonderful person. Her family were Viennese, so, *of course*, they knew our restaurant." (Jasper felt the proud quality of the place in the way she spoke.) "Papa put me in her charge before things got too difficult." Her small voice brisked up again, "Maman is in the sister house here. It's a quiet safe place for her."

Safe from what? Jasper wanted to ask, but he left the question vacant.

"She's an old woman," he said. "She's a blind old woman. No one could . . . . after all this time. . . ."

"It took us quite a time to catch up with her friend. Maman got uneasy. She can smell things, so she turned him in – to me, actually."

"You hunted them out?" Coming from Jasper a question so definite sounded almost melodramatic.

"I'm an Israeli." In the way she said it he felt there was a two-edged sword flaming and turning every way in the air of the big faded room smelling of primroses.

"Maman will be quite all right," her voice sobered back into neat practicality, "if she stays inside her convent. Blind or not, I can't be sure of everybody in my lot. They've taken a few wanted ones out of Southern Ireland before now."

There was a pause while Jasper swept crumbs off the table with a small curved brush into a small mahogany tray, belonging to butler days.

"So, you see how it is." The little woman took a few steps towards the door; then paused to say apologetically: "I don't want to hurry anyone, but we ought to start soon. It's a long drive." She pushed up her cuff to look at an ugly watch, "and I must make my flight tonight."

In the last words Jasper heard hesitancy change to a tone of unalterable determination. She sounded a person from a different world, as she had when she said: "I'm an Israeli."

"I'll make you some sandwiches for a picnic." A tin of anchovies, scrambled eggs, mayonnaise, no butter. After the wild talk and the terror that moved, unspoken, behind it, the idea of sandwiches was a solace and an escape.

"Oh, you *are* kind," her polite acceptance clipped down a curtain on anything that had been said, or understood, in their talk.

In the hall, on his way to the kitchen, Jasper passed April. She was putting down the telephone. That she should use it at all was another of the morning's surprises. When she turned from it he saw how beautiful she was looking, almost radiant.

"Leda is leaving us," he wrote on the telephone notebook. He felt rather pleased that no arrow from the past had struck into her contented beauty.

"Quite right too," she answered, and sped upstairs, light on her feet as she had always been. When, he wondered, would she be her age? Never, he supposed. She wouldn't hear it coming; or Time's Chariot, or any of that stuff either. Alone in the kitchen at last, he set himself to the construction of the perfect sandwich of his imagination. Leda didn't deserve it, of course, but who did? Besides all that, everything is best forgotten. When he put down the flat anchovy tin of oil for Mister Minkles he felt he was back with realities again: "For you, old man," he said.

In the hall, a departure was imminent: suitcases, dogs suspicious of desertion, and now the beautifully packed sandwiches. Jasper felt as though someone was going back to school, the same cruelty was in the air, unhappiness painfully swallowed, even tears. People waited about to say goodbye. May, silent even with her dog, sat on a wooden hall chair, her knees together, her head down, holding Gripper quietly in her arms. Baby June, back in her wellingtons, was talking to the strange woman about butterflies, and looking at her watch covertly and often. She was longing for May to take the weight of politeness off her shoulders. A peacock butterfly, restored to life out of due time raised and dropped its wings in a pool of dusty sunshine.

It was a relief when Leda came down the stairs, sure-footed, her beautiful coat moving with her. Nobody knew, Jasper was glad to think, whose death had bought it. He felt ashamed of the dramatic thought and denied it to himself immediately.

"I do hate leaving you all," Leda stopped punctually at the bottom step of the staircase. "It's been a lovely, lovely time. I promise to be back. I do promise."

"Yes, Leda, come back." – "Come back when the weather is warmer." – "Come in the summer." – "Next summer." In turn they came and kissed her, their good manners inviolate.

"But April," she said, after the third cold cheek and touch, "where's April?" Nobody knew and it was no use calling. "We must go," the daughter said, "it's my flight. I *must* make my connection. Come along, Maman, please."

"Say goodbye and kiss her for me," Leda laughed, her first laugh of the morning. "No more tisanes, no more bran breakfasts."

She was put into the car, suitcases in the boot, sandwiches in a cool place, when April – beautifully dressed for a journey, the right people never travel in their best clothes – joined the group round the car. Tiger, wearing the jersey that matched up with her tweed ensemble, was on his lead. In one hand she held a feather-weight pigskin case, in the other a neat rotund parcel.

"Don't worry, Leda. No goodbyes. I'm coming too. Of course I'm coming with you." Her voice was full of comforting cadences.

Leda put her hand over her mouth, a gesture of despair. "Oh, no. Please not." Her protest went unheard and unnoticed.

"And we shan't have your good nuns interfering with our diet sheet." April turned to Jasper. She put a cheque in his hand. "And don't worry about my packing. I rang Ulick. He's going to see to everything. His Japanese boy is so skilled. Give Ulick this, please." She handed the parcel to Jasper and got into the car as elegantly as if she were being photographed. When she had settled herself and Tiger she waved, smiling and distant as royalty.

Leda's daughter put her cropped head out of the car window: "Watch your steps," she said seriously, "don't forget. I've warned you." Gravel, unraked for years, shot up in spitting showers as she turned the car fast and drove off down the avenue, heedless of fissures and potholes.

9 ✒ *Time After Time*

The three Swifts stood together on the steps, the rhythm of their day disrupted. Leda had gone and a flame of excitement had died in their lives. Even June had been singed a little, but May had been burned through. Everything that mattered to her was now black paper fragments, a flutter of nothing on a biting wind.

Jasper, denying all regret, unfolded a cheque in his hand. "April's," he said, "we're going to be rather on the breadline without her."

"Ah, she'll be back," June said easily.

"She won't, you know," May looked away down the empty drive.

"And another thing," June went on. "This horse should win the fourteen stone and upwards in Cork Show. Well, anyway, he'll be placed, you'll see."

Jasper turned his back on her, not unkindly, and returned to the house and to washing up breakfast plates in his kitchen. June said to May, "If you like, I'll keep Tiny in for the day."

The concession, implying sympathy and pity, was so mortifying that May's stomach contracted in a shiver of pain. "Don't bother," she said coldly, "I'll keep Gripper with me." She went upstairs to her bedroom and, before she made her bed, she put on one bar of the electric fire, saying to Gripper as she did so, "We'll have a little fire, just for the two of us – won't we, boy?" unaware that she was speaking the loneliest words of a lifetime.

For June, life, this April morning, had returned to something near its proper level. Leda's shadowy and absurd
accusation linking her to Christy she regarded only as angry
ravings, seething in a foreign (dangerous word, "foreign") mind.
Now, with complacent relief at the foreigner's departure, she
called Tiny to her and set off down the drive to organise her
own and Christy's work for the day – an ordinary day. She
would be on the tractor most of the morning while Christy
mucked out the cowsheds and the Wild Man's box and loaded
manure into the trailer. In the afternoon they might give the
horse a little school and, with Cork Show in distant prospect, a
short introduction to dressage. She felt relaxed and affectionate
towards Tiny, and pleased to see Christy looking sharp and able
in clean jeans and blue jersey. He was even wearing a tie, a pretty
picture indeed, as they met for their morning conference.

"I got delayed," she apologised.

"I have my horse done and mucked out, and my cow milked.
God bless her, I think she's getting very anxious for the
bull."

"I'll ring the AID man," June promised.

"The Holy Father is very averse to that class of thing."

"He's only strict with humans," June assured him, "so get her
in at dinner time."

"I mightn't be here for my dinner." Christy sounded
curiously sullen. "And I have to get the eleven Mass."

"What Saint's day is it today?" June asked dubiously.
"Matthew and Mark?" she hazarded.

Christy looked his lofty disdain at such Protestant ignorance.

"If it's not them it must be Peter and Paul – those two haven't
had a holiday together for a long time." June was sorry she had
hazarded the joke, as surprise and shock were evident in
Christy's silence. "Well," she gave in hastily, "if you must you
must, I suppose. Put up a prayer for me, won't you? And you'll

be back to give the lad a little school after your dinner. A dash of the dressage would do him no harm, or yourself either."

"I mightn't be back in any case after the dinner. My mother has an appointment arranged."

"Couldn't your mother put it off today – with the horse to exercise and the cow bulling." June's sense of two urgencies overcame her endless patience with Christy's religious exercises and obligations to his mother.

"It's for me she has the appointment made." He paused. "My mother is of the opinion I should get married. I suppose it's the will of God I to be so unlucky."

"Marry? Who does she want you to marry?" June asked, awed by the calamitous tone of his announcement.

"My mother says I'ld be a long time before I'ld drop on such a good Catholic girl. She says the most of the girls going now are no bloody use."

"Well," June considered the matter as perhaps less of a disaster than she had at first thought, "you won't have to get married this afternoon."

"No. Marriage is horrible. A horrible thing. If you thought of it you'ld go mad."

"Don't think about it," June advised. "And if you must do it, I'll get Mr Jasper to put the roof back on the gate lodge and you can live there."

"It's my mother's opinion I couldn't offer a girl less than the electric light and an indoor toilet."

"I don't think we'll get a toilet out of Mr Jasper," June said helplessly, "but he's promised me he'll lend you his old Huntsman jodhpurs for the Cork Show."

"Thanks, Miss Baby, I prefer the blue jeans, they're less remarkable. And I should go now, I have to get the eleven Mass."

"All right. Don't be too late coming back. We might have

time to get in a short school now the evenings are longer."

"I won't be coming back today, Miss Baby, or any other day either," Christy bent solicitously over the handlebars of his bicycle, rather as though looking down the fore-leg of a lame horse. "I'm giving you in my notice now this minute, and I'll see you again for my money and my insurance."

"Christy!" A chill of despair went through June, and her crying out of his name came from her shocked heart; while through her mind sped a vision of all the impossibilities confronting her with his departure.

"God Almighty – you can't do this – your religion could tell you that much."

"Who are you to accuse me of my religion?" Angry and defensive he leaned his foot on a pedal, ready to ride away.

June put her foot in front of the wheel and a hand on the handlebar. "And what about the cow now?" she said. "And you could spare five minutes to show me where the hens are laying out, and in God's name what will I do with the Wild Man?"

"You'll only have to get some other one to ride him, Miss Baby, for you're not fit. You'd never be able for that sod yourself. He's a proper scourge of a horse – he's waiting his chance all the time, he's as clever as a man. He thought he had me at the caravans yesterday."

June sickened a little in a new panic. "There's only myself to get up on him, and you know it."

"I wouldn't advise it, Miss, for you're not fit for the likes of him, or any other horse at your time of life."

"And the hours I gave schooling you to ride in a show ring."

"I could be at that too," he smiled shyly. "The lady was with my mother yesterday have a horse entered in Dublin, never mind Cork, and I'm to be over with her at three o'clock today. So, if you'll excuse me, Miss Baby," he looked politely at her detaining hand, "I must get Mass first. There's a house and electricity and a toilet going with the job, so I wouldn't doubt you'd give me a nice reference." He raised a hand to his pretty bare head and rode away without a further word.

All sense of order in the day's work left June. Her mind was pitifully confused by the size and complexity of Christy's disloyalty. Her fury with the robber-lady who had tempted him away was only equalled by her contempt for the act. She could think of no one who could have done her such a wrong, until she remembered Alys, May's friend, who had been with them the day before. And May had wanted Christy out, so who but May had alerted Alys to his special skill and usefulness, that even she could not deny?

Remembering all she had taught him, all he could do, and all he could leave undone, June, who should have been on the tractor an hour earlier, went fumbling round the yard, inspecting Christy's morning's works. There was a cool farewell in the perfection of their accomplishment; a righteousness showing forth his ability, as though to cloak the traitor behind the mask. He had slighted nothing. The cow, milked and carefully enclosed, was bellowing for love. The hens were fed and creaking away about their unlaid eggs. Sweetheart lay in a ray of sunlight – very Morland – suckling her young on a clean bed; he had even cut the nettles round the dark mouth of the duck house. "What will I do without him?" June wondered, "I'm sweating, Tiny, I'm sweating to think of all we have to do on our own." She did not admit it fully to herself, but every time she thought of the big horse waiting for her and his daily exercise, she squeezed her fingers into her wet palms before she dried them on her jeans. "We'll be OK Tiny," she promised, "I'm just only nervous. We must get the old tractor going anyway." Thankful to postpone her marathon she set off for the fields in the harsh roar of the tractor's engine. When she saw that Christy had failed from his usual custom of having a line of three gates propped open along the farm track to the five acres awaiting her labour, tears for his forgetfulness filled her eyes.

In the bathroom May was cleaning her teeth. Leda was gone, she thought, and still I have to brush my teeth. In the same way she knew that nothing would ever stop her proceeding bloodlessly, tearlessly, meticulously with her previous plans and commitments, lifeless as wax flowers seen through a window now. But no wax flower was lifeless to May.

Back in her bedroom she decided on a complete change of clothes – it would be a therapy. The least favourite suspender belt must have its turn. So must the brassière with the slipping shoulder strap. She decided against discarding her thermal spencer.

Her bedroom, as she undressed and dressed again, was warm, and smelling a little of happy comfortable dog. Within its order May realised the static frigidity of her own continuing life. Though she might never change her habits, all achievement and all praise would be empty of satisfaction. She knew now that all praise was owing only to her sad repulsive hand; while it was the hand she had controlled and trained which owed all to her; a cold welling of dislike rose in her as she pulled her arms through her sweater and saw her hand again, as she would do till she died. But with May, although she might never escape from her present limbo of distress, habit would prevail, assuaging the bitterness of disaster. She lit a cigarette, hung it in the corner of her mouth – one of the few louche tricks she allowed herself – and proceeded to make her bed, turned back before breakfast for its Spartan airing. She made it up with her usual exactness, giving to it the same attention that she gave to one of her tweed pictures.

In the past happy weeks it had been her privilege to make
Leda's bed and tidy up her room; at the same time enjoying an
informative chat about herself and her activities, useful or
artistic, or both. Today it was her sense of order which brought
her across the landing to the room that had once been
Mummie's. As she stripped the bed and laid the blankets back to
air, she felt it would exorcise Leda's tenancy if she remade it
properly with Mummie's pillowcases, big and little, freshly
washed and ironed. No visitor need ever again interrupt its well
tended privacy – provided that Jasper would keep his cat out
of the Yellow Room, and see to the leak in the Magnolia
Room.

As she shook pillows out of their cases and folded sheets May
noticed a sweetish smell in the room – April's scent, probably,
always heavier and more potent when Leda wore it; but there
was another, a curious under-smell. May thought of asparagus
and looked underneath the bed for the po – which Leda had been
arrogantly obstinate about not using. The po was quite empty.
She crossed the room to open a window, and as she passed the
dressing-table she saw something that made her stand still. To
restrain her shock she pressed her left hand with the other, using
the strong finger and thumb without a thought of their
maiming, the first time since breakfast that she had touched it
without hatred.

A silver photograph frame – it belonged to the days before
leather and talc – lay on the flowered carpet, empty. Its smashed
glass was scattered in stars and angles round it, together with the
torn and twisted pictures it had held of Mummie and Daddy.
Horrified at the extraordinary desecration, May picked up the
pieces one by one and considered the possibility of sticking
them together again.

Careful for Gripper, she was scrupulously clearing up the
broken glass when she noticed him sniffing interestedly at the

base of the wardrobe. She went over to him at once, worried that glass splinters might have flown across the room. Then, she too paused and sniffed, curious and unbelieving, before she opened the door and looked into the spacious half of the wardrobe where she had hung Mummie's lovely dresses closely together in order to leave room for Leda's few belongings – so soon supplemented by April.

Shocked and rather frightened, May drew back from the cupboard, to stand and sniff in excited disbelief, before deep anger at the violation took its place. Folds of satin and chiffon, beaded corsages, strict pleated tweeds, all had been soaked and smeared. May caught her breath in dismay for a mauve brocade shoe with its diamanté buckle. Her love of beautiful things, her efforts and ceremonies in caring for them, doubled the horror she felt at this crazy desecration. At the same time as it axed any remnant of the devotion she had given to Leda, it revived her doctor-like sense of order and restoration.

Jasper met her leaving the bathroom, a dripping evening gown swinging on its hanger at the full length of her raised arm. "It's no good," she said, "soap and water are useless."

"I don't know why you think so," he tried to pass on his way, ducking any involvement, "but I'm sure you're right."

"Just a minute." She stood in his way, with the strange, waving dress. "Come into Mummie's room. See what she's done."

Jasper was reluctant to share May's probable criticism of Leda's untidiness. He felt almost on Leda's side, as he was totally on the side of his cats when May protested at their unseemly habits. However, after all the unnecessary scenes and emotions of breakfast-time, he felt it would be inhuman not to follow her. She brought him to the cupboard and stood, pointing severely, as one indicates to a guilty dog something dirty on the carpet. Jasper leaned sideways to peer with his one

eye before, appalled and embarrassed, he withdrew his head and
put his handkerchief to his nose.

"My God, am I seeing the truth?" he said.

"*And* smelling it," May responded, almost in a tone of
triumph. "Right?"

"So right." Again he tried to escape, and again she and the
dress on its hanger stood in his way.

"It's what one has read about places like Belsen."

"She was never near Belsen, or any other camp." For once
Jasper spoke directly and with disgust. "From what I gathered
this morning, she sold her Jewish friends and kept herself out of
trouble for the duration. Then, Brazil with the Nazi boy-
friend."

"Something to do with the Vatican, I'm sure." May
dismissed the Nazi régime, as for years she had dismissed the
thought of Leda. "But the thing is – what am I to do about
Mummie's lovely dresses? How many years have I looked after
them – moths under control, every shoe stuffed with paper. And
nothing will wash. Look, it rots the chiffon." She displayed a
wet sagging hole.

"To the sword with the lot of them," Jasper suggested
hastily, "or the garden bonfire."

"Mummie's dresses?" May looked really stricken.

"Then take the lot to the cleaners today."

"Why, Jasper, that's a fortune. You must think money grows
on trees."

"I don't care what it grows on. I'll pay, if you'll do
the explaining to the cleaners."

May grew suddenly taller. She was back with decisions, with
capabilities that others lacked. "Good!" she pronounced. "All
this muck to the cleaners today. I'll get it in before my lecture to
the club. Right?"

"Sooner you than me," Jasper murmured to himself, "not my

affair anyway." At the door he turned to say: "And bring that parcel of April's to Ulick. I really can't involve myself there. It's on the oak chest in the hall."

Another importance. And she could be rude to awful Ulick. Quite revived, May set about the dreadful task of packing the defiled garments, between layers of tissue paper, into two large suitcases. On each sheet of paper she sprayed Green Apple deodorant from the bathroom. "Hope for the best. Everything under control," she told herself as she slapped shut brass locks in her own masterful way.

In his kitchen Jasper ran the hot tap rather carelessly in and over the breakfast-time cups and plates. He felt more free and relaxed than disturbed at Leda's sudden departure. Drama of any sort was one of his special dreads. Although he had entertained himself in depriving his sisters of Leda's undivided attention, he was more than relieved to have evaded the deeper waters of last night's visit. He had never been one for midnight rampages in the dorm, and he certainly felt beyond adventure now. The desecrations in his mother's room, which had so appalled May, he was able to ignore, since someone else was dealing with the nastiness. "Very nasty" was his hardest word for what he had seen; he set the whole affair aside; and, along with it, the sad reality of Leda's untempting body. It all belonged to the wild accusations of breakfast time. There might be more than half a truth, he suspected, in those launched against his sisters, but in his own security from scandal he knew himself inviolate – for how could Leda have guessed the first thing about his relationship with Brother Anselm? At the same time he was not without a slight shudder of apprehension over her hint at a hot-line to the Lord Abbot. He must see his young friend today. He hoped the boy would bring the promised load of willow hurdles, one of the monastery's most attractive industries. How he wished they would make liqueurs as well; out of gorse blossom, perhaps; or the berries of mountain ash. His mind chased away after endless possibilities. Bringing it back to the hurdles, and the shelter belt to be constructed from them, he set about preparing a large and luscious sandwich for the strong and handsome Brother.

With April's default there came, of course, a reality to be considered, a reality entailing so much unkindness to Baby June that he lacked the iron-clad resolution necessary for its pursuit. If only some unhappy accident (for which he was unaccountable) might befall, he would be willing to take advantage of it and proceed with – he shuddered – the sale of the land. With the sale of land went Baby June's lifetime's occupations; a welter of uneconomic projects, of which one of the most expensive and least rewarding in practical terms was Christy Lucey.

That problem brought unwillingly to mind Leda's allusions to their great-grandmother, the ex-dairy-maid. Her grace and and good looks had come down to his father and to April; perhaps, in a lesser degree, to himself; might some different inheritance have stirred in Baby June? Leda's suggestions had been preposterous, or course. Still, there was room to wonder. And for surmise, too, at May's stricken look when her turn for betrayal came on. He put the absurd idea of shop-lifting a long way behind Leda's unforgivable allusions to May's hand – a matter always in camera, undiscussed as his one eye, accepted as April's deafness, or Baby June's difficulties with the written word. Mummie had taught them how to grow up with their maiming and how to ignore its different constrictions. His disgust at Leda's undoing of that work, and the throwing of facts in their faces, went beyond his disgust at a vicious slut's revenges for any long-past, or long-imagined, injury. As he threw the remainder of yesterday's Austrian failure into Sweetheart's bucket, Jasper, leaving unsolved and forgettable the suggestions of breakfast time, set himself to unravel his ideas about lunch.

Hard-boiled eggs in a plain sauce, he decided; that ought to show them he was bent on economy. No luxuries to be added. Well, yes, no, perhaps a few mushrooms? No, again. The mushrooms were in the larder – much too far to walk. Mustard would liven things up a bit and the coriander seed was close at hand. Turning from the table to move a steaming saucepan of dogs' dinners off the hot ring of the Aga, he felt quietly pleased that today there was no need for the incense of bay leaves. The girls' protests might sound again over the smells, briefly cloaked for Leda's benefit. Herbs on a shovel, he thought. That silly chapter was ended.

May spent the rest of the morning perfecting and finishing the restoration of the twice broken candlestick. Although delight was absent from her satisfaction with the work, and the usual tide of pleasure in such an achievement was far out, May decided to bring the candlestick to the Flower Club lecture that afternoon – an object lesson in restoration and an example of dexterity. In unacknowledged defence against Leda's taunts, she packed, with the candlestick, her latest and most beautifully executed tweed picture. Both objects went into a capacious Greek basket once given her by a travelled Alys. "And I thought she was pure gold," May bowed her sad head at the memory, but packed up her works of art as though she were still a happy person. A slightly sour note influenced her decision to lecture that afternoon on a Japanese theme; a dried flower arrangement, which some wild parsnip heads, lichened apple twigs, and a few stones would suffice to illustrate.

The time came to give Gripper his run; time, too, for her

eighth cigarette of the morning and for a moment's aberration while she lit it. Then she locked her door – on what? she asked herself again with a sickening recall of Leda's exposures. Standing outside her own locked door, locked on no secrets now, she picked up Gripper, usually treated with proper austerity, and laid her cheek against his. Since he was as heavy as two telephone directories, she soon put him down, uncomforted.

In the dining-room she found June with her head in the drinks cupboard of the sideboard. She stood up with a bottle in her hand. "Shall we have one?" she suggested. "Just the one," she added as though to modify the unusual idea.

"Not for me, thank you, Baby," May refused tightly and brightly, forbidding any necessity for a restoration.

"Well, I will." June poured out a modest drink.

"Not *whiskey*? Before *lunch*?" May was genuinely taken aback, as much by surprise as by disapproval.

"And I need it, too." Baby June sat down and stared silently at the vacant goatskin; she had been as good as her word about Tiny.

May put out her cigarette to fidget, without interest or approval, with the primroses on the table; primroses, like everything else, had lost their quality.

The lift ground its way upwards, followed by Jasper. Surprisingly, in contradiction to his planned economies, the first thing he took out of it was a bottle of wine – cool and fresh in his hands.

Observing it, May ached at this further celebration of sympathy. Kindness again. She could have struck him.

"I wondered if we might? . . . Perhaps? . . . What do you think? After all, a very meagre luncheon. So why not?" He looked up and sniffed disapprovingly as he was about to draw the cork: "Now, who's been stealing to the sideboard?" he asked the air.

"Me," June admitted. "It's not like me, it's not like me at all, is it? But there it is – I needed a little something."

"What's up, Baby? Aren't you feeling well?" Again he skipped any connection with breakfast's rough affair.

"Christy's gone." June could have announced a death more cheerfully.

Although any significant decision was well beyond him, the announcement eased the foremost tension in Jasper's ideas for the future of Durraghglass.

"Anyway, who did half his work?" May could not conceal her pleasure.

"I did not, too," June contradicted.

"Far too much for you, the whole thing. I've thought so for some time." Jasper sounded as if he had actually noticed that June was over-worked. June took him up in the way he had not intended. "So what am I to do without Christy? Who am I to manage a bulling cow without a helping hand?" Her dreaded problem – the young horse – she was too proud and frightened to mention.

"You might manage to keep chickens instead," May suggested.

"I'm killed from chickens. I'm too old for following them into the briars and nettles after their nests."

"I mean, intensively."

"That's against nature. Free run, or nothing, it's the only way."

"Let's face Facts, I –" Jasper looked across the table at June – "I'm snipping the double-leaders in the spruce belt this afternoon," he finished, dodging whatever fact it was that he had meant to face.

"Anyhow, of all the useless, idle chancers I've ever known," May stopped her indictment, suddenly aware of June's face, furious as an angry baby's.

"And I suppose that's why you recommended him to your friend, Alys." June's voice rose.

"Don't be silly, Baby. As if I would do such a thing." There was both anger and surprise in May's denial.

"Oh, great! Great out!" June's disbelief was manifest. "And you'ld have Tiny put down tomorrow if I didn't watch it. And who, only Alys, offered Christy a house and an inside toilet and a ride in Dublin Show?"

"Girls, girls!" Jasper was dismayed at the emotion in the room. He went to the lift for the egg dish, hopeful that even plain food might quieten things down. Only a brooding silence settled. He could have found it in him to wish that Leda with her joyaunce and falsity was there to stir up the atmosphere; or even April to achieve the same, with her absurdities and her money. Thinking of the money, he almost joined the brooders; he was held from gloom only by the prospect of an interesting, and, possibly, rewarding afternoon.

Luncheon was silent, unenlivened by glasses of wine – proffered and mutely accepted. When it was over, and the table cleared, Jasper left all the dishes and plates, varied and beautiful in their designs, to soak; cats hated Lemon Quix, and were even less interested in spinach, so the plates might rest unbroken till evening. He put Brother Anselm's sandwich in a basket along with his stainless steel trowel, fork and secateurs. Then, carrying his heavy clippers, he set out for the rendez-vous. As he went on his way he heard the sound of May starting up the car; forgetful, for once, of the criminal cost of petrol, he was pleased to think that she carried with her those dreadful suitcases to which he had yielded a shudder of recognition and avoidance as he passed by in the hall.

June went to her bedroom after lunch. She brought Tiny the

egg her stomach had refused. The whiskey, fuelling her anger against May, had lost its power now. Even towards Tiny her interest failed a little. She set her mind on the practical details to which she must attend before her ordeal, rather in the way a suicide might measure the length of his rope. "I suppose I must only look out the old cap and the old jodhpur boots," she told herself. "Sense, child, don't ride that lad in your wellies!" After a search through discarded sneakers, espadrilles, and awful sandals, she found them at last – blue-moulded and hard as glass, almost crisp, from age and neglect. Miserably oblivious of the past and lazy days when she had worn those boots, June sat on the edge of her bed and crammed her feet into them; an ankle-strap cracked between her fingers as she forced it into a buckle. Her head felt too large for the faded velvet cap – which, in any case, had grown soft as the boots were hard. She picked up a little bamboo stick from a corner in the back of the cupboard, wondering when, or why, she had put it there; the usual feel of it in her hand lent a glint of old procedure to the nervous trial of the present moment.

In the stableyard she leant the little stick against the wall, and balanced the saddle on the half-door of the loose-box, before going up to the big horse, bridle in hand. Surprisingly, almost dolefully subject, he lowered his head, and with an arm across it, behind his ears, she had the bridle on him without the smallest trouble. Saddling up bore no difficulty for her. How often she had the horse ready for Christy to school and exercise. She had never lost the proper knack, and the right tone of her voice, pleasing and subduing, was changeless. The Wild Man swelled himself against the girths, and she led him out before taking them up two holes. When she pulled down the stirrup leathers she saw that Christy, with almost loving care, had shortened them to the length he thought she might ride. That he should have done so made his defection more than ever calamitous.

Now, bitter and fearful, June faced the problem of getting up on the young horse. "Will I jump up on you, you bastard?" she asked him aloud.

Her strength and activity a myth now, she only saw Christy's cat-like nimbleness, the tidy horsemanship he had learned from her. Sometimes she had held his off leather while he got up from the ground – practice for show rings and elderly judges. But now, she was alone, an old woman, worried sick as a nervous child – "And not one of them, Jesus, to give me a thought!" In the tightening of her nerves as she coaxed and fiddled her horse up to the old stone mounting-block (where so many ladies of yester-year had dumped themselves into their side saddles) she was not sure who she blamed for her horrid situation.

She thought the Wild Man looked round at her foot in a nasty way when she was up on him. Her leathers were just the wrong length. But, as she bent to shorten them, changing her reins from hand to hand, the horse walked quietly round the unkempt circle of grass in the yard, and her mind and body found the old familiarity with the horse she rode. The brown hens scratching in the grassy cobbles belonged now to a world of no import-ance: "Lay, you buggers, lay," she thought with careless venom. Even Tiny, incarcerated in her bedroom, was less of a loved obligation. She was on a horse again. And who was boss? She was.

Under the archway of the yard, and along the drive, all was perfect decorum between them. She was prepared for him to blow and shy and stop at his usual imagined ghosts in the empty windows of the gate lodge, but today he saw none of them. As if in celebration, the sun came out, and Baby June, enlivened, con-fident, almost jubilant, caught hold of her horse's head and sent him jogging, in chaste sobriety, along the grass verge of the narrow mountain road; Jasper's woodlands were on her left, and on her right gorse, under the sun, was smelling like sweet food.

She expected trouble at the tinkers' camp where coloured stuffs were spread like flowers or flags, still in the windless afternoon, on thorn bushes and walls. Empty tins and bottles that had held stout and orange juice and meat (how sad, no more baked hedgehog) rolled about, discarded, in the ditch; a woman jogged two whining babies in a smart pram and shouted at a boy who held a quiet pony by the rope rein of its head collar. To all of this the Wild Man paid no heed or attention. And, as they proceeded on through the lovely afternoon, something bordering on ecstasy re-made for June the mind and body of her youth.

It was when she turned for home, after an hour or longer, that the day changed mortally; spikes of hail pierced the thick cream of the hawthorn flower, a wild west wind, warm, but unmerciful, tore flowers from the most sheltered banks. June stooped to her horse's neck and sent him along faster, correcting his swerves and dodges; the rain had put up his temper. As she steadied and controlled him with all her old acumen, June felt happier and more confident with every passing minute. It's like the old bicycle, she told herself, you can't forget how to do it.

Nearer home, she felt the pulse of his will grow stronger. Once he put his head down, and his back tautened under the saddle, but she pulled the bit through his teeth and growled a telling reproof. Remembering Christy's warning, she sat down in her sadle and shortened her reins as they neared the tinkers' camp – earlier so quiet under the sunshine. She kicked him out of the idea of stopping for the plausible reason of bright stuffs flapping at their anchorages on the thorns. Disaster struck only when the pram, left unattended and empty of its babies, rolled, wind-driven, towards them. She pulled her horse nearly into the ditch to avoid it, but, caught in a sudden gust of mountain wind, the horrid object swerved nearly across the Wild Man's forelegs. Then it happened: he put down his head and, at his first lightning buck, June was gone. She landed on her head in the stony road, where she lay quite still, a solid little huddle under the rain and wind. Then, with another plunge in celebration of his freedom, the Wild Man made off – flying reins and stirrups urging him on into an admirable turn of speed.

As he walked through his groves above the river bank, devising his afternoon diplomacies as he went, Jasper saw a clear way towards his intentions; particularly when he considered Christy Lucey's disloyal defection, and the consequences it must have on Baby June's stewardship of Durraghglass.

Jasper followed the paths, broad and narrow, indifferent successors to the tamed ways and walks through a pleasance of yesterday. Now, most of the paths were choked and impassable; others, narrow and overhung, he kept clear of briars and wild, insistent growths. In an indiscriminate kind of way they went to and fro, linking his various plantings. It was here that Jasper led his proper life. His kindness, his indulgence never failed towards his trees and shrubs. If some rare subject disappointed, he blamed only himself and sought patiently to remedy his ignorance. He went about among his plantings like a hopeful, but not over-optimistic, doctor, pleased by his successful treatment of some patients, while admitting death and disappointment to be the lot of others. The site was all too open for his exorbitant fancies; river frosts and mountain winds had killed off many of his more exotic subjects. Shelter was what they craved; given honest lengths of shelter, in place of scrawny hazel and mean ash-saplings and alder, Jasper's garden might fulfil his dreams and plans.

On the other hand, he was sometimes relieved to think that many of his trees and shrubs might never mature, or not in his lifetime. *Hoheria populnea*, the white witch tree, might never reach the magical ballet-like excitement he knew to be possible.

Capparis spinosa already disliked its situation; and, even if it decided to thrive, its flowering could be well below his hopes. Jasper was a visionary gardener. He could see himself, high on some mountain plateau in China – or Korea, perhaps – where rocks were covered in rhododendron, and ice-blue seas of primula spread out to dazzle him past delight. He would never go to China; again he was pleased to think how disappointing it might prove to be. His expectations were the best part of his gardening, changing, concluding nothing.

He wandered on, pausing and peering at cherished groupings, his mind set on the necessity for their shelter. There was to be no hesitancy in his proposed alliance with Brother Anselm, an alliance long delayed by his own enervating talent for post-ponement. Even now he doubted his power to consummate any lasting involvement. He was too early for the planned meeting, he knew, and occupied the time on the slaughter of en-croaching briars and nettles. He stopped for a minute near the double white cherry he had planted years ago; full of buds now, and lavish in its still unflowered grace. He thought of some un-demanding woman on a summer's evening; perhaps with a white umbrella. What a pity that women could not grow old gracefully, like a tree. Not that it mattered to him: fortunately.

In contrast to such imaginings, he saw, beyond the bare screens of trees, June riding down the drive on her young horse. He had not seen her on a horse for many years; the sight brought back her triumphant youth, and his own unhappy one. Was he about to betray her? Was it, curiously, a belated revenge he was taking? It was a worrying thought; but one has to have one's worries, he knew; they gave one something to think about, and led the mind away from major disaster. He refused to feel guilt towards her useless devotion to a ghost cause and a hollow prospect. He stopped his nettle-slashing and stood for a minute watching Baby June. Time dissolved as he noticed how her contact with a horse still had its own truth and balance – a rhythm of yielding and control. Baby June was no longer a stuffed toy. She looked as strong, and as lonely, as she did at eighteen, neat in her colours, riding down to the start of a race; today, a Husky jacket and a bare grey head. As the evocative sound of a horse's hooves was lost on the grass verge of the mountain road, that whisper from the past ceased to irritate him.

Jasper passed easily on from the thought of Baby. Other, more interesting ideas sifted and changed in his mind: which subject might make good progress in such a situation, when shelter matured; what vista could be created draughtlessly, and how, and where. There was a great deal to be discussed with Brother Anselm this afternoon: Brother Anselm, the strong young friend and ally. Jasper continued on his way through the torn woodland, between Durraghglass and the monastery lands, to the point from which he saw the monastery tractor waiting – a clean and opulent object, redolent of good care and good money. On this afternoon there was to be no wavering, no saving temporisation and postponement; no delays; no side-stepping of issues. In a torrid state of determination, foreign to his entire nature, Jasper advanced; his walk, sure and unalterable as his melodious voice, did not betray the tumult within.

A monk – a strong, middle-aged, ugly monk – got off the tractor, and walked down the road to meet him. His habit, although the same, had none of the grace and flow of Brother Anselm's; it looked tougher, shorter, more workmanlike. His approach was determined, and, in some way, authoritative – as though he had an unwelcome message to deliver. If it was difficult, he was the man for the job.

As Jasper stopped and waited easily (the ex-landlord, and gentleman at ease on his own property) a dreadful supposition assailed him; a remark of Leda's blew through his mind again, and with it came the memory of a sour and silly riposte of his own, made to May, on the subject of a handsome – no, a "pretty" – young monk. Linking the two, a wild possibility became credible.

"Good afternoon, Brother."

"Good evening, Mr Swift." The monk's bulk in his habit seemed to fill the little roadway with menace. He was turning over in his mind what he had to say.

"Rather a wonderful afternoon." Jasper spoke to bridge the gap of silence.

"Beautiful, thank God," the monk agreed. Then, accepting the conversational opening, he went on: "I think, Mr Swift, you were expecting Brother Anselm. You meet frequently, I understand."

"As our lands touch, it would be rather hard to avoid meeting quite often – and," Jasper went on hardily, "I very much hoped to see him today. We had urgent business to discuss."

"I'm sorry to have to tell you, Mr Swift, discussions are an impossibility. The Brother is in heavy trouble for transgressing the Rules of our Order. The Abbot has him back in Silence."

A horrified disbelief, beyond any discreet evasion, became for Jasper a reality to contend with. Present and future dreams expired into nullity; gone as utterly as the dream at waking goes. "Oh, I am sorry," was all he could find to say; perhaps it was appropriate to his feelings.

"It may seem a small thing to you," the old monk was eyeing Jasper's load of garden tools, "but it's the rule. It's Obedience."

"Well," Jasper hesitated, "we only talked about it."

"If you'll excuse me, Mr Swift, there was a lot more than talk to it."

"Brother Anselm certainly brought me several loads of hurdles for my wind-breaks."

"Never mind the hurdles. Hurdles are neither here nor there

in the case. This is a serious thing. Did you, or did you not, give Brother Anselm a ham sandwich? Or any other class of a sandwich?"

What next? Jasper wondered. What was coming next? "Of course, I did." He felt sandwiches were a long way from any nasty implication Leda had contrived to convey to the Lord Abbot. "The boy looked desperately cold, and hungry too, working all day on the mountain. What is more," he continued, with an artist's defiance for his oeuvre, "*my* sandwiches are the proper sort. I hope he enjoyed them. I think he did. He should have."

"The Lord Abbot saw no harm in a sandwich – ham or any other kind of a sandwich." The monk paused portentously, a stern, habited figure, stolid in disapproval, unafraid to speak, Sin his subject matter. "The Rule does not forbid the acceptance of a cup of tea, or a sandwich itself, provided the little refreshment is outside of the monastery. But, to bring it back with you, in among the Brotherhood, and to eat it, solitary in your cell – that is the sin of disobedience to the Rule of the Order. And the Abbot is strict on that one; oh, very strict indeed."

Jasper seldom – almost never – laughed, but the waves of pleased relief that swept through him on the tides of so perverse an absurdity was such that its suppression brought a flow of tears to his eyes, both the blind and the seeing. Brother Declan arrested his lecture on the niceties of disobedience as Jasper mopped his eyes. When he saw the black patch shifted, the better to stem the rivulets coursing down Jasper's cheek he averted his eyes, politeness forbidding comment, and gave all his attention to Jasper's armoury of gardening weapons. Then, with beautiful manners, he prolonged the conversation by a change of subject.

"We hear up at the monastery that you're a great gardener, Mr Swift."

"Oh, I think I'm more of an old weeding woman," no sooner spoken than Jasper hoped his deprecatory description was not going to be misunderstood.

"Ah, there's a lot more than that to a horticulturist." The old monk's eyes lit. "Brother Anselm was telling me you have a very rare subject well established down there. And from his account I can only think it should be *Hoheria populnea*. And if you can flower that – it should only put you in mind of the Bride of God. Now I always considered *Hoheria populnea* as an exotic. How do you winter it, at all?"

What was this? What new road had been opened – and by Leda's treacherous mischief – for the hopes she had vilified to follow? Would the dream shared with Brother Anselm, an ardent but limited horticulturist, be near now to practical solution? The scheme they had discussed was dependent on the sale of the last lands of Durraghglass at a low price to be agreed as exchange for perpetual labour in his groves. In the still undrafted agreement shelters were to be planted – drear conifers, of course, but supplemented by screens of ash, hazel, alder, oak – all to be cherished into maturity. And in this haven from mountain winds the right sites should be prepared for delicate subjects, their individual likings in soils imported from no matter what distances. Below the groves, the river bank and its boggy margins were to be planted with every rarity found in Waterers' Catalogue, suitable to the situation. Here groupings of dogwood and golden willow would shelter the dammed pools on which water-lilies and swans might float together. Only the harsh problem of Baby June's heartbreak had come between Jasper and the blissful consummation of his designs. Today that problem had gone a long way towards solving itself, for, lacking Christy Lucey, how could June contend with the work? A successor might be found for the farm labour, but what postulant could there be for the role of that centaur she had trained and made? It was strange that Christy's defection was most likely due to Leda, and yesterday's desertion of their cake making for the sake of more fun with Alys: again, the dancing class; but not again the gloved hands clasped beneath the carriage rug.

Pocketing his handkerchief and picking up his tools, Jasper felt that this new-comer from the monastery might prove to be a far more stable agent than Brother Anselm. "If we aren't breaking any rule," he said with real hesitancy, "may I show you what I've tried to do? All a miserable wilderness, of course. But some of my plantings may amuse you."

In the hour that followed Jasper found his perfect companion. Brother Declan was an ardent and knowledgeable horticulturist. Before entering the religious life he had worked in the Botanical Gardens at Glasnevin, and he had once refused an offer to go to Kew; "Now, when it's all only in the mind," he said, "it can't get in the way of your religion."

"What about the gardens at the monastery?" Jasper asked. "You ought to propagate unusual herbs. They ought to make liqueurs – something like that."

"Not a hope of that, son. I suppose I'ld be too happy to be at it. I'll only have to offer it up," he said in his most practical voice; then he stooped down over a sickish camellia to instruct Jasper on its treatment and revival. Mentally hand in hand and seeing eye to eye, they walked together. The sun shone through the glades they envisaged, they changed the nature of the soil for the species they discussed; they might have been talking about women, their ardour was so restrained.

Then, the rain came, and the wind changed, whipping through Jasper's meagre belts of trees. They sheltered together in the hooded cab of the tractor and it was while Brother Declan was eating the ham sandwich that Jasper (June's heartbreak properly isolated) put his proposition about the sale of the land.

Brother Declan screwed up the foil that had wrapped the sandwich into a neat ball, and aimed it out into the rain. He screwed up his face too, even his hoodless tonsure wrinkled as he shook his head. "With the depression and the inflation the money isn't in it. The Brotherhood haven't it to give," he said.

"Brother Anselm was rather hopeful." Jasper looked sadly down between his thin knees.

"That's the way with the young," Brother Declan sounded like a nannie closing the book at the end of a bedtime story. He looked out into the blinding rain and back to Jasper. "It's not to say," he went on, "there's not a middle way in everything. That narrow strip, now, between us and you – all rushes and ragweed – if we had that it would be like a little convenience getting stock back to the road; we have two gates and around the world to go the way we are situated presently."

"What sort of financial arrangement would you suggest?" His heart beating as at first love, Jasper seemed only mildly interested.

"Oh, finance! If that has to come into it, we're done . . . . I was just thinking we might come to some little arrangement . . . . if the monastery supplied you with a bit of labour, yourself and myself could direct it." His face expanded, almost illuminating the rain-beaten interior of the cab. "We'ld make a lovely job of it." He waited.

"Well, I'm not saying yes and I'm not saying no. I'm saying, well, but, perhaps. . . ." Jasper could only teeter on the edge of accepting what he wanted most in life.

"Take your time," the monk said patiently. "I'll be here again on Thursday. You can let me know then if I'm to put the notion to the Lord Abbot."

Jasper got out of the tractor cab. He stood in the rain like a heron at the water's edge, a heron about to miss its fish. Just before Brother Declan started up his engine he opened the door and pushed his head in, past the tall window. "Tell him I like the idea very much. Tell him tonight," he said. He shut the door before Brother Declan could answer, then opened it again to ask: "Do you see the journal of the Royal Horticultural? I can let you have my back numbers."

"God bless you," Brother Declan said sincerely. He let in the clutch and the tractor roared away to its proper labours.

Standing alone on the stony roadside, Jasper looked through the falling rain into the possibilities open to him now. Without the sacrifice of Baby June, the unsatisfied appetites of his life were at last to be gratified. His struggles against rabid Nature, battles so often lost to the meshed briars and nettles that overtook his clearings, would be won now with the gift of obedient, monkish labour. With the power that this promised him he could accomplish his vision; slice away the mountain winds; create the garden he had seen for so long as far beyond any horizon or reality. Possessed by his delight, Jasper experienced, for the moment, some of the emotion he could have known, perhaps, with an undemanding bride, had love not been so aborted in him when he was young. Now, his resigned, dispirited face was lighted in a brief glory of acceptance. His happiness was now, and for the future years when the stored love of half a life-time should find its true employment. Rain on his face, graceful coat clinging, indifferent to discomfort, Jasper was in love; age forgotten, no age he; overdraft whistled away; over his shoulder went every care.

Jasper was not one to thank God, or any lesser power, for this benificence. Sourly he agreed with himself that the break had come through horrid Leda. However she had done it, she had alerted the busy Abbot's worst and most reluctant suspicions. Or, Jasper's inmost vanity suggested, it was the inspired ham sandwich, proffered in ignorance, that had been the catalyst for such a providence. The thought of Brother Anselm, back in

Silence, affected him not at all: the silly fellow had been, in any case, rather an eager bore. Beyond his own exhilaration – which he soon tied grimly into place: never exaggerate – was the lightening of that tiresome sense of contrition towards Baby June which would have loomed had the sale of the land gone through, as he had intended. Obviously, as he had seen so lately, she was still able for a difficult horse; and, perhaps, Jasper thought, a holy brother on a tractor would be a valuable substitute for that spoilt Beauty Boy, Christy Lucey.

Soaking wet, but light-hearted, he turned back towards the kitchen, going with him the happy thought of the strong hands so soon to be at work on his briars and thickets. After a quick inspection of a group of gold mottled *eleagnus*, to check on May's depredations (from the back, as usual she had cut some promising young growth) Jasper's mood changed to its ordinary state of vengefulness. "I'll put the Monk Pack on to her," he promised himself. The idea of a new tease was always satisfactory and added to the blessed sense of a return to the usual. This was especially so after that preposterous interlude when he had seen himself through Leda's eyes that could not see. A delicious, villainous moment was thankfully over. It had been a brief entertainment, ridiculously exciting – for vanity, he owned, outlives all the handicaps of the ageing. Although the climax to the charade had been monumentally embarrassing, Jasper, slashing at young nettles, felt that he had escaped something worse than death with decorum and tactfulness.

He could not feel the same about that dreadful breakfast scene with its illicit exposures of each to each. He retreated now from any understanding of his sisters other than the way in which he had always known them. He had no wish to be made an intimate of their secret behaviours. He would put all that aside, as he trusted (but doubted) that they would put aside Leda's suggestion of his possible perversity. Not that he cared; such fancies had never been one of his worries. "I just wish I was more of a Human Being," he sighed, but comfortably and with no regrets. A crooked gratitude was what he felt for Leda now. Perhaps a faint sympathy as well, because she had deaf, devoted April for ever by her side.

Back on the road and nearer to the gates of Durraghglass, he heard the sounds of a horse coming towards him – sounds sharp in the distance, harsh and hollow as they came closer: Baby June on her way home. He had news for her, but he would not hurry himself in its telling; no further delays in the rain. He felt very kindly towards Baby June since he had been spared the accept-ance of those drastic ideas for change favoured by May. In his present euphoria he could put aside the exigencies of the situ-ation and allow life to pursue its accustomed downhill course. He was ready to give a nod and a smile, perhaps a little greeting when Baby June should overtake him. He turned to make his pleasant little gesture as horse and rider came round a bend in the road behind him. But his gesture checked and failed in his surprise when he saw that the rider was not Baby June, but a wild red-haired tinker boy who held his reins as if he drove an ass in a cart, looped his long legs inwards far below June's short leathers, changed his ash-plant stick from right to left hand to smack it down along the horse's ribs as he turned him, with a wild shout, from the gates to his stableyard, and sent him back the way he had come, crying out to Jasper, as he hit the horse twice more: "There's a woman dead below – hurry on till you see her. Hurry, or you'll be late."

Like a bad fairy with a fatal message the boy could have come from the blackened heather and grey mountain stones, where the gold of the gorse was sodden back into its heart. Dread and annoyance possessing him equally, Jasper dropped his tools and ran, his long spider's legs weaving, his breath catching. "How unpleasant, how tiresome," was how he phrased the fear that

shook him through at the idea of life at Durraghglass without
Baby June.

Only an imitation of her particular sense of order gave May the
resolution necessary to set her afternoon in order. Her true sense
of loyalty to her own art-and-crafty skills and to the expectant
flower Guild ladies moved her delicate testing of the newly
assembled piece of porcelain. Would it, or would it not endure
transport? Quite a question. Packed by her, she decided "Yes".
It would be a pity if her recreative genius was not seen at its
finest moment. After the return of the candlestick to Alys, any
further exhibition would be out of the question. It never
occurred to May that to smash the piece to irreparable atoms
would be a fitting revenge for Alys' disloyalty and cruel dis-
paragement of herself to Leda. Small, beautiful objects were, to
May, far more important than the breakage of her own self-
respect and confidence – established with so much discipline and
difficulty.

She put the materials for her afternoon's lecture together with
a cold lack of interest, a sense of duty quite unlike the bustling
certainty in which she usually made such preparations. Her
latest tweed picture – cottage with geese and chickens – a little
masterpiece of its kind, evoked in her no pleasant anticipation of
the moment when she would display it before the ravished eyes
of her disciples. Lessening every accustomed importance that
came to mind were Leda's sneering words and the all too recog-
nisable quotations from Alys. She knew that, together, they had
laughed at her, insulting the hand she hated and cherished,
spreading the fungus of their persecution into the roots of her
life – and why? She could see no reason for it. They had undone
her trust in the country women and in the flower ladies,
whose appreciation and admiration had stayed her self-

confidence for so long against any tease or gibe from Jasper, any idiocy of June's or April's, holding her above the rot she could not remedy at Durraghglass. Coldest of all these realities – for, indeed they were factual miseries to her – was the unacceptable impact of unspoken pity and overdone politeness with which the air was loaded. June's awkward gentleness was hard enough to take; but, when she thought of the wine Jasper had produced (so unnecessarily) for luncheon, her resentment, and her pain, were absolute.

In spite of all this unhappiness, her practical intentions guided her religiously through her preparations for the afternoon. Fragile, paper-thin spokes of wheel-like flower heads, preserved intact, along with teazles and seedheads and apple branches, went into the sturdy Renault. The basket holding the wrapped candlestick and the tweed picture had a safe place by her side. The suitcases containing darling Mummie's desecrated clothes, and the parcel April had left to be delivered to horrid Ulick were in the boot. With Gripper, rigid in disciplined obedience, on her knee, May reversed the car carefully through the jungle of discarded household junk that half filled the garage – once a coach house, where clean carriages waited under great dustsheets for the ladies' afternoon drives: for parties and pleasures, and for the long roads to those legendary balls given by dead soldiers in long-forgotten garrisons. Only April could faintly remember the very last of these festivities. April too was gone, May thought with a pang, first of relief, then of regret at the passing of another certainty: no more squabbling as to who should drive.

Down the avenue she drove, missing most of the deeper hazards, one of her perfected skills; but as she dodged and swerved her way along she felt no satisfaction, only the persistent miasma of loss. Beyond the shade of the trees, the mountains on her right, and the fields, dipping to the river valley on her left, were equally endowed and blessed in the change of the year. Larks should have been singing; the strong spring sun required their celebration. The lovely day found no response in May; the dead flower-heads in the back of the car matched her mood far better than sunlight; the suspicion that she had a flat tyre fitted in perfectly with the day's disasters. When she stopped at a bridge over the river to verify the matter, she was almost disappointed to find that she was mistaken. Changing a wheel had no difficulties for her. It would have been some assertion of her capabilities, which far exceeded Jasper's in any mechanical direction. Looking down the river without much interest she saw a swan, nesting solitary between reeds and willows. May watched while the swan bent her cold neck double to nuzzle eggs farther beneath her. "That's right, girl, keep your secrets," May said aloud. Secrets? At the word a blush rose in excited shame for the secret that should never have been told; for the betrayal of her hidden strength. Colour streamed down her neck; her breasts sweated. When she got back into the car she put Gripper's welcome aside, all values lost.

Passing the monstrous gates to Ballynunty she thought how once she might have made of the exquisitely restored candlestick a reason for an afternoon visit, a cup of tea; stretching that hour to the time for sherry; then home again through the enlivened evening, fortified by the glamour of Alys's friendship, and ready for any tease from Jasper. Now, such a gap had been torn open through all that mattered to her that she drove past the gates – cold to their familiarity as any stranger. If I had a car crash today and broke my leg, she thought, I wouldn't tell them to carry me in there.

Rain came down, violating the afternoon; rain fell into the dark river beside which she drove, rain almost defeated the power of her windscreen wiper; it streamed before her on the wet, black road; rain possessed the day, and a stormy wind buffeted the car and the steering in her hands. Common-sense had failed her for once; no umbrella, not even a mackintosh. There she was, muttering her annoyance, in her neat trouser-suit, hatless, scarfless, when she came to the town where her afternoon's activities waited for her – the suitcases full of filthy clothes for the cleaners; the Flower Guild meeting, and the delivery of April's parcel to Ulick Uniacke. She had put that commission last on her list, hoping that his shop might be closed, and Jasper could do the job on a different day.

It was the rain that changed her plan. If she put Ulick first on the list, she could at least potter in shelter until the downpour lessened. She parked her car opposite his shop. Rain slapped against the flat old windows, sustained on their trumpet-shaped uprights – an original shop window, no gothic glazing bars or manufactured bow to vulgarize it towards any pretension other than being a shop window. Today the window was filled with a deadly dull display of barometers and weather vanes, all looking too large for their setting. Looking in through the sheets of rain, May knew how much more attractively she could have arranged it. Silly old queen, she thought, as she shut the car door on Gripper's imploring face. "*Sit*," she said with some shred of authority, and scurried for shelter, April's mysterious parcel in hand. Suddenly struck by a fear that Gripper might do some accidental mischief to the basket containing the candlestick and her tweed picture, May delayed, while the rain was sticking her smoky grey hair to her cheeks, to open the car door and take them with her.

Today the shop was crowded and choked, a mouth too full of food, with pieces of furniture strange and diverse, good, bad and indifferent. She thought there was some sort of coarse purpose in their disarrangement as if a voice had said: I refuse to make a pretty display. Find your own interest and purpose. There was no one there to sell, or prompt a purchase. Huge pictures were leant against mahogany Victoriana of vast solidity. She was looking, with unfashionable distaste, at the portrait of a fat little boy, wearing red velvet knickerbockers and standing with one hand on a pedestal and the other on the head of a deer-hound, when a voice from behind the cupboard on which the picture was propped, said: "Lather fun," and a really hideous Japanese dwarf in a very expensive velvet coat – black, with frogs – followed the voice. "Les?" he said enquiringly.

Here was the sort of quiet indecency one could expect to find among Ulick's macabre collection, she thought with dull acceptance, rather than with the interested disapproval and condemnation of a happier day, when she would have noted every nasty detail for relay to Alys. "I have a parcel for Mr Uniacke," she said.

The tiny idol shook his head as if it nodded on a wire spring. His flat yellow face was closed firmly against any wish to please or assist. He eyed the round parcel with oriental disdain. "We don't buy any lubbish here," he said.

To be treated by a yellow catamite as though she had come into a pawn shop with a piece of indifferent plate made a further hideous turn in May's misfortunate day. On any other occasion she would have found a ready reply to snub such insolence. Today she only said, "Mrs Grange-Gorman sent this parcel. For repair. Not for sale."

"Mrs Glange-Gorman," the dwarf repeated in his small hissing voice. "The lady who lang this morning orderling *me* to pack her tlunks – I deny."

Through a filter in May's memory came the recollection of April's morning telephone call. No doubt she had assumed that Ulick was its recipient. "Where is Mr Uniacke?" she asked, explicit in her denial of the familiar "Ulick".

"Ulick? Gone to Dullaghglass and leaving me to move all this ugly lubbish into place. Who does he think I am? A White Witch? To move gland pianos by myself? Oh, he is Bad News. A load of old lubbish himself."

May looked away from the furious Oriental, and out at the teeming rain. There was nearly an hour to fill before her meeting. She could shelter here for a little longer since an encounter with horrid Ulick seemed remote. "I'll wait for a few minutes," she said, "if that's all right?"

"Oh, feel flee," the boy said. "You'll excuse. I have my own tlunks to pack, my leservations to confirm." He was gone, clattering away up some staircase in the remote bowels of the shop.

May could see absolutely nothing to interest her in the shop; nothing to envy; nothing to excite. That the interior atmosphere of the old Fisherman's Bar had been so well preserved – the bar counter for small disarranged objects (none displayed), the bottle shelves behind it, the half circular corner of the snug (room for two and confidences) – seemed to her affected and untidy. She sat sadly down on a bench in the snug, cushioned austerely in cracked buttoned leather stuffed with horsehair – like pony-carriage seats of long ago – and looked out at the rain through gaps in the barometers and weather vanes. There was not one busy, trimmed-up thought in her mind; absolutely nothing to which she might look forward with her usual lively spark of interest or criticism; nothing to wake her again to the artistic achievements she recognised so clearly and respectfully in herself. Because she felt their recognition was halved and quartered to nothing by a macabre and greedy interest in her deformity, now, she told herself, whatever she did was deprived of its rightful values. Jasper's sceptical acceptance of Leda's dreadful betrayal followed by his simmering kindness would stay with her always. And for how long would he be kind? she wondered. With such advantage as he now had over her, how could she ever hope to put him down again? She would see it in his eye; she would hear the unspoken "poor thing", that belittled all she knew herself to be. April and June she could discount. One had not heard Leda's wild revelations, and the other, she was sure, would neither understand nor believe in such an adventurous travesty of dull morals.

That her passionate confession to Leda had been made subsequently to the afternoon's tête-à-tête between her own two dearest friends, seemed to May the only mercy granted her in the whole tragic affair. Every prop but that one had been struck from under her. Alys didn't know. Not yet. The two words choked her with their presage.

Anything to dispel the mortification – she was unconsciously arrogant in her lack of repentance: who repents adventure? She would face the horrible weather after all, and transfer the subjects for her lecture to the hall where they were to be displayed. But, when she had picked up her bags, ready for departure, a further consideration of the torrential rain reminded her of the frailty of last year's dead heads and bog flosses. True to her feeling for all pretty things and the importance of their preservation, she delayed again, and stood irresolute, pining for any activity to disturb the fixed depression of her mind and mood. It's not like me to feel like this, she thought, genuinely surprised by her reaction to catastrophe: it's not like me at all. Not a bit like me. In compensation to her more proper self she set out on an inspection of the large boring objects which represented Ulick's present stock in trade.

Mahogany curtain poles, with their rings, lay about on the floor. Why should he have been stupid enough to lumber himself with a really elephantine brass fender? she felt pleased to wonder. Only three bedside steps and their candle box, the piece covered in dry chicken manure and without its properly secreted po, struck her as interesting. The gothic window panes, torn out of some ruined gate-lodge, had no charm for her. There was no trivial elegance to amuse: not a papier-mâché tray, not a blotter nor a lonely ink-pot – only one pretty chair, its cane seat broken, most of its mother-o'-pearl chipped and lost. I could have done something with that, she thought, her lips pursed in disapproval at so much anonymous neglect.

She pursed her lips again, disapproval restoring some interest and confidence, as she surveyed a kitchen dresser, painted bluer than blue – she could not see that stripping and restoration would do much for that. Why buy such stuff, she wondered, and rather agreed with the Jap about loads of old rubbish. An enormous brown enamelled tea-pot, black bottomed from smoke, stood on one of the dresser shelves. Loose notes, two one pound notes, three five pound notes, and a wad of others, held together by an elastic band, were clustered like leaves in the dark circle of their container. May replaced the lid and put back the tea-pot. What a silly place to keep money. *Too* obvious, was all she thought. Enlivened a little by such an absurdity, she tried one of the two deep drawers; all it contained, besides old crumbs in cracks and corners, was a small note book; in it accounts of other days were carefully noted: 1 doz. eggs – 2/–, 1 lb. sugar – 4d., Leg lamb (7 lbs.) – 15s. 8d., 1 gal. paraffin oil – price indecipherable. She put the book back thinking regretfully that times were easier then.

The second drawer was half open, obviously shoved in at an angle. She suspected the angry little Oriental of that piece of carelessness. Although she saw that the rain was now stopping, May's innate sense of order made her delay her departure and put down her bags so that both her hands were free to set the matter of the crooked drawer straight; it would have been unnatural for her to have done otherwise. She pushed and coaxed for a minute without success; then, determined to do the job properly, she pulled the drawer out as far as it would go. It was full of broken pieces of china. Entranced, May peered, then picked them over – small pieces, all broken, or with cracks grotesquely riveted – a mute swan, both wings gone; a saucer dish, three times riveted through its strawberries; an enamel bird that had been the lid of a snuff box, perhaps comfits? she wondered; a bantam hen, russet-backed, beakless, legless; not a rabbit among the lot. Though interested, she envied nothing. She straightened and shut the drawer, then tried it again to see if it slid and ran easily. She never left a task unfinished. As she gave a last quick look before the final closing, a small parcel caught her eye. Not like me to miss anything, she thought again, upset by an inattention to detail so unusual for her.

Cold sunlight came streaking through clefts in the groups of furniture. The rain was over, and she must not be late for the Guild. But a ray of sun, piercing like a spear into the small bleak contents of the open drawer, held her for a moment. All the pieces were fine porcelain, the sudden light changed them into small, jewel-like objects. Their forgotten beauty aroused her old interests enough to make imperative an examination of the parcel, there could be some pretty discovery within; a pity to neglect it. A minute or two more or less would make no difference to her flower ladies. Let them wait, she thought. Her affectionate indulgence towards her disciples had waned piti-fully since the morning. She unwound the first of the wrappings, in which something that felt like a hazel nut had been carefully screwed up. A tiny piece of china, shaped like a thimble, a tasselled thimble, was in her hand. She put it down, and went on unwrapping. Whatever the further contents might be, they had been most meticulously cocooned and sellotaped into their parcel. May picked carefully at the beastly sellotape, now curious to find out what broken piece deserved so much more care than the other bits and oddments rattling round in the drawer. There was so much paper and sellotape to deal with that she felt like unpacking a Christmas parcel, or disembowelling a Russian doll; her excitement rose to a blush along her cheekbones; she stooped to her hands, intent only on what she might see.

Bared at last, she set out on the dirty dresser the wish of her heart – a rabbit, flowered gown to his feet, seated on a chaise percée, his nightcap lying in the dust beside him. Here was the mate and pair to her own precious ministering nurse, wife, or mother, complete even to the blue medicine bottle, star piece of her collection. No question, the two must be united. Gently, as though bed clothes for a baby were in her hands, she was about to lay him again between his wrappings when she heard the sound of voices, far in the dark caverns of the shop; first a disgruntled hissing, answered by a second voice, assured and dismissive: Ulick was back.

Ulick would have ideas about this treasure, pricey ideas; or ideas about keeping it. Beyond all doubt she knew it had to be hers. Now, as always when she had known risk to be greatest, she felt her hand empowered and tautened, the missing fingers daring their survivors towards a sensation that must be placated. So, gently and quickly, without a rustle of paper she wrapped up her figurine and thrust her package deep down in her basket, between the wrapped candlestick and the tweed picture. As she turned the well-considered wanderings of her footsteps in the direction of escape with her plunder, the surge in her blood sank gently to rest as though succeeding the climax to an act of love. Calm in this peace, nerve unshaken, May sauntered, unhurrying, towards the door, delayed once in a blind alley of dark mahogany. It was only when she turned the refusing handle of the shop door that a very slight uneasiness, no more than a wish to be punctual for her meeting, came over her. She tried the lock again, adding her left hand to the job. Then, looking down to enquire into her difficulty, she saw that a very new type of lock had been fitted to the old shop door, in place of the original heavy mortice. In very poor taste, too, she considered, before calling out in her clear upper-class voice, "*Would* someone, please, open this door." No answer came; and, when she turned unwillingly to retrace her steps, she saw Ulick, smiling and softly threading his way towards her through gaps in the Victorian bulwarks.

"Something seems rather wrong with your door," she said.

"Oh, yes, it can be awkward. I've been playing with my little Black Box, and I don't really understand it yet. It's a ray, and it's supposed to lock and unlock from a distance."

"How interesting," May said, without glancing at the cassette he was showing her. "I'm rather late for an appointment. Do you have a back door?"

"This locks both doors," he said, "it's Japanese, of course. My assistant understands the cypher perfectly, but I'm afraid he's in one of his moods. Do sit down," he indicated the snug, "until he's calmer."

May looked with total disapproval at Ulick – her scarcely known, least favourite man – wondering again at April's taste for him. She had to admit that his clothes were remarkable, without absurdity, and he wore them with the style of a bull fighter. Perhaps it was because he had the right kind of voice that she allowed herself, muttering protests, to be enticed towards the snug; she was only surprised when he sat down beside her like an old friend.

"Another gadget I've just installed," he went on pleasantly, "are these two-way mirrors. We're often so busy with our restorations in the backroom, it's nice to know what's going on in front."

A chill numbed May's hand – that was where she felt the impact of fear. To still panic and restore potency, she opened her handbag, took a cigarette from her case and flicked her lighter with total ease. "Well," she drew on her cigarette and looked round her, "not very easy to get away with any of this stuff." She surveyed the Victoriana with a cold eye; then, turning back to him: "And, by the way," she asked politely, "did your Japanese friend give you a parcel from my sister?"

"A nice bit of Leeds," he said, "I'll look after that. And would you let me know when to collect all those 'baggages' she rang about. Some day this week? My assistant's a marvellous packer – clever oriental fingers – but he's a temperamental little bastard. I'll come along myself."

So this was what the delay implied: an opportunity to spy out the possibilities of Durraghglass, a typically unattractive ambition. Jasper would never let him in, and, for once, she was in agreement. "Thank you," she said, "all her suitcases will be packed and ready in the hall on Thursday. I suppose my sister is paying for the transport? Or would you like it in advance?"

His face darkened. "April's rather a friend of mine," he said. "I'm quite glad to be useful."

"Oh, how *kind*." May's acknowledgement sounded so unreal as to have a pitying quality.

"Perhaps," he said, "I might be useful to you, too. You've forgotten something, haven't you?"

May drew deeply on her cigarette and looked about her vaguely. A perfectly assumed "silly me" expression superseded all the resolute certainty of a natural decisive briskness. "I don't think so." Her memory seemed to hover. "Could I have?"

Smiling again, he opened his hand and laid a scrap of china, no larger than a wren's egg, on the table between them. "What about this?" he asked. "His nightcap. Rather of the period, wouldn't you say?"

A different excitement rose in May's blood, colour crept up her neck. "I can't imagine what you're talking about." Past any panic in her situation was disgust at her own forgetfulness. Her inadequacy shamed her cruelly; she pushed out her half-smoked cigarette, maimed hand reprimanded on the burning tip. "And now," she said, "I really must go."

He picked up the little piece of china and looked at it carefully. "Sorry about the locked doors," he said, "I didn't want a scene in the street. April's quite a friend of mine and she *would* rather hate this kind of thing."

First Jasper with his denigrating understanding. Now April's turn.

"For Heaven's sake," she said piteously, "you can't tell April."

"No. Let's keep it to ourselves. And now, if you don't mind," he smiled towards her basket, "or perhaps you'ld rather unpack it yourself?" His good manners never slipped.

Pulsating, as before an operation without anaesthetic, May groped in her bag and put the little parcel on the table between them. He undid the wrapping as carefully as she had done, and was about to fit the china cap to the china head, when May let out a scream of protest. "Don't," she said, "please, not like that – you'll chip the edges, you'll ruin the restoration."

They looked at each other with a sudden understanding. "Thank you," he said. "Stupid of me."

There was a pause. May was shaking now – shock and anguish undelayed. He looked at her with something near interest, and far from sympathy. "You do understand," he said, "I really must. . . ." and he tried to take the basket out of her clinging hands. Her last refuge was its rightful possession. "Let go," she ordered, "at once. Everything in this basket is my own private property."

"Our ideas on private property don't quite match up; I don't want to ring the police," he sounded quietly considerate.

May loosed her grip on the bag. She bent her head. Her need

for a cigarette was beyond endurance. And, at this moment of her greatest need, her hand failed her. Her thumb and finger were shaking so shamefully they were past any obedience; they could not open her cigarette case; it was as if their life was ending. She laid her cramped hand on the edge of the table and stared at it, and touched it with her left hand, inattentive to what Ulick meant to do to her, or say to her. Or say to others.

"Christmas morning, isn't it?" Ulick said cheerfully, undoing a parcel busily as he spoke. First the tweed picture came to light. He examined it for a full minute. "Hideously good. Quite a gem of its genre. Where did you 'find' it?"

May was silent.

"Do say. Tell all."

"It's mine."

"Yes. But whose was it? Before it was yours. It's perfect tourist stuff."

"It's my own work," she said.

"Mmm." He didn't look once at her hand, but she knew he must be thinking of it. If only she could name a reputable witness to confound him. Alys? Nevermore. He put the picture down and started to unwind the candlestick from its paper. "This is really very fine," he said, "pity you didn't get the pair. An incredible bit of restoration. I suppose you'll say you did it. Don't disappoint me."

May didn't answer. Humbled, she waited for the next insult. No tears. All her distress was in her hand, immobile and useless.

Ulick took out his cigarette case. "Let me light one for you," he said; and still he kept his eyes away from her hand. She took the cigarette from him with her left hand, and drew in a lungful of something strange.

"Perhaps a cup of tea," Ulick got to his feet. "I'll ask my man to make us a cup of tea. Perhaps he will."

"Oh, please," May said, "will you open the door. I'm late already. It's my lecture."

"What's your subject?" he asked incuriously.

"China restoration and what to do with dead heads."

"Fancy!" Ulick's disinterest and disbelief were equally manifest, as he glided away through his furniture.

When she had sat for a few minutes, inhaling the smoke of the cigarette he had given her, the non-importance of the Flower Arrangers Guild invaded and quietened her. Let them wait, she thought. Let them wait for me – che sera sera – right? Of course I'm right.

Ulick came back with two mugs of China tea, milkless. "Had to make this myself," he said. "He's packing. He's really going. Almost gone. A bit worrying. He's the best I've ever known on marquetry – but he's such a scold." He put down the mugs and picked up the candlestick.

"Oh, look out!" May screamed again. "Be careful! I only did that this morning. It's hardly set." As she spoke her shocked hand flew out to protect her work – its stillness over.

"Am I seeing the truth?" Ulick asked himself, and he kept his eyes from her hand. "I think I am. This too?" he asked her, looking disgustedly at her tweed picture. "You ran up this cottage pie? Very crafty."

"You don't have much of an eye for quality, do you?" May said. "Not if you call this canvas 'craft'."

Ulick smiled at her, not so unkindly. "Have you ever worked in wood?" he asked.

"No. I've always longed to get into marquetry," May found the discussion of her own subject too tantalising to avoid.

"There's a little Dutch ruin in the workroom now. Would you like to have a go at it?"

Resistance spent and curiosity awakened, May followed where he led her, through the jungles and labyrinths of furniture and past a door leading into a glass-roofed workroom – a room full of delicate pieces, all in some degree broken or marred, all of wonderful quality. The room was equipped with every possible device for their mending, it was as tidy as a hospital and lighted as expensively as an operating theatre. . . .

When, an hour later, they came back to the shop together, May and nasty Ulick were hand in glove, and heart to heart – in a manner of speaking.

"And that is the best money I can offer you," Ulick was saying. "Of course, there'll be a small commission."

Unaware, uncaring that she was about to accept a wage far beneath her abilities, and half that earned by the Jap she supplanted, May walked through the giant furnishings as though she went through cloud-capped towers and glorious palaces. "Only one thing," she hesitated. "Jasper can be very selfish and unpleasant about the car."

"I supply the car," he said.

May reeled. She sat down. This was past belief. "And the petrol?" she had the good sense to ask.

"Just enough," his eyes narrowed, "to commute."

"Jolly good!" May's own language was reviving. "Ten o'clock to five – Saturdays free."

"Unless there's a sale – you wouldn't mind an occasional rampage in the sale rooms, would you? And they don't have two-way mirrors at country auctions." In perfect understanding they both lowered their eyes. For the second time that day May picked up the *Malade Imaginaire* and re-wrapped him. Ulick took the package gently from her hands.

"I must restore him," May said. "I'll do him at home."

"No, dear. You'll do him here. And what's more, he's going to cost you your first month's wages."

"If you get a better offer for him, you won't take it, will you?"

"I might," Ulick said. May recognised the careless truth-fulness of his tone; and she knew that she had met her match. In a curious way, Ulick felt the same. After the first rampage, however meagre the loot, they would be in each other's hands.

It was late in the afternoon before May drove home. She knew she had never given so inspired a lecture. And, in her demonstration, her hand had been almost officious in dexterity; each stem, each cartwheel of seedheads took the air, floating their ghostly shapes obedient to her direction. When she had set a piece of white driftwood in front of her creation, May knew that she deserved even more applause and congratulation than she received. The delightful thought: how they are going to miss me, gave power and kindliness to her little speech of resignation as their President.

"Much as I'm going to miss our meetings," she had said, "and I hope that in my own small way I've been a tiny help and a bit of inspiration through my demos, I don't feel it would be fair, now that I have undertaken such a full-time job in the Antique World. . . ." Later on, over cups of tea and affectionate protests against her resignation, she had put it to them with quiet practi-cality: "You do see my point? I could be at a Sotheby sale on the very day I had promised to give you one of my special demonstrations. You get the message? Right? Am I right? Elect your new President, and I promise to come and watch her demonstrate." Her fixed smile sent a shudder of anticipation through each postulant for Presidency. "So you do see, it's not goodbye, only au revoir."

May had parted from her Flower Guild and turned the car for home before she remembered that the suitcases with their dread contents were still in the boot. Flown on the afternoon's successes she had little doubt of her ability to deal with this last ugly matter, difficult and embarrassing as it could prove. "Pick yourself up," and "get back on the highwire," were two prin-

ciples that had sustained her determination through many
a difficult encounter. She parked the car neatly; put Gripper on
his lead ("runny-runs for good boys"), and walked towards the
cleaners, first suitcase in hand, refusing to admit to any sinking
feelings about the nearing moment when its contents would be
revealed. The phrases she rehearsed – "*Very* naughty little
dog," or, perhaps, "some horrible cat," – seemed every moment
less convincing. Although sure, as ever, in the rightness of her
actions, May felt almost overwhelmed by the flood of relief that
swept through her when she saw that the cleaner's premises were
shut, windows darkened for the night; her awful mission
aborted. Back at the car she unclipped Gripper's lead, replaced
the suitcase, and lit a cigarette. As she expelled her first deep
inhalation a new resolve, difficult to implement after her long
years of loving, sentimental care, rose within her. "Right, am I
right? I know I am!" In the garden, in Mummie's garden, every
rag of Mummie's desecrated clothes would burn to ash on a
funeral pyre of rosemary and lavender, apple-wood and sweet
geranium. May's fortune had taken two such strange turns in
as many hours: perhaps it was that which provoked the
sharp sacrifice of a long sustained dream, and empowered her
practical decision for tomorrow. Once taken she put the resolve
away – a concluded matter – and allowed her memory to revert
pleasantly to the bits of her speech that had particularly pleased
her.

The hour was much lighter than it had been when she and
April had driven together to find Leda at the end of the day:
Leda, the magical nightmare, blind and bereft of all beauty.
Leda, who could construe love out of her cruelties. Leda, in
whose faithlessness had lain the origins of May's spectacu-
lar afternoon. Thinking like this, May hummed and sang,
punching her foot down on the accelerator as if she kicked a lazy
horse along. Her mind skipped across the days until there would

be a car, her car; to the days of the pay packets and the times for
bonus. Those would be the days when she would return to
Durraghglass with the week's shopping, paid for by herself –
only the account shown to Jasper, shown to him with a careless:
that's OK I've paid. Don't worry. It would be a way of
keeping him in his place. His proper place.

From Jasper and his kitchen came the thought of her garden;
of the vegetables she grew with no labour but her own, and a
very occasional day stolen from Baby June's schedules for
Christy Lucey. "I shall have my own garden boy," she told
herself, "two days in every week. And he shall never go into the
farmyard unless to fetch a load of manure – well-rotted manure.
And I shall pay Baby June for that, too," she decided magnificently. She took a breath of happiness as she passed the bank of
primroses, so lavish this evening. Tears for their beauty, or
gratitude for her own wild success, filled her eyes; while a
frisson for the future shook through her with even finer
intensity than the shudder of pleasure and relief earned by any
previous escapade.

The evening belonged to May, and May exulted in, and
explored the evening. Every sight along the road charmed her,
bright with interest and suggestion for her future artistic
successes. A quiet old man leading his pony through a stony gap
would be in her next picture. Cattle grazing on the side of a hill,
steep as a bank, assumed, for her, a primitive quality. The
unseen legs must be shorter than those visible. While she noticed
everything, no dreaminess overtook her strict road-sense. The
memories of scarifying journeys with April came back to her;
journeys when April, deaf and immune to all sensible advice, had
swerved on her way, regardless. Her departure with Leda today
was somehow linked up with those terrible road risks which (so
unfairly) never ended in disaster.

Happily relieved by April's absence from the driving seat,

May drew carefully closer to her proper side of the road as she heard the distant sound, a sound uncommon on any road, of a horse galloping; nearer and louder and still unseen, came the thrilling measured spaces of the galloping stride, until a horseman came riding round the bend – on the wrong side of the road, and nearly into the car, before, shouting a wild command, he pulled his horse across, and, laughing in pure delight, rode away.

One of those ghastly tinkers, May thought angrily. I shall have to get after Jasper about that camp. It's a must. That fellow could have killed me. No control. Good thing April wasn't driving. The idea that, had April been driving – driving, as usual, on the wrong side of the road – she would have escaped the danger, did not strike May. She drove on, more to the left than before, and ten minutes later she approached the untidy encampment of the people she preferred to call tramps and tinkers, avoiding the vulgarly respectable word: itinerant. She sounded her horn authoritatively at a man who stood by the roadside, raising his hand to slow her down – as though she was the kind of driver to kill a dog, or even a child. Before she could drive on, ignoring his signals, he stepped out into the middle of the road and she saw that it was Jasper who had caused her to brake so suddenly as to kill her engine. "So like him. Not at all like me," she thought as she let down her window and waited for him to speak.

It was more than an hour since Jasper had gone running, stooping into the wind, a tall old gentleman, bent forward in dread expectancy – grace gone, age apparent in all its sad inadequacies. He who, to conserve his energies, would avoid crossing the kitchen floor for a tin of mustard, now expended his tired strength in panic hurrying towards a disaster he was too old to mourn. Regret, regret, and a house companionless was all he was able to feel. Beyond regret for Baby June lay the horrid prospect of teasing May without an audience. The boredom of the prospect weighted his stumbling feet on their heron's legs. Why can't I be more of a Human Being? he asked himself again. No answer came.

A little boy wearing an expensive anorak was leaning on the handlebars of an expensive little bicycle near the steps of the largest caravan. Occasionally he kicked one of a posse of yearning dogs crowding with lolling tongues and lifted legs round the caravan wheels. Their guarded hostility to each other indicated a bitch on heat within.

"She's within," the little boy said, aware of the hour's drama.

Jasper had a foot on the lowest step, and a hand on the rail, but good manners delayed him.

"May I go in?" he asked.

"My Nana's with her," the boy said. He flung his leg across the bicycle and rode away followed by the screaming curses of a little friend, obviously the owner of the bicycle.

There was no reason for further delay and hesitation. Jasper climbed the four steps and, when no answer came to his knock on the door, he pushed the craving dogs aside and opened it. He looked down a warmly heated tunnel of darkness – a darkness broken by the glitter of mirrors, the cut-glass bowls of old oil lamps, and the naive splendours of Staffordshire figures. An old woman with dyed red hair came down the dusky warren to meet him.

"Shut the door, if you please, sir. My son will choke me if one of them curs gets at his little bitch, Fairy, he calls her. Excuse me," she pushed by him to the door. "Begone! Begone!" she screamed, leaning out menacingly.

"How do you do?" Jasper said, taking off his cap, when at last she turned to him.

"Come on in till you see her," the change of voice from a tone of rage to quiet solemnity held its own presage for him. "I have her in on the divan," the old woman pointed towards a further partition.

Infinitely embarrassed and infinitely sad at the picture he foresaw, Jasper went towards the more exclusive apartment. It was nice of them to have put her out of the sight of curious eyes.

Baby June was sitting up on a padded bench that could transform itself into a divan bed, drinking tea out of a china cup.

"Hullo, Jasper," she said, "what a fool I was to part; I'm sorry."

An immense surge of gratitude stilled the air and hovered for a moment in and over Jasper, until relieved by annoyance. "My dear girl," he said, "how silly can you get?"

"It was only the shock quenched her out," the old woman took over the conversation. "And don't worry yourself at all. My little boy have the horse re-captured, he's sorting him up, now. You'ld want a good jockey for a start, and the Holy All about it is the lady's past that class of work. It's the age knocks you. What she'ld want is a quiet little animal could travel the bogs – a donkey is light, you know. We have a Spanish breed, they came from Spain, they have a long mane like a horse. Would you buy a little donkey, my lady? Take a cup of tea, sir. Take a little cup, dear, it's nice tea. Take a seat, sir. Forget about the horse, now. Don't think about him at all. My little fellow will take the short way back across the mountain and he'll have the horse civilised. I'm bloody sure he will. He can charm warts and he can stop blood too. His uncle, God rest his soul, was able to stop the flow of blood even if it was only a goat itself was bleeding. . . ."

Only the subdued, tamed sounds of a horse, walking quietly, interrupted her flow of tea-time talk. It happened to be just the sort of conversation Jasper approved, leaving no gap for

answers. Now he could get to his feet and ask June how she felt
about getting home.

"I'm going great," she said, "only a bit shook, that was all I
was. I'm great now, after the tea. I'll ride the bastard back." She
got up and took the old woman's hand.

"And you'll take a look at the little ass in the morning." Careless and polite as any great hostess she followed them out with
easy goodbyes, before shouting abuse at the craving dogs and
shutting her door.

Outside the warm gypsy cave there was a late shudder in the
evening. The boy dismounted and waited, the reins turned over
the horse's head, expectant of a good reward.

"And how did you like your ride?" June asked him, while
Jasper searched for his note-case.

"Great out, m'lady, that's the lad watches his chance to fire
you. Head him for home and he's gone into the air with buck,
lep and kick."

The innocent realism of the words recalled, for Jasper, the
despair and agonies of nerves which had once been his own cruel
affliction and alerted him now to the reason for June's delay; for
the crumpling of her little face when she turned the Wild Man's
reins back over his head; when he heard the shake in her voice as
she said: "Catch my foot, boy," and held out a leg to be thrown
up. Some long abandoned collusion with the days before she
had shot and wounded him told Jasper how distant was the June
of this evening, even of this afternoon, when he had watched as
she set out, unchanged, as he thought, by her years, to the Baby
June of long ago.

"Stop a minute, Baby," he said, catching at the sleeve of her
muddy Husky. "Let's just see how useful this boy is."

June put her foot back on the ground. Gratitude beamed, an
aura round her stout little body, while she tossed the boy up,
light as a feather, into the saddle. "Take him easy, now. Walk

on. Jog on. That'll do." After ten minutes she turned a radiant look of expectancy to Jasper. "Well, what d'you think?" he asked her.

"He does it like an Indian, a Red Indian, what they call a Brave." June had the illiterate's long memory for books read aloud to her in childhood. Books such as *Tales of the Blackfoot Indians*. "I'd say he'll do. I'd say we should chance him." She said no more. In silence she waited for Jasper's answer, afraid to hope for a future when a new companion would wait for her in the mornings, do her bidding, and accept her kindness through the length of the day.

"I'm no judge," he said doubtfully. "You decide."

"Come over here, child," June called to the boy who waited in careless unity with his horse at a little distance from them. "Can you milk a cow?" she asked.

"I can. Or a goat. Or a donkey mare, itself."

"Ride on up to the big house, so," she said, "and we'll have a talk. And mind you don't bring that horse in sweating."

Was June fit to walk even the short way home? Jasper, feeling that he had already overstepped discretion, and commonsense too, by his implicit agreement in the employment of a flighty young tinker, was not in the mood to burden himself with any further worry or decision. But it was a latent care for the chubby figure, trudging off so urgently in pursuit of horse and rider, that made him stand firmly in the path of the car he recognised at once as the Durraghglass Renault 4.

"Jasper," May leaned her cross little face out of the window, "how typical! I could have killed you. I suppose you want a lift. Get in. Get in. That door's locked. Don't touch it. Please, leave it to me."

June out of sight, Jasper's always solicitous feelings for his own comforts urged him to get into the car and drive, rather than walk, back to home and tea. As he opened the unlocked door, Gripper, after an afternoon of boredom too long for his patience, shot out past him and, ignoring May's cries, scurried across the road to join the pack of longing dogs round the caravan wheels. As one, they turned on this fresh postulant for Fairy's favours. The frightening turmoil of a genuine dogfight (so different from the morning's little fracas) tearing at his ears, Jasper's nerve failed him utterly. Unashamed, he leapt into the car, slammed the door, and shut the window. As quickly, May was out, and across the road, embroiled at once and dangerously in the heart of the matter. She flung dogs, ravening for blood or sex, or both, off her darling, and was in the proud act of unclenching Gripper's teeth from the neck of the fiercest combatant, when the old tinker lady, so lately the polite hostess, leaned down from her eyrie. "Bring him in, lady, bring him in," she called, "bring the little fellow in before they choke him, God bless him. He's the very article my son would pick for Fairy."

"Have you got some clean water?" May asked.

"Spring water, my lady, I wouldn't use any other."

It was on Gripper's account, and not for her own bleeding hand that May climbed the steps leading to the squalor that she expected and deplored. As the door shut behind her, she was surprised to find herself in a smugglers' cave of old lamps – their bowls ruby glass and clear glass, milk glass, pink and blue and white glass; some of the lamps were still mounted on their brass pedestals; legless bowls, flowered and plain, sat, sitting ducks, waiting for her skills. May swallowed a gasp of wonder and delight at the prospect of such an exchange and mart at her gate. Near to dreaming, she considered how, one by one, these peerless objects might be bought, re-conditioned and re-sold, by her to Ulick. So absorbed she was, that it was only when she heard a magnificent ribald shout of laughter and saw toothless jaws agape to laugh again, that she realised a mating was being consummated, happily, and beyond interruption in the back of the caravan. The old woman stared engrossed in its contemplation, a bucket of water swinging and slopping unnoticed from her hand. "And did you ever see a donkey's wedding, lady?" she asked, ready with a reprise of the tea-time conversation.

May hesitated; if tolerance of Nature's horrid ways was the way to business, that way must be kept open. "No. Actually, no," she said, "but what I'm really interested in is your collection of oil lamps . . . Now this one, with the cracked base, would you let me have it in exchange for –?" She indicated the continued nuptials.

"You wouldn't sooner take a little pup, lady? My son bought those lamps very dear. He travelled every little house when the people had them thrown out, for the electricity. He has the lot priced. Seven pounds for the blue."

"Dear at the price," May turned away smiling and shaking her head. She foresaw that the bargaining would be long and enjoyable.

Jasper, crunching up his long, cold legs in the inadequate spaces of the car, slid back his window in response to May's imperative tapping. Considering all that had come to light that morning, "saucy" seemed to him the best description of her present manners.

"Well?" His tone conveyed a disinterested rebuke, tinged by present martyrdom. "Are we ever going home?"

"Afraid you'll have to walk it," May smiled brilliantly, then snapped her smile shut. "I've got some business to do in there. It may take a little time."

"Business with the tinkers? Your favourites?"

"They've got some quite pretty things. Stolen property, obviously."

Jasper stared at her. How, after Leda's revelations, could she pronounce the word "stolen" in a way suggesting that it was only tinkers who stole? When, in the miseries of breakfast-time, such meagre sympathies as he had to spare went out to her violated privacies, how could he have foreseen this speedy resurrection of all her assured perkiness of manner? It was at this point that a nasty misgiving struck him – the remembrance of the mysterious collection of coloured glass eyes, big and small, all arranged provocatively and accessibly along the shelves in the caravan. How to play this safe? How to avoid a scandal with the tinkers?

"You'll want some money?" he said, his hand going towards his note-case. "Oh dear. How much?"

"Thank you, Jasper. I'm full of money. Actually, I landed rather a paying job in the Antique World, today."

"Not with Ulick? You can't have. What about the playing fields of Eton?"

"Someone has to make up for April's departure. Right? So there it is. Anything's better than the bread-line. By the way, there's a bottle of wine in my basket – quite a good year. Take it back and warm it for dinner, would you? I may be some time."

He saw her bend her head into the weather and light a cigarette expertly, before she turned to walk back across the road, heels down, toes out, in her natural and determined style. As he watched her disappear (without knocking) through the door of the caravan, he reached into the back of the car and felt for the bottle in the basket. When he looked at its label, the vintage year surprised him pleasantly. He wondered, as he walked home through the chillier evening, whether it would be worth the trouble of transferring its contents for his own future enjoyment and substituting a lesser wine. Despite May's silly patter on the subject, neither she nor June had any sort of discriminating palate. Perhaps the search for the silver funnel, through which butlers used to fill decanters with the best of clarets, would be too arduous and time consuming a task for him. He put the idea aside as he reached his derelict gates and empty gate-lodge.

When, as he walked down the drive, he saw the tinker boy, a foxy shadow, slip out of the dark Portugal laurels, he accepted the fact of another Christy Lucey in the failing years of Durraghglass. Another boy, pretty and useless, and always needing one of June's stealthy sandwiches, was what he envisaged; a ghastly mistake, allowing June to engage him. However, nothing like a new worry to keep the mind off worse things to come.

Worries put aside, permitted, or ignored, Jasper's mind went back to that happy hour – previous to the shock and anxiety he had experienced over June's tiresome little accident – that he had spent in Brother Declan's company: an hour pervaded by garden visions far more ambitious than any of his previous unattainable dreams. Now, as he walked back to his kitchen, underneath the cold bare trees, doubt, as usual, took him over. The prospects, discussed in that euphoric hour with Brother Declan, were so vast as to be nearly unacceptable. Jasper sighed, sniffed disparagingly, and trusted that, given more time, he would grown accustomed to the idea. He hoped Brother Declan – perhaps rather a talkative fellow – would not urge him on too fast. There was no hurry. Autumn plantings were best. As he neared the house, he was only glad to think that life at Durraghglass, lately so intemperate, could now return to its accustomed importances, their establishment unshaken by Leda's appallingly embarrassing behaviour.

June and Christy Lucey were clenched in argument outside the closed door of the Wild Man's box. Christy was putting undue emphasis on his virtuous return to employment. "I have Sweetheart fed, and my hens in, and my cow milked, and I would think, Miss Baby, if you'll excuse me, you should know more than allow such a little tinker near my horse." His voice rose with emotion.

Vengeful as any victim of a betrayal, June answered him. "Your horse? Thank you very much. Whose horse was he when you walked off this morning? To your indoor toilet, and your electric light, and your ride in Dublin Show?"

In the relentless memory of a wrong done, June was as deeply unforgiving as her peasant ancestress, the regretted dairy-maid. Her lack of education left her without any false leanings towards diplomacy or convenience. How often, when she was shielding Christy's frequent failures from duty in exchange for his value to her as a rough-rider, an able substitute for her own lost courage, had she indulged the pretensions to a religious discipline with which he excused his early departures and late arrivals. And today, in his worthless betrayal and light departure he had not only justified May's endless spyings and steely criticisms, but, without a thought, he had left June to chill and sicken in a bitter wind of fear.

Now, when deliverance from fear and new hopes had come to her, brought by such another postulant as Christy had once been, he was back to reclaim his position as lightly and confidently as he had whistled away to brighter prospects in the morning. He was ready, too, with a shamelessly pathetic answer.

"And how should I know," he asked her, "the Brigadier would throw me out? After all, the lady promised my mother; and my girl-friend in a condition I don't like to mention."

"Christy – you never! What about your religion?" June's voice was almost respectful in its incredulity.

"When an accident like *that* could happen to me," Christy spoke with real distress, "it could happen to the Lord Abbot himself."

"It's no good putting such things on the Lord Abbot," June said with literal conclusiveness, "and my new little boy has done his horse down quite nicely, before he went." She stretched up her child's height to peer over the half door of the box. "And he's engaged now for the job you threw up when you pedalled away this morning."

"Pulling favourites at Flapper meetings and riding donkeys on the strand is all he knows," Christy said with angry jealousy.

"I'll teach him," June answered with quiet certainty, "the same way I taught yourself. So now, goodbye."

"My mother'll only kill me," Christy stooped miserably over his bicycle.

"Watch yourself, your girl friend might be cross, too." June gave the caution seriously.

Looking round him at the shelter of the stableyard, Christy made his last appeal: "Miss Baby," he said, "I was never one to let you down."

"Oh no, never-ever," June laughed nastily, "and you can pedal off to her ladyship in the morning, for you're not wanted here." Pain and temper were joined in her stubborn reply.

"Ah, Miss Baby, you'll say a little word for me to the Brigadier," Christy persisted, confident as always of winning his way through to her kindness. "The words he used to the Lady today when he knew I was from Durraghglass were only shocking. And" – Christy spoke with prim disapproval – "what he said to myself for leaving you, I wouldn't care to repeat."

A ripple of warm feeling towards old Hippo who, through his proper sense of behaviour, had put her in power to say or to withold a word for or against Christy, melted the edge of June's resentment; in that faint thawing she glimpsed a little of his predicament, entoiled between his mother, his pregnant girl-friend and the strictures of his religion. All considered, he could be granted . . . perhaps not forgiveness, but a last indulgence.

"All right, Christy," she conceded, "I'll slip in a word to the Brigadier."

As she spoke the quiet, reluctant notes of a distant bell recalled and dispelled the ties between them.

"Do I hear the Angelus?" June said. Her back against the stable door, she nodded towards the archway. Christy bowed his head and crossed himself gently before he rode away towards his church and his mother.

June opened the door of the loose-box, and went inside to stand in deep straw, and appraise her horse for the hundredth time. Warmed in the thought that she need never again ride the Wild Man she made him move over in his box with a commanding admonishment, and an authoritative slap or two. She bolted the door of his stable and left the yard by its great familiar archway. When she reached the front of the house, the sour look on its darkened face did not dismay her at all. It was as she had always known it.

The dear and beautiful young nun who had shown April round the flat for two, complete with every possible convenience, and overlooking the convent garden, paused at the door. "Our last old lady, God rest her soul, was very happy here. You won't mind the stairs, will you?"

"But I do mind," Leda wailed, "I shan't know my way to the loo."

"Your own toilet is here too; you won't even have to ring a bell and wait," the Sister assured her.

"Please, I want my old room," Leda insisted.

"Oh, no, dear, you only think you do. You'll love this nice sunny flat. And your daughter and Mrs Grange-Gorman have made every arrangement, and paid in advance. So you mustn't worry yourself about anything. Now," she took out a note pad and a biro, "what about supper? We have roast lamb, the first spring lamb."

"That's for me," Leda said.

"And Mrs Grange-Gorman, what about you?"

"Lamb for both of us. She can't hear a word, deaf as a post," Leda spoke decidedly.

"Oh, it's no trouble to write it down, none in the world." The pretty nun advanced with her biro poised, patience and understanding written plain on her devoted face.

"French Paysan soup," she wrote in her perfect script. "Roast lamb, spinach, roast potatoes, treacle tart."

April studied the menu carefully. Then: "Spinach, perhaps," she suggested. "Could there be some milk cheese – skim milk? Then a salad and yoghurt. That will be perfect for tonight. I expect my own special nature foods will be here by tomorrow evening. And could our trays be sent up here?"

"Naturally. Of course. No trouble."

The sweet nun straightened her white cardigan and smiled her way out.

"Isn't this nice?" April said, "so clean compared with Durraghglass. I'll have the room with the view," she went on, "because that doesn't affect you, darling." She crossed to the window. "What a nice tidy garden – perfect for pi-pi. I do think Tiger is going to be happy. Are you happy, Baby-Doll? Please say you're happy, little man."

"I'd like to kill you both," Leda wrote in a furious indecipherable scrawl and handed the message to April.

"You know I can't read your writing." April handed back the envelope. "Anyway, it's time for our breathing exercises."

"Oh, shut up if you can, you silly old bitch," Leda screamed.

"Take a deep breath and expand your stomach muscles. Do it naturally. Then relax. Just shut your eyes and let everything go." April closed her eyes to concentrate religiously on her own performance. The session over, she opened her eyes, to see Leda groping wildly at the bathroom door. "Wrong door," April laughed a little. "You'll never find your way out, darling Leda," she said, "without me."

Imprisoned, Leda put her hands up to her blind eyes. There was to be no escape.

A NOTE ON THE TYPE

This book was filmset in Janson, a recutting made direct from type cast from matrices long thought to have been made by the Dutchman Anton Janson, who was a practicing type founder in Leipzig during the years 1668–1687. However, it has been conclusively demonstrated that these types are actually the work of Nicholas Kis (1650–1702), a Hungarian, who most probably learned his trade from the master Dutch type founder Dirk Voskens. The type is an excellent example of the influential and sturdy Dutch types that prevailed in England up to the time William Caslon (1692–1766) developed his own incomparable designs from them.

Composed in Great Britain by Photobooks (Bristol) Limited,
Barton Manor, St. Philips, Bristol
Printed and bound by The Haddon Craftsmen,
Scranton, Pennsylvania
Display typography and binding design by Amy Berniker